"With the intellect and comic instincts of Rushdie, the obsessiveness of Percy, and the gritty realism of Bukowski, Syed Afzal Haider has created Ramzan Malik, seeker and romantic, moviegoer and Muslim, who breaks from his traditional Pakistani family to be with the American woman of his choice."

Elizabeth McKenzie, author of *MacGregor Tells The World*

"Much will be made of the rich cross-cultural perspectives and striking depictions of people places and times in *To Be With Her.* Those are certainly among its many outstanding qualities. But like all books that will last, it preserves the palpable texture of its particulars while simultaneously exploring many of the universal themes that are the currency of great literature: love, loss, aspiration, disillusionment, and personal identity."

Donald Whitfield, Director of Higher Education Programs, The Great Books Foundation.

TO BE WITH HER
Syed Afzal Haider

TO BE WITH HER

SYED AFZAL HAIDER

خ جھ ج

Weavers Press
San Francisco
http://weaverspress.wordpress.com

ACKNOWLEDGMENTS

Portions of this novel have been previously published, sometimes in slightly different form in various publications. "Blind Date" appeared in *Manhattan Literary Review*, "Tribes" was first published in *AmerAsia Journal* and was reprinted in the anthology *Leaving Home* (Oxford University Press) and reappears in *Indian Voices*. "From Brooklyn to Karachi Via Amsterdam" was published in the anthology *Sacred Ground* (Milkweed Press), reprinted in another anthology, *Dragonfly in The Sun* (Oxford University Press), and again in *Different Cultures* (A Collection of Short Stories), (Pearson, Longman). "Jhansi Zero Miles" was published in *Life Boat, A Journal of Memoir*.

Many dear friends and members of my writing group have helped nurture this book at various stages. My sincere thanks to Lois Barliant, Hollis B. Birnbaum (AKA Hazel R. Peartree) Valerie Ellis, Anna Maria Hozian, Frank Reckett, Brian Skinner and Eleanor Jackson for their help, support, and guidance. Special thanks to David Penna for the font support and to Natalia Nebel for reading the final draft. Much obliged to my editors, Jane Lawrence and Debi Morris, and for an outstanding work of editorial fine tuning and their wise comments, to Amna Ali, and Moazzam Sheikh and to Caitlyn He, for her editorial support and copy edit.

Heart felt gratitude to Comrade Gary Houston, most generous and giving. Heaven be praised for the friends like Mark Sherman, Allen Steinberg, Olga Domchenko, TVB, Steve Woodhams, Polly Barker Duffy, Les White, and Carl Levin and to my old buddies from NJV High, Anwer, Arshad, Quitb, Sajid, Sibte, and Waji. My heart overflows with love and appreciation for My Dear Gail Hochman for her faith in me, and my work. To the extraordinary Lisa, I'm grateful for more than you know. *Merci, gracias, shukria.* My unconditional love to my sons Sean and Dustin, pride and joy of my life, for their wisdom and support. Admiration, and adoration to Miss Janice Nakao, my wife, for her benevolence and forbearance. You are all lovely people.

For Vicky

To Be With Her

The Journey

CHAPTER 1

I love movies. I see life as a movie. I go to a movie almost every day. My best friend, Kazi, lives in flat number three in Aziz Manzal, the building next door. His father is the manager of the Majestic Cinema on Bunder Road, two blocks east of our home. Thanks to Kazi, I can walk into the Majestic any time for any show— three, six, or nine; and the additional ten o'clock show on Sunday mornings. When Mehboob's silver jubilee film *Andaz* opened at Majestic, Kazi and I went to see it every day at 3:42, 6:42, and 9:42 for seven weeks. I loved the scenes where Dilip Kumar sings to Nargis: *Hum aaj kahi dil kho baihtey . . .*

Ramzan Pervez Malik. RPM. My friends call me Rama. I see myself as a good guy, a main character, a matinee idol, leading man material, not a supporting player, and definitely not a villain. I am like the gorgeous romantic with a studied smile and a dreamy, wistful look in my eyes. More cunning than a villain with bourgeois perturbation in my nature, and like the hero in an Indian movie, I'm ready to spontaneously break out in song and dance.

The year I was born, 1939, *Gone With The Wind* (220 min., Technicolor) won the Oscar for Best Picture and Best Director, Victor Fleming, but most importantly, Hattie McDaniel was the first black actress to win an Academy Award for Supporting Actress. Although the Academy recognized, "regardless of creed, race, or color," a Negro, for her performance, Hattie McDaniel and her escort were seated at a table in the back, near the kitchen.

I was born on the first day of Ramzan, the ninth and most holy month of the Islamic calendar. I was promptly named Ramzan to honor the holy month. The first religious duty of a Muslim is to pray five times a day; the second is to fast for the entire month of Ramzan. From the moment at dawn, when a white thread can be distinguished from a black thread, until sunset, when it is again impossible to distinguish between them, a pious Muslim does not eat, drink or smoke. While fasting, he must also abstain from thinking of or engaging in carnal and other pleasures. It is a spiritual as well as a physical discipline.

Women are not required to fast during their feminine indisposition or when pregnant. My mother is a woman of faith. When not indisposed in her feminine way, she prays five times a day and fasts during the month of Ramzan. She believes the body's ebullition of its beastly nature hinders the perfection of the human spirit. The most effective way to attain perfection is to break the focus on the physical through hunger, thirst, and the renunciation of carnal desire: fasting brings solace and purifies the soul. She thinks that fasting brings one nearer to the Almighty since God neither eats nor drinks. Although nursing mothers are excused from fasting—they can make up the number of days defaulted at a later time—my mother fasted *and* nursed me. My mother is a woman of high spirit. My mother is a beautiful woman.

❦

I am always in love or I'm missing being in love.

Looking back, the first notion of love I remember was when I was fourteen. The object of my love was Tara, "the girl next door." I lived in a yellow brick building, Ali Manzil with large balconies, in Karachi on Mission Road. Palm, coconut, and fig trees grew along the sidewalk. Tara lived across the street in Raja Mansion, on the second floor, in an apartment with an iron grille balcony that was painted green and seemed to float atop a fig tree.

Tara was lovely and sixteen, sensuous and naughty, with the most tempting eyes. Tara was a senior at Cosmopolitan Girls High School. I was a freshman at CMS Christian Muslim School. This is how we communicated: our eyes searched one another's longingly, and occasionally I'd fling a love letter tied to a pebble towards her balcony.

Once and only once, on a hot summer afternoon, a Sunday when my family was away attending a wedding, I managed to communicate with Tara. She came to visit me in my room. Like children in Paradise, we played doctor, innocently and with great curiosity. The rule was to look and touch but do nothing else. I felt lucky. Lying beside me on a faded red-and-green cotton futon, she viewed my young brown nakedness intently and announced that it was not straight. Like the shy one at an orgy, I looked the other way as Tara

10

told me what she had observed.

I was well aware of the bend, at least six degrees, definitely less than ten, but after Tara's observation, I could not forget it. Every time I looked down, all I could see was the bend. My gym teacher, Mr. Khan, used to say that too much masturbation caused them to bend.

"All heroes have flaws; some obvious, some well hidden," I thought.

My affair with Tara ended when I made a wild throw. The pebble tied to my love letter went past Tara's balcony and into her father's room, breaking the window. Her family moved to Gulberg, a suburb of the city, soon after. I wonder if my handicap will cause me intimacy issues. Sex I can have with anyone I find attractive, but can I love and be loved by someone I find attractive, can I love and be loved with all my handicaps?

※

Living *is* love, I believe. I still live with my family in flat number two of a yellow brick building on Mission Road, two blocks from Dow Medical College in one direction and one block the other way from the Empire Cinema. Mission Road runs east-west, a large block of shops and buildings that stretches out from Mohammed Ali Jinnah Road to Lawrence Avenue, where you can catch a train to Gandhi Garden, the city zoo. Flat number two has a kitchen, a lavatory, and a large balcony. There are four rooms, all equal in size, laid out like squares on a chessboard. In one room sleep my mother and father on separate cots. In another room sleeps Yasmin, who is eighteen now and attends the women's college. The third room serves as the living room and my father's studio. My fourteen-year-old brother, Kamran, sleeps in the fourth room that also doubles as the dining room. I sleep in a six-by-eight-foot storage room between the kitchen and the bathroom. It has a small window that looks into the large indoor courtyard between our building and my best friend Kazi's, next door. I sleep on a faded red-and-green cotton futon that I roll up during the day and put under my desk by the window. I used to think I would die young, like my brother Rahman; he was eight when he died, and I was three.

11

It makes me sad to think how little I know about Rahman. It was raining the day he died. Or maybe it rained later. Uncle Aftab took me to the river—we lived in India then, in a city on the banks of the River Betwa. Uncle Aftab had always taken Rahman to the river—they'd go fishing—so I thought it was to be my turn at last. On that day it was cool; dark clouds covered the sky. I remember walking in the water till it was knee deep, holding Uncle Aftab's hand. I was happy. It was a long time ago, when for one paisa you could buy ice balls, hand shaved, on a bamboo stick, and flavored with sweet red, green, yellow, or orange syrup. You could really taste raspberry, banana, lemon, and orange, and for two *paisas* you could buy a large glass of cold sweet yogurt lassi.

The dark clouds began to drizzle. We waited under a large neem tree for it to stop. After a long, futile wait, Uncle Aftab took me home in the falling rain.

At home, all I can remember now is the heavy rain. The water cascaded down the stairs that led to an open terrace. I still feel sad and lonely when it rains, even when I have what I ask for and I am with the one I desire. Somehow something is always amiss on a rainy day.

My mother talks about Rahman a lot. She remembers him with tears rolling down her cheeks. Baba, on the other hand, never mentions his name. But one day, two months after Rahman's death, a custodian at the school where Baba taught brought him home on a tonga. He had fainted in the class he was teaching. Everyone said it was from grief.

ॐ

I was four years old when I had my first big disappointment. A friend of Baba, Uncle Sattar, came over one afternoon in a horse-driven carriage, a Victoria. The Victoria and its driver waited outside our front door while Uncle Sattar waltzed into our living room. Baba was taking a shower. Uncle Sattar was a professional hunter, who worked for Nawab of Bhopal and told tiger-hunting stories. A good hunter shoots and kills the tiger before it attacks the goat, used as the bait. Baba walked in, dressed in a blue-and-white striped shirt and beige gabardine pants. He smelled of perfume. When Baba and Uncle

12

Sattar walked out the door, I wanted to go along with them. I began to cry. Baba, who was almost always calm and giving, refused to show any patience, but Uncle Sattar finally gave in and told me to join them in the Victoria.

Amazed at my success, I perched on my knees, watching the wheel tracks disappear behind us in the dirt road through the rear window until we reached the Datia Gate where a tarred road began. Uncle Sattar told the driver to stop at a sweetmeat market and bought two pounds of my favorite sweets. I accepted the gift with stunned surprise. The carriage traveled another short distance to Nurya Gali. At the corner, under a neem tree was a *paanwalla's* stall. Along with paan, he sold bidis, cigarettes, and boxes of matches. From a tree branch hung a long length of rope that smoldered on the unfettered end to provide a quick light for the customer who bought individual bidis or cigarettes. Here the Victoria stopped again, and Baba and Uncle Sattar got out. Before I could react, Baba paid the carriage driver double the fare and asked him to take me back home. I sat, dumb with betrayal, clutching the bag of sweets in both hands, all the way to my home by the banks of River Betwa.

Later I learned that Baba and Uncle Sattar visited Akhtari, a floozy, troll, a *fille de joie,* a Delilah. Akhtari would sing and dance, and then Baba and Uncle Sattar would visit Akhtari's young cohorts in private chambers.

Not eating a single piece of those sweetmeats is my first regret; after that, the list goes on. Brown shadows, pink sunshine. Time passes and I come to the age when I no longer fear *jinns* and *bhoots*— shadows and phantoms—nor the elderly members of neighboring families. But I have dreams. I want to go to America. I want to study civil engineering and I want to build bridges. But most of all, I want love. I must have love. In the end I'll marry my love and live happily ever after, just like in a movie. I know I've already told the ending, but it's the song and dance—just like in an Indian movie—and the journey there that matter. And sometimes the irony of life is that one gets where one wants to go and then regrets it.

1956 is a schizoid year for the Oscars. Best Picture: *Around the World In 60 Days.* Best Director: George Stevens, *Giant.* Best Actor: Yul Bryner, *King and I.* Best Actress: Ingrid Bergman, *Anastasia.* Best

Supporting Actor: Anthony Quinn, *Lust for Life*, and Best Supporting Actress: Dorothy Malone, *Written on the Wind*. The Best Director did not direct the Best Picture, nor did the Best Actor and Actress star in it.

I am seventeen now. I guess I'm not going to die young after all. It's nice to think of dying young when you are young. It adds mystery to life. Instead of Indian movies, I now watch American movies. Lying in the storage room before falling asleep, I fantasize late into the night of sailing away to distant lands to seek knowledge, fame, and destiny. I look out my window and watch the coconut tree dance in the wind, shape-shifting in the moonlit breeze.

I wake up early every morning, hungry. I am an athlete, tall, slim, and lanky. I play cricket, and I'm good; in fact I am captain of my team. I'm an all rounder, someone who is a good bowler, batsman, and fielder. I am a fast bowler. A fast bowler runs a mile in frenzy to the bowling line, where he hesitates, swinging his arm up over his shoulder in one continuous motion, and releases the red ball. Then in his own momentum he keeps running toward the other wicket, where a man fully protected with pads and guards stands with a bat in his hand, ready to hit the ball any way he desires. I have a rather awkward delivery, but I think all fast bowlers do. And as I said I am very good. Last year, my junior year, in the High School Ruby Shield Tournament, I set a record for getting the most wickets and allowing the fewest runs: 101 wickets in 307.5 overs, allowing only 204 runs and scoring 302 runs.

When it comes to sports, I am excellent. I am now a senior, and as always, I am in love, I'm in love for real and for good, hopelessly. This time the object of my desires, my *arman*, is Leila. I am lucky in sports, but I think I am not lucky in love.

I remember the night the Imperial Cinema on Hospital Road caught fire. It was after the nine o'clock showing of *Aag*. Some kind of electrical problem, they reported. It was good that it started after everyone had gone home. From across the street, by the permanently overflowing public urinal, my sister and I watched as the theater burned down. Flames shot off the exit sign on the second-floor balcony. Yasmin cried and I comforted her. The Imperial reopened two years later, fully air-conditioned and renamed the Ritz Cinema.

14

CHAPTER 2

Karachi has four definite seasons: summer, when it's ninety degrees Fahrenheit with the ceiling fan running; fall, eighty-five degrees with intense humidity and the skies always threatening rain; winter, eighty degrees, with people running around in sweaters to insulate themselves from the Quetta winds; and spring, eighty-five degrees and dry and dusty. Every two hours during any season, like the disposition of the adored, the Karachi weather changes so that no matter what you are wearing, you're never dressed right.

On a warm day in early March after cricket practice at Fire Brigade Ground, I walk into the Rainbow Restaurant across from Ritz Cinema. With me is Kazi, the wicket keeper, which is like the catcher in baseball. He is vice captain of our team and my best friend. We order tea for two and four biscuits from Jacob's Bakery. I have so much on my mind that without wasting any time I ask Kazi, "I love falling in love, but how can I be sure that this time I am in love for real?"

"Love happens a hundred and one times," says Kazi, "and it's always real when it is happening. But in my view, what's more fun is *kama*, which is desire/love/pleasure/sex, all in one, the sensual gratification and enjoyment of love with all your senses: seeing, feeling, hearing, tasting, smelling, and touching, love in sync with your body and soul." With a wink, he adds. "It's *making* love that's full of pleasure, not *falling* in love." The waiter serves our tea and biscuits.

Pleasure and lust are different from the joy of love. I shake my head in disbelief.

"You don't touch the one you love, your true love, until you marry her." He looks at me curiously, like I have dropped an easy fly ball. I continue, "What would you know about making love anyway? But that's not even the issue. The problem is, I can't fall in love with Leila. She is of a different kind of people."

"All people are different," comments Kazi.

"Don't be a wise guy," I say, taking a sip of my tea. "I am talking real differences, people with different values and backgrounds. She lives in Civil Lines in a mansion. She is gorgeous, with glitzy confidence, looks book straight without wearing glasses and street

15

smart without looking tough, qualities that capture my imagination. We are people of different tribes. They are served tea at four by servants dressed in white, and they go around town in a chauffeur-driven car, and they speak English at home, and she goes to a men's college."

"You have no imagination and you need to find your soul mate," says Kazi with a smile dunking his biscuits in his tea. "Love has no boundaries. In America, Rockefellers marry their maids. You must fight barriers and rebel against unjust ways, unfair values." He looks me in the eyes and continues, "Or marry a woman of your parents' choice."

"She is two years older," I say, "already in her second year of college, on her way to medical school."

"We all need a mature woman in our life, a mother figure," he replies. "And it's nice to have a doctor in the family, they come pre-scented in antiseptic."

"Kazi," I snap, "you are not being helpful. This is serious. Why is it important to know that the one you love, loves you as well?"

"I don't know," says Kazi. "Why is it important? In America, they say, 'Love them and leave them.'"

"This is the situation," I say.

"Do I have to listen to stories of your loves and longings?" says Kazi, laughing.

"Yes, you do," I reply. I signal the waiter for more tea. "I am paying."

"In that case, what's the scoop?" asks Kazi, smiling with mock interest.

"My sister Yasmin met Leila at some intercollegiate event, and Leila came to our flat in her chauffeur-driven black Mercedes-Benz, and the moment I saw her, the moment our eyes met, I knew it. It is love at first sight. The cupid had pointed his arrow, she and I are now pierced by the same arrow. She is beautiful, like Kamni Koshal, and she smiles at me, like, you know, she likes me. She comes and visits Yasmin on Tuesdays in her car, and occasionally on Wednesdays on her ladies' bicycle . . ."

"Do I have to hear all these details, Rama?" asks Kazi.

"I know she is coming to see me as much as she is visiting

16

Yasmin. On the days I miss Leila's visits, Yasmin doesn't have to tell me that Leila has been there. She leaves all kinds of signs, like writing her name all over the newspaper—sports page, movie page, right over the front headlines, signed and posted, 'Leila was here.' Other times she'll forget a book, a scarf or her white handkerchief with a pink border. I know all this is for my benefit. 'Look, I was here and you missed me.' And when I stay home waiting, she doesn't show up for days, sometimes weeks."

"RPM, you are seeing too many Indian movies," says Kazi.

"I'm seeing more and more English movies now," I tell Kazi. "The other day I saw *Roman Holiday*, 118 minutes, black and white. Released in 1953, in America. Audrey Hepburn won Best Actress for it in March of 1954. It finally opened at Palace Cinema, in March 1957."

"Is *Roman Holiday* a stag movie?"

"I am serious," I insist. "I've looked in her class folder and learned her schedule. I've gone by her college, stood behind the mulberry bushes, and watched her leave in her car, and I know every Wednesday she rides her bicycle."

"Maybe it's time you come out from behind the bushes and jump in front of her bike."

"As a matter of fact, I've done exactly that, but all the while she remains perfectly casual and patronizing. She'll ask, 'So how is your cricket coming along?' As if cricket is a pet or book. On other days, when I'm dressed for a cricket match, she'll comment. 'These days it's becoming fashionable to dress in a cricketer's uniform'." I shake my head. "No, she couldn't love me."

"I think you're right," says Kazi.

"But when I stop running in front of her bike, she comes to visit Yasmin just to see me, and if I am not there, she leaves her mark. Last week she left a poetry book in my room, on my study table, with a bookmark at Walt Whitman's 'Are You the New Person Drawn Towards Me?' What shall I do now?"

"Have you tried talking to her?"

"Saying what?"

"Saying something like, 'There is an uneasiness in everything for me now. I wake up in the morning with certain anticipation, yet I am uncertain about everything. I think about you all the time, I spend sleepless nights without you, and it's you I love.'"

I shake my head.

Kazi continues, with an optimistic smile. "'In the quiet solitary evenings, I hold unending conversations with myself, saying *I said, you said.*'"

"Thank you, Kazi," I say. "You've been very helpful."

"Why don't you write her a letter if you can't say how you feel?"

"I've thought about it, but I'm afraid she might throw it back in my face, or show it to her mother, or my mother, and make me an object of laughter and shame."

"That can't be helped. No risk no game. But to protect you, I could write the letter expressing your sentiments," Kazi offers, like a good friend, "and if Leila makes your letter public, you could say you never wrote it."

"If my sentiments are being expressed, then I shall write the letter," I say seriously.

Kazi nods in agreement.

❧

The following day, dressed to kill in my cricket whites, my team's worsted wool blue blazer, a scarf around my neck, my hair greased and combed meticulously, hearing music in my head—Lata Mangeshkar singing, *aayega aayega* — I jump out of the bushes and in front of Leila's bike. "What a coincidence," I say. "I walk back from cricket practice at the same time you get done with your chemistry lab."

"What a coincidence, indeed" she says, smiling knowingly. I put my hand in my blazer pocket, feeling the envelope. She adjusts her books in the basket hanging from the bicycle handles.

Without losing a moment, I say, "There is something I have to tell you. I am madly in love with someone." Every day I read the serialized comic Tarzan in the *Daily Jang*. Sometimes I wish my life were as simple as his. Mr. Tarzan wakes up every morning pre-shaved. He has no final exams to worry about. He travels from tree to tree, and

18

each time the current branch reaches the limit of its arc, the next branch magically appears, or a convenient lion or elephant's back presents itself. His wardrobe is simple and perfect for all occasions, and when he needs to defend himself, his trusty knife will do. About the only thing I share with Tarzan is his habitual paralysis when his sweetheart appears.

"Would you care to tell me the name of your victim?" she asks, her dark brown eyes focused on me. I look at her: *How beautiful she is!* For a moment, I can't say anything. I deliberate, although I have rehearsed many a time what I was going to say.

Leila and I cross the street and enter Noor Jahan Garden. A cool breeze is blowing, and the scent of *raat ki rani* is in the air.

You are my Kamni Koshal, my raat ki rani, I am madly in love with you, I want to scream.

"I'll tell you her name," I say in a low voice, "if you promise not to tell anyone else or laugh at me."

"I don't like making promises," she says, looking away. "I can't say anything until I know the name."

"I've been watching this person for a long time now," I say, looking at her. I want to hold her in my arms. "She is a good friend of my sister."

"That limits the possibility to about half the girls at Women's College," she says with a smile.

"She doesn't go to Women's College," I say. "You know her the best."

"You'll have to tell me her name," says Leila, shaking her head. She no longer smiles. I want us to sit down on one of the park benches in a secluded corner, around the rose path. But she keeps moving, almost at a hurried pace.

Before I can say anything more, we are at the other end of the park. I hold the metal gate open so she can walk out with her bicycle. She is quiet. She does not look towards me. *I've confused her sufficiently,* I think. From my pocket I take out the blue envelope; inside, on a lighter shade of blue-ruled paper, with blue-black ink, I've written:

Dear Leila:

19

Thorns and flowers,
All is vanity,
I love you,
Do you love me?
Rama
Wednesday, March 15, 1957

1957 is the year *The Bridge on River Kwai* won the Oscar for Best Picture. Its director David Lean won Best Director, and its leading man Alec Guinness won Best Actor. Best Actress went to Joan Woodward for her performance in *Three Faces of Eve*—Judy Garland and Jean Simmons both passed on the role.

After due consideration, I sign my name. *What's the sense of writing a love letter and not signing your name?* I hand her the sealed envelope perfumed with Yasmin's Evening in Paris. A cool breeze blows in March, a car moves at high speed on Polo Ground Road. I want to flee.

Leila takes the envelope from my hand. She leans her bike against her waist, her hip slightly tilted. She holds the envelope, and with the precision of a surgeon slits it open gently, carefully, with the long nail of her index finger. I think of the first Indian movie I saw, called *Najma*. In one scene, the hero is called to save the husband of his beloved.

"Doctor," begs the heroine, "please save the life of the master of my house."

"Allah saves lives," replies the hero. "I am just a doctor."

Leila removes the folded blue sheet and holds it to her nose, as though it is a rosebud. "Evening in Paris," she announces. She unfolds it, reads it quietly to herself, her thin lips closed firmly. Then she folds it and puts it back in the envelope. She leans forward, opens her microbiology text with the red cover, puts it somewhere in the middle and snaps the covers back together. She looks up into my waiting eyes, smiles, gets on her bike, and moves away without saying a word, not even her usual "Ta, ta."

"What do you say?" I call out with anticipation.

"What are you asking?" she replies, stopping her bike. She

looks back with controlled indifference.

I walk towards her. "I am in a bit of a hurry," she says. "Papa has passes for a six o'clock showing of *From Here to Eternity.*" She gets on her bike again, but before she moves away, she ruffles my hair. *From Here to Eternity* was the Oscar winner for Best Picture in 1953. I want to let her know, but I say nothing. *She touched me! She loves me!* I shout to myself. I'm attracted to her like a man loves a woman, and I know that she is attracted to me like I am her man, but I need to contain that kind of attraction. Real men don't have sex with the woman they love, and plan to wed until they marry her. Someday we'll experience together that which will make us both one and whole. I know we are both looking at the same scene in the movie of our life.

I watch Leila ride across McLeod Road until she makes her turn toward Governor General Road.

I walk back through the park, elated. Red roses and white jasmine and huge snowy hibiscus bloom everywhere. Their fragrances mingle in a perfume so heady that I am stunned with intoxication. *She loves me!* I shout out loud. On impulse, I snatch up a full-blown rose and begin to pull off the petals, leaving a trail behind me like a character in a fairy tale. *She loves me,* I chant. *She loves me not.* By the time I walk out on the other side of the Noor Jehan Garden, I am more confused than ever.

⸭

Thursday after school I skip cricket practice, anticipating that Leila will come by our house to visit Yasmin. I am elated. I can't do anything. Afternoon turns into evening, but Leila does not show up. I feel miserably low, sad and lonely.

Friday, warm and windy, moist and salty air blows from the sea. I walk home from school in a hurry, hoping to find Leila's Mercedes parked under the neem tree in front of my apartment building. I sit in the living room reading an excerpt from Dutt Bharti's *Jalan* in *Shama* magazine. On the radio is *Apki Farmayesh,* a radio program where people request the songs they want to hear. Today I listen to the names more carefully, thinking I'll hear Leila ask for *Mujhe ho gya tum say pyar—*

I've Fallen in Love with You. No such luck. My situation is hopeless. I wait and I wait, lonely is life, long is my journey. Leila does not care for me—*she loves me, she loves me not*—everything is uncertain. Pretty Leila does not return.

On Sunday, during a match against Sindh Madrassah, I keep looking towards the pavilion to see if a black Mercedes has pulled in. Not that she has ever come to any of my games in the past, but I keep looking.

We win the game. In fact, I am the player of the match—six wickets for fifty-seven runs, I bat fifty-two runs not out. After the game, I tell Kazi about my letter to Leila and my dilemma that she didn't say that she loves me and hasn't come to visit me.

"Did you write your letter in English or Urdu?" he asks.

"In English, of course." I say, frustrated. "What does it have to do with the price of fritters in Belgium?"

"You write your English as well as your Japanese, maybe she can't understand what your message is."

"Very funny."

"Maybe you shouldn't return to the scene of the accident," Kazi advises.

CHAPTER 3

A week has gone by, and it's Wednesday again. I asked my teacher Mr. Noor-ul-Huq to excuse me from tutorial class on account of feeling sick, a stomachache. I don't have cricket practice in the afternoon. Do I go and visit Leila at her college? Or should I stay away? I wander in and out of Noor Jehan Garden, unable to decide if I want to go and run into Leila at the college gate at four thirty.

I am behind the mulberry bushes, waiting for Leila. I pace nervously, in the blowing wind, my moving lips rehearsing what I'm going to say. Promptly at four twenty she appears, dressed in her college uniform, sky blue *shalwar* and *kamiz* under a white lab coat, looking her usual self. She smiles at me. I feel hopeful. I want to hear the magic words.

"Do you have an answer for me?" I ask without preamble.

"One should be patient in love and war," she says with a detached calm. She keeps walking. We cross Burns Road dodging hordes of students on their bikes and so many chauffeur-driven cars. She acts as though everything is the same, like I never gave her the letter professing my love for her, she never read it, and all is normal. I should have stayed away from her today. Leila walks ahead through the park hurriedly, her bike wheel clicking. I follow. "So is it love or is it war?" I ask. I should never have said a thing. She says nothing. I have a sinking feeling.

It's a beautiful day, warm in the sun, cool in the shade, all the trees moving in unison. In a movie, it would be cold and raining. I wonder if she saw my photograph on Sunday in the sports page. *Rama loves Leila. Leila does not have to love Rama. I am not the hero. I am the other guy.* When we get to the other side of the park, without smelling the roses, she reaches into the basket on the handle bar of her bicycle. From her biochemistry book with a green cover she removes a rose-colored envelope. She hands it to me wordlessly, and pedaling away on her bicycle, she ruffles my hair, bids me, "Tata," and pokes the tip of my nose.

I feel no need to rush to open the envelope. It probably says, "Leave me alone, and get out of my life." I re-enter the park and sit on a metal bench, still warm in the setting sun. There is a waning breeze. I open the envelope carefully. On a sheet of pink paper, beautifully scripted and scented with *raat ki rani*, it says:

> *My love of loves, my beloved,*
> *What I think, words cannot say.*
> *What I feel, I cannot express.*
> *My pen doesn't have the strength to write the sensation I feel.*
> *My heart races eighty miles a minute,*
> *I perspire like it's 122 degrees in the month of July.*
> *You are all I think of, want, and ever desire.*
> *I adore you.*
> *Forever yours*

She has not signed her name. Did she write this letter or have a friend write it? Is an unsigned love letter even a letter? I am neither happy nor sad to be alive. Now what? *My love of loves, my Beloved. . .*

Spring is in the air, a beautiful day in April, cool and uplifting. Life is worth living, yet it's too early to start living happily ever after. This is just the opening act.

I should be happy now, I think, and for a brief moment, I am.

On Wednesdays, the slaughtering of fauna and fowl and sale of meat is prohibited, and meat dishes may not be sold in restaurants. I don't have cricket practice and Leila doesn't have to be picked up at the college gate by her chauffeur, so the meatless day in the city becomes our day to meet. Instead of meeting in front of the college gate, we decided to meet inside Noor Jehan Garden, on the other side of the rose bed by the wooden bench under the banyan tree.

Today, with a red-and-green Waterman fountain pen on a light-blue ruled sheet of paper with blue-black ink, I have written:

> *My Dear Leila:*
> *Now that you love me, I hardly know who I am or who I'll be tomorrow. But do you love me like I love you, is the question.*
>
> *Ever and forever, truly yours,*
> *Rama*
> *Wednesday, April 8, 1958*

I seal my note in a blue envelope and put it in my pocket. I arrive at the appointed place before the appointed time dressed in my blue cricket blazer with a scarf around my neck. I walk around like a hero in an Indian movie. I stop by a bed of roses. A large rosebud dangles over a sign erected on two wooden posts. On a black board with white lettering in English and Urdu, it says PLUCKING OF FLOWERS IS STRICTLY PROHIBITED. I think of a scene from an Indian movie: in black and white, our hero stands in a lush garden with blooming flowers, singing a sad song. In the gusts of heavy wind, the flower petals tumble and flow across the screen. When the song is finished, at final cadence, the garden is barren, and now our hero stands in front of a sign that reads "Plucking of flowers is strictly prohibited." I guess the wind cannot read.

I look around. A gardener kneels in the distance, pulling weeds. I pluck the rosebud carefully, without being seen. The art of stealing is in not getting caught. A young thorn, still green, pricks my index finger. I take my white handkerchief from my pocket, wrap it around the stem, and put the rosebud in the inside pocket of my blazer. I walk to our corner of the park, caressing the tender sting on my finger. I find Leila sitting on the bench, her bike leaning against the banyan tree.

She smiles at me. I sit down beside her. We gaze into each other's eyes. I don't know what to say. What do lovers talk about? But we are not lovers, we are merely in love—or at least I am. *That ought to help.* But I am lost in an Urdu movie and she in an English movie. I think, *If I were in an English movie like* Love is a Many Splendored Thing *or* From Here to Eternity, *it would be time to kiss her.* A passionate kiss, perhaps. We talk of our favorite movies; we don't agree. She likes comedies. I prefer drama. We talk favorite subjects; She likes chemistry and biology, I mathematics and physics.

"I really must be going. I have to get home before Papa arrives from the office."

"They are showing *Beju Bavra* at 10:00 a.m. on Sunday at the Regal Cinema," I say. "Maybe we could go?"

"Indian movies are such rubbish," she says. "They are all so predictable. They all have the same story—boy meets girl, they sing four happy songs, misunderstanding evolves, boy loses girl,

25

intermission. Afterward, four sad songs, misunderstanding resolves, boy marries girl. They live happily ever after. Indian movies steal scenes and copy stories from English movies. We don't see Indian movies."

Beju Bavra, *is the story of a real man, a musician in Emperor Akbar's court,* I want to inform her. Beju went mad when he lost his love; even his music couldn't comfort him. I know my movies, but to her I say nothing. The first English movie I ever saw was *Thief of Baghdad* (1940, 109 min., Technicolor). I liked it, but it was dubbed in Urdu. Even the song "I Want to Be a Sailor" was translated and sung in Urdu. My favorite was Abu, who said to the old King, "I am Abu the thief, son of Abu the thief, grandson of Abu the thief, with ten cents for the hunger that yawns day and night." The wise old king said, "This is the Land of Legend, where everything is possible when seen through the eyes of youth." I liked Abu, played by Sabu Dastagir, an Indian, a former stable boy at the court of a maharaja, but I wanted to be John Justin, the hero.

"Being the Chief of Police," Leila continues, "Papa gets all these passes to movies, and I love Sunday morning shows, but not this Sunday, perhaps another week. In the meantime, I'll have to think of an excuse regarding where I'll be, what I'll be doing, and with whom." I nod my head.

We smile at each other. She gets up and walks to her bicycle; I follow. Together we stroll toward the rose bed. She reads the posted sign, loud enough for me to hear, and smiles to herself.

"One of my favorite opening scenes in a movie was in *The Wind Cannot Read,*" she says. "It shows a lush garden in Technicolor— red, yellow, blue, pink, and white flowers surrounded by green leaves. There's a sign posted that says 'Plucking of flowers is strictly prohibited.' A heavy wind begins to blow, blowing all the flowers and leaves away, and then the title comes on the screen: *The Wind Cannot Read.*" The film is set in India and Burma, the story of an English flying officer, Dirk Bogarde, who falls in love with a Japanese language instructor, Yoko Tani.

I smile, sharing her amazement. *How did they open* Written on the Wind? I want to ask her. Outside the park, before she rides away, I take out the blue envelope and the handkerchief-wrapped rosebud from my blazer pocket and give them to her. She takes the letter from

26

me as if she's taking it from the mailman.

She smells the rosebud then casually puts it and the letter somewhere in the middle of a thick green-covered book. She rides away on her bike. I wait until she makes her turn. I walk back through the park toward home.

❧

On Monday when I return from cricket practice, I know that Leila has been there. In my room, I find my white handkerchief, washed, pressed, folded, and perfumed with *raat ki rani*. I pick up the *Merriam-Webster Dictionary* from the reading table, and from underneath the green rexene tablecloth, I pull out a pink envelope—a letter from Leila. What joy! A love letter straight from her heart:

> *My love of loves, My Beloved, My Very Own Rama,*
> *After reading your letter, I felt sad. I wished I was with you so I could have held you in my arms, put my head on your shoulder and cried my heart out.*
> *Dear heart, you don't know how I adore you. I long to see you even when I'm with you. I love to hear you talk. I am drawn to you. I wish I could sit across from you and look into your deep, dark, hypnotic eyes for the rest of my life.*
> *I miss not talking to you. I miss not listening to your voice and I miss not being able to look at you.*
> *You are a man and you are my man. Men are strong and capable of accomplishing what they want. I am frail and I am a weakling. I am Miss Nothing. I hope you'll try to know me and to understand me.*
> *Only yours,*

She didn't sign her name again, I notice. These love letters are certainly addressed to me but who is writing them, I wonder. I return the letter to the envelope. I take out a blue-and-gray Jacob's Biscuits tin from my desk drawer. Inside it, I place Leila's letter on top of her first letter.

I finish my trigonometry homework. I am fascinated by the mathematical ways to measure distances. By knowing one side and one

27

other angle of a right angle triangle, one can measure the distance from here to the moon. I look out my window into a moonless night. Like the dreams of an insomniac, sometimes you receive signals that are never sent. The palm tree in a grey night looks ghostly, shadow like. I think of our home by the river Betwa.

On Sunday mornings, Baba would wake me with kisses on my forehead and a rub of his unshaven beard on my cheeks. Before sunrise, Amaji, who prayed faithfully five times a day, would offer the morning *Fajr* prayers. Baba and I would set sail to our fish hunt. With his gun in its case on his shoulder, his hunting bag securely fastened to the rear carrier of his bicycle, his dark hair neatly combed back, dressed in a loose white shirt and trousers, Baba pedaled his bike uphill with me perched on the crossbar. We would arrive at the bank of the River Betwa as the sun rose.

Carefully, Baba parked the bike on its stand, removed his gun from its case and cleaned the single-barrel ball and muzzle-loader with a ramrod. Then he packed in black powder, a homemade lead bullet, and a scrap of rag. Standing at the edge of the river, I watched him aim at bubbles like pearls, ripples in the water. Baba cocked the gun, placed a cap on the nipple, aimed, and fired. What he did next seemed performed in slow motion, although it must have taken only seconds. He put the gun aside, laid his glasses carefully next to it, kicked off his moccasins, and jumped into the river.

In those moments when the river covered him, I always held my breath. Then suddenly, always in a spot I could not anticipate, he would burst from the water with a fish in his hand, the river streaming from his hair and clothes, his brown face shining in the morning sun. Baba was a sure shot. He thought there was nothing in life that couldn't be done or undone.

Afterwards, we would coast leisurely downhill—Baba smoothly peddling the bike, his cool wet white shirt flapping against my head—to Amaji's Sunday morning breakfast.

※

In 1947, at the partition of India, I was eight years old. We took a refugee boat from Bombay to Karachi. Baba had decided

28

against a train to Lahore, fearing the massacres on trains crossing the newly formed India/Pakistan border. Karachi, I was told, was a large city with streetlights and homes with running water. This didn't excite me. I loved the oil lamps on our gravel streets and the deep night shadows. I loved the walk around our house to the well under the *chronji* tree to fetch water.

On the day before our night of exodus, my mother and Yasmin packed our furniture and Baba's bicycle into a large bedroom and locked it. On her grindstone, Amaji ground spices for our last meal in that house and for the food that would sustain us on our trip. The salty rain of her tears mixed with the spices as she worked. She couldn't part with the stone. Baba wanted nothing to do with it. He kept telling her it was nothing but a slab of stone—there would be plenty of stones in Pakistan. When he walked away, she and Yasmin packed it in a large trunk along with our quilts.

That afternoon, I had walked out towards Datia Darwaza, to the big wall erected centuries ago to protect the city from invaders. In 1858, Lakshmi Bai, Rani of Jhansi, led her own armies in a cavalry charge against the British artillery. She died holding the reins of her horse in her teeth and wielding swords in both hands.

Walking one way then the other along the wall, talking to myself, I picked *bir bahuti*, tiny insects that looked as though they were made of red velvet, from under the green grass. I watched farmers plow fields on the other side of the wall. On summer days when the high wind blew heat and dust in the air, all the children of my village would run out of our homes. The gusty wind would blow ripe tamarind fruit to the ground like pennies from heaven. We'd fill our pockets with tamarind, and then rolling the front of our short-sleeved shirts into sacks, we'd collect all the rest as fast as we could. I'd run back home with my pockets full of sweet and sour tamarind fruit.

Walking back from the big wall, I saw my friend Kuldeep. I wanted to tell her we were leaving for Pakistan that night, but Baba's instructions were to tell no one. Besides, how could I say goodbye forever? Kuldeep and I walked to the *mandir* across the street from my house and played on the steps. Then Amaji called me, and I went home. Yasmin's friends, Zohra and Batool, were there. They all looked very happy; they were laughing.

When evening began to show, I left the house unnoticed and sat on the *mandir* steps. Roshan Lal, the light man, was cleaning the chimney of the street lamp. I watched as he filled it carefully with oil and lit it. He picked up his ladder and canister to leave, calling out, "See you tomorrow."

I'll not be here tomorrow, I wanted to shout; I said nothing. My mother called me for dinner, like she did every night. I was not hungry, but I ate. After dinner, Ramchand Cha-Cha, our next-door neighbor came to see Baba. Baba gave him the keys to our house and to the room where we stored our belongings. Again I left the house. With the dim light of the street lamp behind me, a lake of darkness lay between me, and the *mandir* steps. A flicker of light from an oil lamp was barely visible inside the *mandir,* and as long as I kept my eyes on it I was not afraid. *I will walk into the* mandir *and piss on the gods,* I told myself. I made my way slowly. With each step into the blackness that lay between the two points of light, my heartbeat grew louder, and beads of sweat blossomed on my face and neck. When I reached the steps I blinked, and in that instant lost sight of the light inside. The darkness was total. I ran home for the last time.

At midnight, two tongas arrived to take us to the train station. With her green embroidered shawl draped over her head and shoulders, Amaji looked graceful and dignified. Baba wore his felt hat, a tie and a beige silk suit. He always looked dignified. I sat in the back seat with Amaji and Yasmin. Baba sat in front with three-year-old Kamran. Our luggage was loaded in the other tonga. As we moved slowly away from our house, I gazed at the street lamp, then at the light coming from the *mandir.* Without warning the tongas turned by the big wall, and we were in total darkness.

There were no street lamps until Sepri Bazaar Road. Listening to the jingle-jingle of the bells on the trotting horses, I peered ahead into the distance. I heard the whisper of my mother's prayer and that comforted me. I thought of Rahman and wondered if, left behind, he would go to a different heaven than the rest of us. I saw only darkness. "There is only one heaven," Amaji said gently, touching my hair.

I was jolted by the brightness of the light at the Railway Station. JHANSI, ZERO MILES said a sign. "Jhansi is a junction," Baba said.

30

"Trains go in more than two directions from this station." *Which way were we going?* My cousin, Farooq, was at the station. He worked for the railway and had arranged for our tickets. I was glad to see him. He took us to the first-class waiting room. The bathroom had a flush toilet. *Where does it go after one flushes it?* I wondered. Baba's friend Sattar joined us with his two wives and their troupe. Uncle Sattar, a hunter for Nawab of Bhopal, had a license to carry a gun. He was carrying one now on his shoulder. Like other Muslims, Baba was forced to surrender his gun at partition.

Now I live in a large city by the sea. When the high wind blows, the only thing that falls from heaven is tumbleweed and yesterday's newspaper. I look out my window into a moonless night. Rainwater cascades down the open stairway leading to the terrace. I see myself pick a red *bir bahuti* from the green grass. A palm tree in a gray breeze outside the window changes shape. *I'll go to America and study engineering*, I remind myself. I'll learn to build bridges. *And then one day I'll marry Leila, and we'll live happily ever after.* But I feel empty, like something is amiss.

CHAPTER 4

When I arrive at the Palace Cinema for the 10:00 a.m. showing of *Love in the Afternoon* (1957, 126 min., bw), Leila is already there. She is dressed in a pink silk sari and a black satin blouse. Her dark hair combed back, her eyes lined with *kajal*, and red lipstick on her lips. She looks taller in high heels. This is first time I've seen her in civilian clothes, and she looks like she just walked off the screen of an Indian movie. She stands beneath a poster of coming attractions: *An Affair to Remember*. She smiles at me. All smiles are not the same. There is the smile of Buddha when he achieved nirvana, his head bowed, eyes downcast. And there is the smile of Mona Lisa—a smirk perhaps? Looking you directly in the eye, Leila, my Mona Lisa! In the background, from a radio somewhere in the distance, Lata Mangeshkar sings an appropriate song.

"I got the passes," announces Leila.

We are ushered to our seats in the grand dress circle, back row center. The grand dress circle is mostly empty; only the third and second-class sections look fully occupied. I'm not used to sitting on the velvet-cushioned seats in the dress circle. I usually sit up front in second or third class wooden bench seats. An Anglo-Indian couple sits two rows down. An usher closes a red velvet curtain under the exit sign as the lights dim and die. When they start showing the previews of coming attractions, Leila puts her hand down touching my knee. It was no accident. Despite the air conditioning, heat explodes through my body as though I've been touched with an electric current. Danger, high voltage! After a moment's hesitation, I cup my hand over hers. Her hand is warm. I caress her fingers; her palm is moist. I contemplate leading her hand to my manhood, but it doesn't seem right. Leila is my dream girl, the one I will marry one day, she has to be pure, someone who has not touched it or been touched by it. We hold hands all through the movie, all 126 minutes of it, until the lights come on again at the end. Then we act, as though we had not touched at all. Outside the theater, Leila says that this was the best movie she has seen so far this year.

I'm not sure it's the year's best. It was an ok movie, two stars:

slow, exhausting, a romantic sex comedy, way too long and totally miscast. I fell in love with Audrey Hepburn the moment I saw her in *Roman Holiday*. I also saw myself as the hero, and to me Gary Cooper is no Gregory Peck, but then Gregory turned down the role in *High Noon* (1952, 85 min., bw), which won Gary the Oscar for Best Actor. And *Love in the Afternoon* had a happy ending—I guess happy endings are possible. I want us to go for coffee at Café George, but Leila has told her mother she was seeing the movie with her girlfriend Jamila, and Leila was being picked up by her chauffeur, he will be here any second. Into my hands she pushes an envelope scented with *raat ki rani*; from my blazer pocket I hand her a blue envelope scented with Evening in Paris. I put Leila's letter inside my blazer, she tucks my letter into her black leather purse. Then without so much as a lingering parting glance, she walks away. I walk in the other direction.

Leila and I remain strangers. The distance between us remains the same as before we began to meet in private. Other than our school work, our favorite subjects, movies, and my cricket, we don't talk about much. We look at each other a lot and we always smile. She never utters the words "I love you." Neither do I. I like to look at red lips, but I don't like kissing lipstick. I have fallen in love with writing to her and reading her letters, more to the process than the person. It feels nice to be loved, and it is nice to be in love. When we talk, not once do our hands touch, and sitting next to each other on our bench in the park, our bodies never touch. Contact of any kind outside of the movies is strictly prohibited, and we act like movie handholding or any other sort of touch never really happens. I could never tell, not for sure, how she felt upon leaving me. "Its time to go," she'd announce with her wonderful smile, which appeared both happy and sad. She'd give me her parting glance, and she'd get up and leave.

I stroll pass Hotel Metropole. I gaze at the statue of Mahatma Gandhi in front of the chief court building. Except for the folds of his *dhoti*, it doesn't look like Gandhi. A couple dressed in traditional Goanese white cotton ride by in a Victoria holding hands. Christians are free to hold hands in public as well. A serene-looking old Parsi man crosses the street. I enter Noor Jehan Garden at McLeod Road Gate. It is past noon and the April sun is getting hot. I sit in our corner on my side of our bench. The breeze feels cool under the shade of the banyan tree. I take the pink envelope from my blazer pocket and read:

> *Dear Rama, my life's companion, source of my beautiful melodic memories . . . The other day you looked rather sad at our parting. Dear boy, you have to remember that there is always pleasure in pain, especially the pain of separation from one's love . . . missing and longing for one's love is necessary for love to grow.*
>
> *I have been observing you keenly for a while and I know you very well. I know you better than you would think. Look at me. Rama, I am talking to you. There is physical love . . . there are men, several of them, who focus on a poor woman, make her an object of their lustful desires, of their sadistic ways, their unnatural ways. They claim love, but it's not true love. It's narcissistic love, a temporary condition. It's deception; it is duping, and using others. I don't see you as that kind of man. I trust you completely and I always will. You don't have to worry about returning my letters, but we must be very careful, there seem to be too many eyes upon us.*
>
> *You shall tell me anything and everything that's on your mind, no formalities, no hesitations. If you avoid telling me what's on your mind, I'll know it and I'll feel that you don't love me enough, you don't trust me and are distancing me, and that you are being careful with me. People in love don't have secrets.*

Another letter from my anonymous admirer.

On my walk home after cricket practice, it begins to rain, a rain so light that if I watch my steps carefully I can walk between the raindrops without getting wet. Behind silver-gray clouds I can see the sun. A single cloud raining follows me home like a full moon. I love rain; it makes music, sings songs. The rain says nothing, it empties my mind, it echoes in my head. Rain or sunshine, I'm fine.

After dinner I sit in my room. Now it is raining hard. Water from the fourth-floor drainpipe drums the concrete floor of the back yard. Children, talking in loud voices and singing, take turns showering beneath it. They sound delighted, full of joy. There are few pleasures equal to walking barefoot on naked earth in the rain of a hot

34

summer day.

My mind wanders as evening draws down. Shadows begin to disappear. Now is today, and like an idiot at the gates of Paradise, I have already accounted for my tomorrow. Sitting on my study desk, I read Leila's letters again. I listen to the rain and write:

My Dear Leila:

I favor the underdog, and I always provide unnecessary details. I am going mad with joy. I am not sure if I am awake or living in fantasy, a dream land. Why does a rosebud always look at you so shyly?

This leads to what? Will our love today be our love tomorrow? Is forever here already, and if there is no never, then there is no ever either.

Are we not too young to be in love like this?

> *Yet leave me never, beloved.*
> *Never, I own, expected I*
> *that life would be fair.*
> *Do you love me like I love you?*
> *—Thomas Hardy*

Ever, truly yours,
Rama
Sunday, April 1958

CHAPTER 5

I receive through overseas airmail an application and other admission information from Indiana and Oklahoma State University. Sitting at the kitchen table, I eat my favorite meal, split pea lentils over rice and pickled mango. I eat with my fingers, sucking on the mango seed, and daydream about sailing on a steamship, and meeting beautiful American women, like in *An Affair to Remember* (1957, 114 min., Eastmancolor CinemaScope), in which an ex-night club singer, Deborah Kerr, falls in love with a rich bachelor, Cary Grant, aboard a luxury liner on a transatlantic voyage. During my voyage to the land of the Americas, I intend to have my own pink champagne slice of Hollywood romance, a CinemaScope shipboard romance, followed by a lot of fun and frolic until, brilliantly and effortlessly, I complete my education and return home to the woman I love, whom I shall marry and live with happily ever after.

Amaji brings me cold water. She sits beside me and fans me gently with a straw fan. *Something is not right in this picture,* I think. Everything seems too perfect: a devoted mother at home and a secret love in the park. After the death of Rahman, I have become the number one son by default. My mother, who is protective of all her children, has become even more protective of me. And my father, who never expected much before, now expects much more.

After dinner I go to my room to do my homework and labor over the essay questions for the college applications. Amaji brings me a cup of tea and seats herself beside me once again. She has a graceful, elegant face with a beauty mark above her lips. Her head is covered, as always, with a *dupatta*. She never wears makeup and her jewelry is simple: her wedding band, a gold stud in her left nostril, and six bangles on each wrist. My mother is the essence of modesty. Right now, she wears a faint expression of sorrow.

"I know you want to go to Amreeka to study," she says, "and I'll have to let you go, when it's time." She dabs at her wet cheeks with the end of her cotton *dupatta*. My mother cries easily. "I've lost Rahman," she continues, "That was God's will. But I worry that you'll get involved with one of those *goris* and never come back."

I feel a boundless love from my mother. She would do anything for me. I know I'll do anything for her. I'll obey all her wishes. I respond with an indulgent smile. I know my family thinks I fall in love easily and could therefore be taken in by beauty. The thought of meeting those lovely, pink-skinned women does excite me, though. *I may fool around a little,* I think, *but I'd never marry one.* "Don't worry," I laugh. "I won't marry a *gori.*" I take a sip of my tea. It is delicious sweet.

Assured, Amaji looks at me lovingly. Her smile casts a ray of warmth on me. "I'll leave you to your studies," she says. She kisses my hair and exits, closing the door softly behind her.

I focus on the overseas forms again and make notes for the essay question:

There are several reasons I would like to study engineering. Engineering is the study of applied science based on knowledge. A knowledge that is exact and specific: things work if calculated, designed, and built right. America is not only the land of opportunity it is at present the Mecca of technological advances and know-how. I'd like to learn to the best of my capacity, and I would like to study in the best possible school of learning, in order to one day return and help build bridges, build homes, serve my country, develop an underdeveloped homeland, and marry a woman of my mother's choosing. I've heard and seen a great deal of America through American movies I've seen and also the movies at United States Information Centre, and the journals I've read in the library . . . the land of freedom, equality and opportunity.

I love movies. I like American movies better than Indian movies. I also like reading short stories. Shafiq-ur-Rahman is my favorite Urdu writer. I also like Dutt Bharati and Qurat-ul-ain Hyder. I've not read many American novels, but I've heard of American writers like Hemingway, O'Hara and Allan Poe. I've read a few of Erle Stanley Gardner's Perry Mason mysteries. I love poetry and I've read Longfellow. "Mezzo Camino" is one of my favorite poems. Hopefully, half of my life is not gone yet, although I've let a few years slip away. But I still have aspirations and hopes of what I need to accomplish yet. I long to travel, to learn, to see, to explore, to experience. The prophet Mohammad, may peace be upon him,

37

has said: "Travel to China, if you need, in pursuit of knowledge." Although I don't consider myself a religious person, I'll travel to Timbuktu in pursuit of learning. I want to see this great land of yours—New York, Chicago, San Francisco, Los Angeles, and Hollywood. P.S. I am an excellent cricketer, but in America they play baseball. Maybe I should be applying to Oxford University, instead. Only kidding, like they say in America.

I look out the window. The color of the evening has changed into night. New stars beckon above the palm tree. I take Leila's letter from my desk drawer and read.

Dearer Than Life Rama,
Every word of your letter has left a permanent impression upon my heart. The thought of being with you tickles me to a silent smile.

Don't ever be unhappy. You must find the joys in your life and draw from them your reason to live. When I see you unhappy, it makes me sad. You must struggle, you should study hard, and when you study, be at peace with yourself and stay focused.

You must pass the matriculation exam in first division with distinction in every subject. I pray to Allah for your success and I wish you to accomplish all your higher goals. You say you'll have to work hard to get me. I've never thought of it that way, although there is some truth to what you say. You don't have to do anything to get me—I am already yours, but I am afraid of the expectations of others, the world around and what society requires. A word of caution: watch out for my cousin Yousuf. On the way home last week, I saw him by the Hotel Metropole. He said he had seen me walking around before, but hadn't said hello. I think he is up to something. I don't trust that man.

My love for you is real and is forever, but true love is one that is shared between lovers only. The wind blowing or the third person a heartbeat away should not know of it. Our love remains our secret, please know it, please keep it,

is my only request.
With all my hopes and all my wishes I remain,
never to forget you.

I write her back:

My Dear Leila:
    Shall I begin by asking if love is for once only? There is first
love, and no other. Does it stay? I never want this feeling to
cease, escape or slip away, but sometimes I get scared of my own
self. I feel like something is about to happen. There have been
too many peaks of late and no valleys. The bubble has to burst;
it can float above the sea of joy only so long.
    In any event,
Into my heart's treasury
Is the safe-kept memory
Of a lovely thing.
—*Sara Teasdale*
    I get sad only when I think that this will pass.
    Ever truly yours,
    Rama
    Wednesday, 13 May 1958

On a day that looks as though it belongs to the monsoons, with gray clouds hanging low and the air heavy with moisture, Leila sits next to me under the banyan tree in our corner of Noor Jehan Garden. I am dressed carefully, as always for our rendezvous, in my cricket whites, my team's blue blazer and an ascot around my neck. Also, I've allowed a few locks of hair to fall across my forehead. Leila wears her college uniform, a sky-blue *kameez* and *salwar*, under a white lab coat. Her eyes sparkle. She looks heroic and beautiful like a doctor in an emergency room, and I love this girl and she loves me and we love each other. At most I shake hands with her, but we feel good in each other's company, we could have long wonderful talks about love, intimacy, and long-term relationships. Our love is platonic, yet titillating, something could happen, but it will not.

My thoughts are jumbled up. I study hard, play good cricket, and swim and run every day. My chest and shoulders are muscular but trim, tidy and strong. I am no longer plain and lanky; I am tall and taut. Life is living. It is wonderful to be young. I ask her to sing me a song. What cannot be said in words is somehow easier to express in song. In fact, you can buy a movie songbook for two *annas* from the bookstalls outside movie theaters.

I half-expect that she'll be coy and protest that she doesn't know any songs from Urdu movies or can't carry a tune. She smiles into my eyes and pleads that she can't sing. I insist—in Indian movies, the hero and heroine always break into spontaneous duets after asking one another to sing. She walks to the banyan tree, and in a picturesque gesture, places her hand on a low branch. She sings:

> *Barsat may*
> *Hum say milay tum*
> *Tum say milay hum.*

She didn't do the chorus, "*Dhum, dhuma, dhum.*" I hoped Leila would sing a song of everlasting love and never parting from one another, but nevertheless, I'm pleased. She has a good voice; she carries a tune well. Standing under the banyan tree, now it is Leila's turn to insist and my turn to sing to her. Unlike Leila, though, I really can't carry a tune. That's why they have playback singers to overdub Indian movies. I tell her that I don't even sing in the shower. But she insists as she is supposed to, and I comply like I am expected to. Sitting on our bench I sing back to her:

> *Ye rataen*
> *Ye mausam*
> *Ye hasna, hasana*
> *Mujhe bhool ja na*
> *Inhen na bhulana*

She smiles at me and I walk to her as if in a trance, she puts her head on my shoulder, we embrace. I feel her warmth, my warmth, and certain stiffness. Up close, Leila smells just like her letters.

Someone is walking towards us. She abruptly steps away.

This must be the second song before intermission, I think. Two more happy songs and then comes the misunderstanding, confusion and parting.

We walk back to our bench. Once again she talks about how

lonely it is to be an only child. She always tells me how lonely it is to be the only child. I think she doesn't share much because she is used to being alone. She thinks that the parents of only children don't get along well and that's why they don't have more children. Both my parents are in good health, and if they wanted, they could have had other children. She is who she is because she is an only child. If she had a brother or sister, she wouldn't be the same person. She has a complex about it. She believes everyone thinks that she is spoiled and self-centered. I think there is some truth to the generalization—only children are sometimes spoiled brats. Although she whines and complains a lot, she always has a smile on her face, and I like her smile. It calms me. She acts tough on the surface, but I can tell she is fragile inside, someone who is hiding, ready to be found. We talk about our upcoming finals—her second-year science, my matriculation exam— and the Ruby Shield Tournament, which will occupy me through the next five or six weeks depending upon how far my team goes. Because we both need to pass our exams with high marks and distinctions, we agree not to see each other until finals are over. But we will continue to exchange letters. When Leila visits Yasmin, she'll leave her letters on my study table under the *Merriam Webster's Dictionary,* where my letter will already be waiting for her.

My high school, the Christian Muslim School, has not won a championship in eighteen years, but this year, during the Ruby Shield Cricket Tournament, CMS is unstoppable. It is June; we are in the semifinals, and to my amazement, I play with authority. I am having my day in the sun, my hour of glory. We are to play the championship game, and then, two weeks later, we will take our final examinations. *Too much to do and not enough time, but I must go on. I will not dwell on it,* I keep telling myself. I wake up full of energy at dawn. I jog three miles and study an hour and a half before leaving for school at 8 a.m. Life is good because I am in love and I am loved in return: in love, you give something and you get something back. The pleasure is double sided. I feel free. I can do no wrong. Everything falls into place magically, seamlessly, without any struggle. On the field, when I'm playing cricket my delivery is natural, my fastballs defy the laws of physics, my bouncers bounce, my cutters cut. I am deadly, un-hit-able. In the championship game, I break my own record from last year by taking thirteen wickets in two innings, allowing only seventy runs in forty-eight overs. When it comes to batting, I score sixty-six runs not out in the first inning and a half century in the second inning. I single handedly win the championship for CMS. I am immortal.

CHAPTER 6

Now that Leila and I aren't seeing each other, our letters have taken on a life of their own:

My Dear Leila:

Life may offer very little, our love may vanish like fading shadows, but I think there is light somewhere. I feel like I am a lucky guy, a hero in an Indian movie. I've experienced a certain joy. But thoughts of a happy ending I find unsettling.

Leila, dream within a dream; tell me how shall it end? What will become of us? What is my fate? What is our destiny? I am too happy not to believe that you'll always be with me, for me, yet I know that it cannot be. How shall I remember you, love? Love that is or love that was? If we go on living, they are both one and the same. I beg to differ and I beg to remain, to live in love, and/or without it.

Escape me?
Never
Beloved!
While I am I and you are you.
—Robert Browning

A scent of jasmine, the shadow of a mango tree on the unpaved alley, a yellow rose in the silver moonlight on the terrace, open eyes of a dead soldier, all that eludes us, all that is gone, moments of reflection that pass me by, the scent of perfume released from your pillow. Breathe softly, love, it dies easy.
Ever yours truly,
Rama
Tuesday, June 9, 1958

My Dear Rama,

I wish you much happiness forever. I've not written you in a few days. No reason, I just couldn't put my thoughts together the way I wanted them. I would begin to write and the words would just slip away. Other times I'd write the whole letter, but when I read it over, it would not reflect my true heart and so I'd tear it up. Once I did that, I would be more uncertain about where to start and what to say the next time. This has gone on for a while now. With this letter, though, I've decided that regardless of how I sound, I will not tear it up.

You have given me a photograph of yourself. How thoughtful, how kind you are! But a photograph is not you. I've been seeing your photograph in the paper—the Daily News, the Sunday Times. You took the trophy for best all-rounder! I am so proud of you and I let everyone at my college know who you are and who you are to me, my hero,

My fast bowler, I can't wait for examinations to end so we can meet again, have our movies and picnics and our simple secret pleasures—and we both know what they are.

Rama, you can be so mischievous at times. I love you for it. You keep me at my wits' end. You keep me guessing, you keep me alert. You keep me alive. You know how to strike lightning, thunder and rain on a tender heart.
Truly yours,

Dear Leila:
I would never want to see you sad, and I would never want to make you sad. I don't know how to say it. My mind is confused, the words slip away, and it is hard to explain. What shall I say now, and how shall I say it? Yes, I love you, and I shall always love you. The life of love is as long as you remember it. I'll never forget you. It's you I have found. It's me I have to discover. If I seem heartless, it is not I. It's my state of mind.

Meeting you is cause for joy, yet I remain mellow. I hear a soft, sad melody. Loneliness, the inner solitude of being, is like an illness, and I am afflicted with it. I am lonely by nature. I'm a solitary man and there is no cure for it. Why I am this way, why it is my fate to walk the lonely mile, I do not know. Yet now, since I've met you, I've stopped asking myself that question. Now I need nothing more, I can walk that lonely mile. After meeting you, I can live in my solitary only-ness.
Well, thou art happy, and I feel
That I should thus be happy too.
—George Gordon Byron
And I am ever truly yours,
Rama

Sunday, June 21, 1958

My Darling, My Hero, My Dear Rama, My Man:
    It's only been a short while since I've seen you, but it seems like an eternity. I want to see you so badly. I wish I had wings so I could fly to you, but I am helpless and my situation hopeless. I'll have to live through this examination to see you.
    Reading and rereading your letters over and over again keeps me alive. The other day in our compound, on a tamarind tree I carved a heart and put your name in it, with a Cupid's arrow. I was going to put my name under yours, but I got scared. I carved "Rama, I love you" on my heart instead.
    The way you express yourself, magniloquent. The way you stand, tall, the way you move, smooth, the way you talk, charming, the way you are, magnificent, the way you look at me, unforgettable — do not change, never—ever.
I desire you like the moth seeks the flame, my wanting you is like madness.
    Every time you turn away to leave me, my heart skips a beat. I wish I could hold onto your hand and keep you.
    Yours and only yours,

On a sweltering July day following final exams, I walk briskly towards the Rex Cinema. Dressed in a white shirt and loose white trousers with a letter in my pocket, I am eager to see Leila. I like getting there before she does, so I arrive ten minutes early. Leila is already waiting for me, dressed in a white silk sari with a rose blouse. She looks cool on this hot day.

"Something terrible has happened," she announces, without wasting a moment. "Follow me." She walks ahead. "I'll tell you everything."

I walk behind her silently. I have arrived at the movie theater ready to walk into air-conditioned coolness. The heat is suddenly unbearable. Leila leads me to Cafe George. We sit across from each other at a table in a family room. When our waiter arrives, Leila orders tea and pastry. Before I can even open my mouth, she signals me not to say anything. After our waiter serves us and closes the green-and-brown plaid curtain behind him, Leila begins.

45

"Your letters have been discovered by my mother," she says without showing any emotion. "My mother forbids me to see you, or else she will show the letters to my father." She gives the appearance of a shiver. "My Papa, the chief of police, is overly protective. I'm Daddy's girl, his only child. I am afraid if Papa finds out that I've been writing you love letters, he will deny the existence of me."

I eat two pieces of almond and vanilla pastry to keep myself from talking. I drink three cups of hot tea, one after another, hoping to find solace. "It's just like an Indian movie," I tell her finally. "This is the intermission." I smile as Leila cries into her tea. "After intermission, all the misunderstandings will be resolved and the boy will get the girl."

Leila catches her breath, another tear rolls down her check. She takes out a small folded pink handkerchief from her purse. I smile again. We look at each other, not knowing when we shall meet again. *Something was bound to happen,* I think, *except maybe it happened a little too soon.* There should have been at least two more happy songs before the intermission. What does the script call for now? What do I say to a lover in parting? In the movies, the men gather courage and perform noble deeds.

"Don't worry about a thing," I say, reaching for her hand. "I'll take all the blame, all the heat. Tell your mother whatever will keep you out of trouble."

"I'll be all right, I hope you have destroyed all of my letters," she says, looking down. "I'll find a way to contact you. Through a friend maybe—I'll let you know. I'll find a go-between."

We say good-bye without a hug, a kiss, a handshake, or even a token caress. Leila hands me one last pink envelope, and we part in separate directions. The blue envelope in my pocket remains where it was. It is too late to give it to her.

For a while I wander aimlessly from Elphinstone Street to Frere Road. There I turn left and walk to the rear entrance of Noor Jehan Garden. This is not the dawn of the day I've been waiting for. I sit alone on our bench. Under the shade of the banyan tree on this hot sunny afternoon, I open the pink envelope.

Dear Rama,

Longing of my life, I've so much to say. I do not know

how to anticipate what's coming, how I'll survive the promises I've made. I love you today and I'll love you always, this distance is temporary, this parting will end. I am your Shereen and you are my Farhad. You are my Romeo and I'm your Juliet. If the ending must be a sad one, I'll die rather than live without you. I love you forever.

I am enclosing a photograph of me with this letter; my hair is not right and my eyes look too far into the distance, but this is the only recent picture, taken for my medical college application.

Now I am sitting in my room, alone, my heart in sync with yours. I put my head on your breast, feeling your heartbeat. Dear love, never forget me!

After you finish reading this letter, please tear it up. It may be difficult, but please do it right now. Our love is our secret.

A thousand kisses! I am waiting. I am waiting! When will you come to claim me?

Yours forever,
Sincerely,
Leila

At last she signed her name! I am happy. This is my moment of joy. I press my lips to her signature. I take my black leather wallet from the hip pocket of my trousers and put Leila's photograph under a clear plastic window. I look at it for a moment, then put the wallet back in my pocket. I read her letter again. I take out the letter to Leila from my pocket, the one I did not give her. I read:

Leila, Dear Love,

Something tells me that I'll never win, yet stay with me another day.

In secret we met,
In silence I grieve
That thy heart could forget,
Thy spirit deceives.
If I should see thee
After long years,
How should I greet thee?
With silence and tears.
—Lord Byron

47

Yours forever,
Sincerely,
Rama
Thursday, July 23, 1958

I put my letter on top of Leila's and tear them in half, in fourths, in eighths, in sixteenths. I walk toward home on Mission Road, tearing the pieces into smaller and smaller bits. When I can't tear them any smaller, I roll the pink and blue pieces of paper into tiny balls and, one at a time, I throw them as far as I can into the summer wind. Tiny paper balls scatter like bad wishes into the heat and dust.

CHAPTER 7

The matriculation results are announced; roll numbers of the passing candidates are printed in the local morning newspaper. I pass in the first division with distinction in mathematics, physics and chemistry.

In the same paper, on the back page under the rural news, there is the report of a drowning. The details are sketchy. The article is brief. Kazi Karim has drowned in the River Indus in Sukkur. No body was recovered.

"This can't be true," whispers my mother, drying her tears. No one wants to believe it, but I know it is true. I dreamed of Kazi last night. In my dream, Kazi and I are at Paradise Point Beach in Karachi. It is a hot day. Sun, sea and sand blend in a golden mist at the end of the horizon. Kazi is dressed in a loose white shirt and white pants. His feet are bare. We walk and walk on the wet sand, dodging the approaching tide. When we are ankle-deep, a deep red sunset blazes and I can't go any further. I say to Kazi, "I'll die if I take another step."

"All deaths are by drowning," Kazi says. "Your lungs get full of fluids, your breath gets shallower and shallower, and you drown." He walks into the water toward the sunset. When he is waist deep, he dives into the oncoming tide. As the tide passes, he emerges above the crest and waves at me one last time. Then Kazi swims smoothly away from me. I see a halo of radiance around his head against the setting sun. I did not wake up from this dream; I didn't remember it until just now, reading the newspaper.

The last time I saw Kazi was after our final examinations, before he left for Sukkur to visit his grandparents. It was Tuesday, a hot, sunny day in July with a dusty wind blowing south toward the ocean. We sat in the Rainbow Restaurant, drinking hot tea and smoking Stork brand cigarettes. The ceiling fan churned the hot air and swirled our smoke, blowing it every which way. Kazi thought all college-bound men should smoke—it added character, like the way Humphrey Bogart smoked in *Casablanca*. I don't enjoy smoking; I can't inhale. He said it wasn't any fun smoking alone, so I kept puffing along without inhaling. Kazi sat there, big, tall and muscular, built like

49

a wicket keeper, one of the best, a prospect for the national team. He had told me we would win the Ruby Shield this year and we did.

"You don't go through a long, dark tunnel when you die," said Kazi, taking a drag, looking bright and intelligent. There were happy shouts from the other patrons in the restaurant.

"In fact," he continued, "you go nowhere."

I took a puff of my Stork and blew it out immediately. "Until you die," I said, "you can't say. No one knows what death is like."

"I know," said Kazi. "I've experienced it. It's a wonderful feeling. Actually, you don't lose anything when you die. You remain alert, fully conscious." He inhaled again before continuing. "The bad part of dying is that you no longer fall asleep and consequently no longer dream."

When Kazi talked that way, which he frequently did, I just let him go on. I thought he did it because he was a poet.

"Other than that minor drawback, things go on as usual. You can smell, you can touch, and you can have sex, you can copulate only with the deceased, but you can mind fuck only the living."

"Kazi," I said, "you are getting ridiculous. These cigarettes are going to your head."

"No," he said, "for that effect, you need to smoke *ganja*." I said nothing. He continued, "Let me tell you. The other day I was floating—levitating would be a better word for it. It was late and dark. I needed rest, to lay my head down. But when you are dead, you can no longer close your eyes. It's one of the first things the living people do, after you die. They close your eyes. But when you're dead, you can still see even with your eyes closed. And you can still hear laughter and the morning breeze still feels good. Death is like a dark, dark night that never ends and you are surrounded by ghosts. I need to dream on, but I can no longer close my eyes." Kazi looked at me, his eyes wide open, his dark brown face smiling.

"Kazi," I snapped, "death is painful for those who are left behind. You scare me when you talk like this."

"From the day of our birth, we learn to die. We learn to leave. We are leaving to find the void from where no one returns"

"Death is what comes at the end of time," I said.

"Death is for certain. How and when is a matter of details,

everyone expects it, and we all accept it as a way of life. Like a good Muslim, I acknowledge every day that today could be the last day of my life. One needs to make peace with oneself before it happens."

"Puff, I am an old man now," I said. "I am gone."

"The simplest thing in life is to lie down and die," he said.

"You are playing with words."

"So what?" he said. "Those gone and departed, they are like gods. They are present everywhere."

"Enough," I said. "Go write a poem or two and stop your madness." I paid for our tea, and we walked out of the Rainbow Restaurant. Heat and dust blew in the wind. We walked on Mission Road, making summer plans. I insisted that, like myself, he should consider going to America so we could study abroad together. He wanted to study Persian literature and play test cricket. We arrived at Aziz Manzil, Kazi's apartment building.

"Puff, I'm an old man now," said Kazi. "I am gone." He walked away from me toward the front gate.

"We'll meet again," I said, turning towards my flat.

Now I look at Kazi's roll number in the newspaper. Just like me, he has passed his high school examination in the first division with distinctions in English, Urdu, and Persian. He will never know. But I believe he'd say, the deceased know all, see all. Maybe Kazi knows. I don't. And I don't care. I just want Kazi back, alive and living next door.

Part of me had drowned with Kazi. The part of me that is Kazi will never be again. I had passed away with my friend. Why are our joys always filled with sadness? The deeper the sorrow, the more abundant, more rapturous is our joy. A thing of beauty is reason for jubilance. I weep with delight. I weep for Kazi. Death demands letting go. Kazi will always be with me. Without Kazi, I'll never watch another Indian movie again.

I see Kazi everywhere: his dark eyes and hair, broad cheekbones, wide forehead, full lips smiling, laughing, sardonic and sad. A chill has fallen over my heart that is never going to go away. Yet even with death, the drama of life goes on. Leila's mother visits our family this afternoon. She arrives in her brand-new chauffeur-driven black 1958 Bentley. She congratulates my mother on my successful completion of high school. I think she is here on a mission of peace. I think Leila must have something to do with her mother's visit. Maybe Leila has convinced her mother that I am her man that our two families should be friends now—maybe there is a future for Leila and me. Maybe Leila and I can become engaged—maybe we will all see each other socially in order to get to know one another. We are going to be a single family one day.

Mrs. Khan Bahadur, a plump woman in a red silk sari embroidered with golden thread and a matching red satin blouse, sits on a large stuffed chair in the drawing room, drinking tea with milk and sugar. After tea and biscuits from Jacob's Bakery, she asks me to leave so that she can talk to my mother alone. Yasmin looks at me from where she sits next to Amaji on the couch, and smiles. She gestures with her eyes, telling me to leave. I wonder if she is thinking what I am thinking. How close sorrow and joy can be.

I walk into the next room, sit down on a dining chair, and listen to their conversation through the partially open door like I do the Friday night drama performance of *Dekhta Chala Gaya* on the radio.

"These are the letters your son has been writing to my daughter Leila," says Mrs. Khan Bahadur in a loud angry voice. "My daughter has nothing to do with Rama or the letters he wrote to her."

I can see her sitting straight up in her stuffed chair. She bristles with righteous anger and talks with fury, rolling her eyes, her hands and head move suddenly and dramatically. "People should marry sensibly. A nawab's daughter should not marry a gardener's son. Leila and Rama, are not a match. We are we and you are you and our differences will only magnify with time." Mrs. Khan Bahadur sounded bitter with an unforgiving coldness. She must be living a miserable life. A content person would not talk this way.

"My husband, Khan Bahadur Sahib will never consider a match such as this for his daughter, his only child."

My mother cries easily and early every time there is an argument, confrontation or feud. She is sobbing already. She says nothing.

"Mrs. Khan Bahadur," I hear Yasmin's fury, "maybe the fire is burning on both sides."

52

"*Array,* Schoolgirl" says Mrs. Khan Bahadur. "An affluent young woman is not going to be happy as the wife of a poor boy, no matter how madly she may have loved him in the beginning."

It is my fault. Don't blame it on Cain. Blame it on me.

"Mrs. Khan Bahadur," says Yasmin. "You are you but we are we, and proud of being who we are. My brother is a young man of high caliber. He is going to America to study Aeronautical Engineering. When he returns, he will be somebody. Any girl will be lucky to marry him, even Leila."

I see Mrs. Khan Bahadur getting out of her stuffed chair. "In the future, I forbid Rama to write or try to contact my Leila, or else there will be consequences."

"That scares me," says Yasmin sarcastically. "Your husband is the chief of police, who loves to exploit and abuse the power of his position."

Without bidding adieu, Mrs. Khan Bahadur hastens off our flat.

Intermission, I hear in my head.

CHAPTER 8

July gets hot and time passes slowly. Even on a sunny day, everything looks grey. I shed many a tear, I have too much time on hand and little to do. Awake or asleep, I'm in agony; anguish, emotional torment. I think of Leila constantly. I guess we were not meant to be. Kazi is a different story: I just can't understand his death nor can I accept it. Yes Rahman died young, but he got sick. I guess we will never have a cure for accidental death. I miss Kazi. I keep thinking that this is all a mistake, a nightmare I'll wake up from soon. At the end of summer Kazi will return home and Leila and I will be the best of friends again. In the meantime, I read poetry to find peace and solace:

Why shall I ask the wise, "What is my beginning?"
I am troubled by the thought, "What will be my ending?"

Disparage him? No. Expect it not from me,
Am I not aware, Iqbal, of my own errant ways?

I'll not cry for peace or harmony, if I could see what I long for,
Among the houris of heaven I should but find your face.

Nothing but death can cure, Asad, the sorrow of this life,
A taper shall burn, regardless, till the dawn.

I also write poetry:

Solitary summer evenings
and thoughts of you,
My heart and mind are fully occupied
by you and only you
No thoughts or feelings for anyone
But you.
In the green of spring
I endure,
Barren weeds of loneliness.

Still housed in the solitary desolation
New leaves sprout
On mango trees

From my window of despair
It is hard to see tomorrow.

I know that my poetry is not only foolish. It is also idiotic. Still, I needed to express my feelings.

Life is no longer colorful. There is no longer any music, not even sad songs. Misery and anguish are the norm. I even dream in black and white. I'm eighteen now, the perfect time to fall into cosmic melancholy. I have lost my best friend and my love has vanished.

My head knows that Kazi is gone forever. The summer my brother Rahman died, I remember catching a butterfly and putting it in a clear glass inkpot, then burying it alive in the back yard. I know what happens when someone dies: you never see that person again. They never grow older. I'll never again play or have a conversation with Kazi. He has disappeared into the fifth dimension.

Leila has promised to contact me, to find a go-between. I wait. I know I will see Leila again. We will probably grow old together. But then maybe we are not meant to be. Although I don't hear from Leila, I hear about her: she is learning to dance, she is learning to play the sitar. She is learning to paint. I am well informed about her. It is Leila this, Leila that. Maybe she misses me a lot, waits for my letters. I write to Leila in the sand at the beach; I write to Leila on the morning mist clinging to a windowpane. I write to Leila in the blank of my mind. I write her name by breaking rose petals one at a time.

※

I walk out of my flat toward the Rex Cinema. A hot, sunny summer afternoon turns cloudy and cool, into a gray rainy day that fills the heart with loneliness even if you are not alone. People walk in a hurry under the green trees. I walk along my old familiar path with measured steps, with a sinking feeling in the moist heavy breeze, sorrow filled my eyes. There is not one place I can go that does not hold memories of Kazi or Leila. It's hard to live in the void of their absence.

By the time I reach Chandni Chock, the sky is pitch black, a thunderous monsoon rain begins to fall. I could have taken a bus at Mohammed Ali Jinnah Road, but the rain feels good. As a little boy, I took showers in the summer rains, standing under the water draining from the open terrace. Those innocent pleasures of childhood!

Soaking wet from head to toe, I arrive at Rex Cinema. I am cold. I buy a ticket for third class, nine *annas*. I sit down just as the lights go off and the curtains are drawn on the exit doors. Previews of coming attractions start. I love movie trailers. That is how I decide which movie to see next. Maybe the combination of being wet and cold and sitting in an air-conditioned room will give me a deadly chill. The thought of being ill is charming. Leila will hear of it and be saddened. When the main feature *Love Is a Many-Splendored Thing* (1955, 102min., Deluxe) starts, I forget all my worries. Movies are my salvation. Just as every life has a story, every life is a movie. Look at my life: love and misunderstanding, the death of a best friend.

I am on the island of love with William Holden and Jennifer Jones. I would rather live in a movie. The movie, set in Hong Kong, Jennifer Jones, a Eurasian doctor, meets and falls in love with William Holden, a war correspondent during the Korean War. Life, both on and off the screen, remains sentimental, melodramatic. The movie has a sad ending. The Oscar wining title song, "Love is a Many Splendored Thing," keeps playing in my ear after the lights go back on.

It is still raining when I leave the theater. The annual average rainfall in Karachi is only about four inches, but today I don't have to read the weather report in the newspaper, I can tell all records have been broken. The sky seems to have collapsed, weeping in grief. The familiar street has begun to look like a river. The sidewalks have disappeared. Crossing Elphinstone Street, I am stunned to see Leila in her car going the other way. I wave and wave at her, but she doesn't see me. Her car was moving slowly. I could have run after her and knocked on the window, but I let her go. At least in this downpour no one can tell that I'm crying. I pass the Governor General's house. The yellow stone building looks massive in the grey rain. Guards with guns stand at the gate under a green canopy. By the time I reach McLeod

56

Road, the water is up to my knees, and my shoes feel like soft velvet. Automobiles stall with water rising past their hubcaps. I think of walking to Leila's house and stand in front of her doorway and sing out, *"Tere dowaray khara ik jogi . . ."*

I laugh at the thought.

This chapter is over. Our story is at a standstill, our love in the doldrums. My life is like luggage on an airport carousel, going round and round, waiting for someone to pick it up. I shout, "Leila, Leila, Leila," into the rain. The watery twilight turns into dark night, and I feel cold. This is a good sign. I am bound to get sick now. Perhaps I'll catch pneumonia. Will I see Kazi when I die?

CHAPTER 9

If you don't die in your sleep, you wake up the following morning, and whatever gets you through, gets you through. The next morning, I do not wake up sick, only sad. I learn from Yasmin that Leila has been sent away to King Edward Medical College in Lahore.

I also learn that going to America is not going to be as easy as I thought. To get admission I'll need to fill out more forms. A paper trail has begun—transcripts, mark sheets, affidavits, letters of recommendation, financial guarantees, medical exams, visas, on and on; a process that may take a year or longer.

After realizing the difficulties involved, I register at Muslim Science College in Karachi. Time passes slowly, but it passes. I go to classes every day. I try out for the cricket team. Not only do I make the team, I get picked as vice captain, an honor rarely bestowed upon freshmen.

Since Kazi's death, I've stopped going to Indian movies. Thanks to Leila, I now see English language movies, mostly American: Columbia, Twentieth Century Fox, Paramount, MGM, and an occasional British, J. Arthur Rank. Instead of longing for Kamni Koshal and Madhubala, I pine for Audrey Hepburn and Marilyn Monroe. I, who once admired Dilip Kumar as the world's best actor and thought I looked a lot like Dev Anand, now think Marlon Brando is the greatest leading man. And, of course, I look a bit like Gregory Peck.

I write letters to Leila at King Edward Medical College, telling her the same things over and again: *I miss you, I am lonely without you, I love you,* and *I long to hear from you.* Every day I go to the mailbox in the student's activity room at my college. Letters to students are posted in a glass enclosure. There is never a letter for me, no news from Leila.

I'm a good student, I study hard, even though it is difficult to concentrate and stay focused. I play cricket and I go to every movie that opens at the Plaza, Paradise, Capital, Rex, and Palace, where they show new and old English movies. In Karachi, an English movie is never too old to be shown again and again. For that matter, the first opening of an English movie is always one to three years after its American premiere. Movie advertisement pages of both the Daily Dawn, the English paper, and the Daily Jang, the Urdu paper, will have seductive ads showing women in skimpy bikinis, men and women kissing passionately. Other than young students like myself, most of the patrons in Third Class are the local camel and donkey cart, or rickshaw, and taxi drivers, who do not understand English but come to see what some call nudity, women in skimpy swim suits and on the screen lip to lip kissing, an activity that perhaps a lot of men do not practice even in the privacy of their bedrooms. I see *The Black Shield of Falsworth* (US, 1954, 99 min., Technicolor CinemaScope), *The Bridge on the River Kwai* (GB, 1957, 161 min., Technicolor CinemaScope), *The Defiant Ones* (US, 1958, 96 min., bw), *Trapeze* (US, 1956, 105 min., Deluxe CinemaScope), *The Harder They Fall* (US, 1956, 109 min., bw) *The Sun Also Rises* (US, 1957, 129 min., Eastmancolor CinemaScope), *The Sweet Smell of Success* (US, 1957, 96 min., bw) and many more. Movies are my deliverance, my other world, escape in time.

It is difficult for me to watch Humphrey Bogart—*Sabrina, The Barefoot Contessa, The Left Hand of God*—who is a good actor but an unlikely movie star, not a hero, an antihero, and what a name Bogart, his real name. Then there is Clark Gable—*Gone With the Wind, The King and Four Queens, Teacher's Pet*—with his big ears like an ape's. It is difficult for me to see him play the leading man. To me, a hero has to look like a hero, like Dilip Kumar, Dev Anand, Montgomery Clift, James Dean. Montgomery Clift—*A Place in the Sun, From Here to Eternity, Raintree County*—is the introspective, sad-faced, troubled hero, a great, gifted actor. I like him a lot, but my all time favorite is Gregory Peck, *Designing Woman, The Big Country,* and *The Man in the Gray Flannel Suit*. I see all of Mr. Peck's films.

And there are leading ladies like the sensuous, sloe-eyed Ava Gardner of *The Barefoot Contessa, Bhowani Junction,* and *The Little Hut*. And Rita Hayworth—*Fire Down Below, Pal Joey, Separate Tables*—is a love goddess, oozes sexuality, and has fabulous legs. I read in the local paper that the Seventh Division Medical Corps voted Marilyn Monroe the sex goddess they would most like to examine. I agree; I'd love to observe every centimeter of her. She wiggles and pouts through

The Seven Year Itch, Some Like It Hot, and *Niagara.* Her husky voice and breathless sensuality drive me wild, but Audrey Hepburn is the one I love; she is my favorite. She has a quality of wounded vulnerability that I would slay entire armies to defend. And because of Miss Audrey and Mr. Peck, and their memorable performances, *Roman Holiday* is my all time favorite movie.

※

After Kazi's death and Leila's departure I don't befriend my new teammates or class fellows. I live a life of seclusion, and being alone, a recluse, suits me fine. With all the movies to distract me from my sorrows, there remains haziness, a nightmarish quality to this terrible summer. I wake up in the hot nights shaking with chills. I dream of being a prisoner subjected to torture with electric wires attached to my ear lobes, nipples, and big toes. The wires send shock waves that jolt my body, and I convulse with involuntary spasms, gasping for my last breath. I want to wake up from the nightmare, but I can't, because it is my life. I am awake. I take Leila's letters from my desk drawer and read every one of them again. If there is no love, there is no love lost. She never signed her name. I don't have to be this naive about love. If you love somebody you let the person know. What makes you think she loves you? Her letters are like those post cards, all the proper emotions expressed, printed in black and white, packaged with an envelope. All you need to do is sign, address, and put it in the mail, except she forgot to sign her name. I feel unloved. I put her letters inside an old black woolen sock, rubber band its length and width, and place it in an empty Jacob's Biscuits tin. I tie the box into a blue cotton handkerchief and put it back in the drawer.

Memories play games with me. Sometimes I do not know what is remembrance, what is real. I lie on the floor on my faded futon, watching a full moon rise above the palm tree. I am not happy or sad, just awake. I feel numb; some might call it peace. "*Que sera, sera,*" Doris Day sings in *The Man Who Knew Too Much* and also in my head. Ghosts of the past flit in the shadows, telling me all is well. Seasons of my life blend in time, but sleep does not come. I get up from my futon.

60

It is late. Everyone is asleep. I quietly let myself out into the courtyard. In the left corner, I sit down on a concrete block by the hand pump next to a eight-by-ten dirt plot where the burnisher arranges a fire in the dirt to silver plate all the copper pots and pans. There is also a wooden post with the proper hook for hanging the sacrificial lamb for *Eid al Adha*. The lamb is slaughtered, the trachea slit, after the proper prayers are said. And while the lamb convulses, the butcher pours a can of cool water over its throat. The diluted red blood gushes and cascades down the concrete platform into an open sewer. When life ceases, the butcher ties its hind legs together, hangs it on the hook, and skins it. The wooden post stands there like a cross.

The full yellow moon is already setting. The top floor of Raja Mansion is covered with moonlight. A ray of moonbeam enters the compound from between Eliza House and Patel Building. I sit in that ray of light; the rest of the courtyard is dark. A few lights go on and off randomly, people waking up to relieve themselves, get a drink of water, comfort a restless child.

It was here in this courtyard that Kazi and I learned to play cricket. Even now, despite the darkness, I can see the outline of a wicket drawn on the back wall of the garage. There we would practice with a tennis ball for hours. After that Kazi and I would take turns at the water pump, drinking thirstily with cupped hands. From a certain angle, I can see the slanting moon. I imagine the days ahead, life abroad. *The yellow moon shines brightly,* I think, *there is still tomorrow.* I feel a surprising joy.

During spring vacation, our college cricket team travels to Lahore to play a series of friendly matches against Punjab University. I take a train along with my teammates. We play two days of cricket—a match against Punjab Commerce College, which we win. Batting fourth, I score seventy-six runs and take four wickets, allowing only forty-eight runs. My photograph, a head shot showing me in my cricket cap, is on the sports page of the *Pakistan Times*. S. A. Subari, the sportswriter, writes that Ramzan Pervez Malik's fastball ranges from 92 to 96 miles/hour. In the photograph, my dark eyes, looking into the distance, look darker, shaded by my cap.

61

The third day, a free day, no game is scheduled. Dressed in my cricket off-whites and my Muslim Science College green blazer with a crescent and star, the college emblem, embroidered in silver on the top left pocket, I walk to King Edward Medical College under a canopy of lined trees. I talk to myself, going over what I'll tell the principal, how I am here to see my cousin.

I think of a scene in an Indian movie, *Jugnu*, where Dilip Kumar goes to meet his girlfriend at her college. With a mustache, beard and dark glasses, he disguises as her uncle. When the girlfriend comes to the principal's office, she doesn't recognize her boyfriend and tells the principal he is not her uncle. I whistle to calm my nerves.

Upon my arrival at the principal's office, I see a peon in a khaki uniform sitting on a wooden stool next to a bamboo-curtained door, smoking a *bidi*. "I am here to visit my cousin, Leila Khan," I say with confidence. He draws long and deep on his *bidi* and holds his breath, then exhales a long stream of smoke. Without a word, he rises from his stool and throws his *bidi* into a large clay ashtray filled with sand, which sits by the door under a sign that says USE ME. He squashes it and walks into the principal's office. He returns moments later and shows me in. Furtively I wipe my right hand on my trouser leg, anticipating a formal handshake.

Behind a massive desk, a middle-aged man with a grey mustache sits in an oversize office chair reading some Journal of Internal Medicine. The ceiling fan reflects on his balding head. M. M. MEHBOOB, M.B.B.S., F.R.C.S. reads the nameplate on his desk. He does not shake my hand and in one impatient breath demands, "Who are you? Why are you here? What do you want?" I notice that he smells pungent, like cotton dipped in ether. I am nervous beyond words, and my mouth is dry. I quickly tell Dr. Mehboob that I am in town on an official cricket tour and would like to visit with my cousin, Leila Khan, a first-year student.

Dr. Mehboob takes off his reading glasses. From his table he picks up another pair of glasses and puts them on. He appraises me silently. Finally he gestures at one of the chairs in front of the desk. He changes his glasses again and takes a Parker fountain pen out of his pocket. He writes on a pad in a quick, continuous motion, like he's writing out a prescription.

When he's finished, he presses a bell on the desktop. The peon appears in the doorway. All in one motion, Dr. Mehboob gives him the note and signals me to wait outside his office.

Outside the office once more, I watch the peon walk down a long corridor. I sit down on his stool and look in one direction then the other. A cool wind blows on this partially sunny day. I smell success and am pretty happy with my performance. I love spring, everything comes alive, I feel glad. Of all the times of day, evening is my favorite though it is the loneliest for me.

Suddenly Leila is standing in front of me. I jump off the stool, smiling and adjusting my blazer. Leila looks most beautiful, as always. I smile again. I can't believe she is here before me after all this time, and it is not a dream or my imagination. I want to touch her, hold her in my arms, and caress her hair. Instead, I say, "Hello, Leila."

She says nothing, not a word. The peon resumes his place on the stool and lights another *bidi*. Leila smiles and nods, she leads me away through a long marble veranda. Bright sun filters through the latticed balcony. We walk down six steps to a garden. Here everything is in bloom, spring has sprung, and man's fancy is love. If this situation were a movie, it would be shot on this set. This is the moment where hero and heroine sing a joyous duet of reunion.

We stop under a fruiting persimmon tree. I look at her, the woman of my dreams standing there like Madhubala in the movie *Mahal*, ready to disappear at any moment. I feel like a stranger, unsure of what to say or where to start. I wonder if she knows Kazi is dead.

"You should not have come," she says, coldly, looking away from me. "This could cause trouble, scandal." She takes a few steps back from the tree, stopping in front of a lattice fence covered with red roses. At last she smiles. "I saw your photograph in the paper," she says. "I wondered if my Rama was going to come and see me."

She thinks of me.

"And did you read the caption under the photograph, 'Come back home, all is forgiven'?" I ask playfully.

There is a pause. She says nothing.

"Do you ever think of our days in Karachi?"

"All the time," she says, "What took you so long?"

I could tell she was mocking me, but I could not tell if it was out of love or because she no longer loves me.

"For some reason, I often wonder about Cary Grant's aunt in *An Affair to Remember*, the aunt that Cary and Deborah Kerr visited somewhere in Italy." I look at her. "Do you remember? When they got off that cruise ship, Deborah Kerr admired the aunt's brocade shawl. And then when the aunt dies, she leaves Deborah the shawl—you know who I'm talking about?"

"Rama," she says with pretend impatience, "I don't know how your mind works, how you find time for these unnecessary details!"

In Indian movies young loves are either flirting in all moments or are being annoyed with each other's idiosyncrasies, lovingly reprimanding the peculiarities of the one they love. "I saw *Suddenly Last Summer*. Great cast, Katherine Hepburn, Elizabeth Taylor, Montgomery Clift," I say, trying to make small talk. "Strange, decadent and ridiculous, but I liked it."

"I've not seen any movies, I don't have time. I am much too busy with in-patient, out-patient," she says. "There is the clinic, grand rounds, operating theater, anesthesiology and pathology, and there is emergency room and morgue duty. I don't know when it is day or when it is night. I never have time to think of anything."

"I am leaving, going to America this summer," I tell her. "All my paperwork is complete. I expect to get an I-20 and my visa soon."

"That's wonderful," responds Leila without any emotion. "I am happy for you."

Why should we be apart? I want our lives to be together, carefree and easy, like Sunday morning. *Say something, Leila. I've been waiting to hear from you, I am yours. I am here.* This is the moment of tenderness. Now she will look into my eyes with love. She will put her head on my shoulder and we will embrace. Leila just stares at me.

"There is something I'd like to tell you," she says, combing my hair back away from my forehead.

"Yes?" I say, eager. I am smiling again. It is so nice to be next to Leila. There is so much to say. "Maybe we will meet for dinner," I suggest. "In Lahore, we are free like birds in the wild."

"Your timing could not have been any more off," she says shaking her head. "Tomorrow morning I leave for Karachi for four

64

days, spring vacation, and I have to work in the emergency room tonight. She pauses, fidgets with the tube on the stethoscope hanging down from her neck. "I don't know where to begin this," says Leila, moving away. I look at her. She looks down. She pauses again and there is hesitation. "I had fun writing those letters to you. Maybe I got carried away. It didn't seem wrong at the time, and it was such fun." She sighs before continuing hurriedly, "Oh, at the time I felt tenderly towards you, and I liked you, but love, we are too young to be truly in love or know what love is. Now, it is all in the past, and what little love that may have been there has faded like a watermark."

It feels like somebody has stabbed me in the heart. "That's all you felt? Tenderly?" I ask. "You can't mean this. A watermark is always there; it never disappears."

"I am sorry," says Leila, looking into my eyes for the first time. "I didn't mean to cause you pain. At the time I thought we were all having fun and I thought we both knew it was a game. And now you are on your way to America and it is time to call it quits, we need to move on," she says, putting her hands into her lab coat pockets. "You'll forget me when you go to America."

Leila's eyes are waiting. I say nothing. She is not sure because I'm not sure. I tell myself.

"There is no where to move on to, I love you more than anyone else in the world."

"Maybe you love me more than I love you," she says, looking down. "I know you are unhappy, so am I. I care for you and it breaks my heart to hurt you. Having someone like you is a source of comfort, but I think it is time to move on."

"So this is the intermission," I say.

"No, Rama, Mr. Movie Hero," she says. "This movie is over. The end. *Fin.*"

I look at her, stunned. "You are mocking me," I say. "You are doing a great job, an academy award performance." The sun flashes momentarily between clouds. Leila turns from me, walks away, and like her shadow, I follow.

"Are you not going to wish me a happy life or something?" I call out.

She stops next to a bush, roses blooming with blood-red

65

flowers and thick thorns. She glances back at me then looks away again.

"I am going to the States," I repeat. "I'll study hard, I'll make something of myself. I'll be somebody worthy of you." I talk like a hero, my chest puffed up like a pompous rooster. "When I come back, we'll live happily ever after."

"In America you will meet blue eyed blondes, your own Doris Day! We are on the threshold of the theater. The drama is about to begin,"

"I think it natural for you to share your worries and concerns. I am most grateful. There is no other woman for me but you." What she is saying is very simple. The pain of breaking up now will be less intense. We are young, we can go and do as we both please and start all over again. She is in a coed school with 60% boys; she is beautiful, and I'm sure she already has plenty of suitors. She has seen too many American movies where boys and girls go out on dates and in the name of *getting to know each other,* do everything. Yes, I may fool around a bit if the situation presents itself, who would not? But Leila is the girl I shall marry.

"So, what do you care to do about it?" She asks. "I think our romance should be over now."

"There is no thinking, and there is no *should* in love. Love is all feeling and wanting and love is all that matters to me. We shall wait and stay committed. In six more years, I'll still be twenty-four. What's the big rush?"

"I'll be twenty-six, and that is exactly my point."

"Which is?"

"I care enough for you to let you go."

"But do you care enough for me to stay committed?" I ask.

"If it will make you happy, we can remain in touch, you can write to me at my dormitory address."

"So, will you wait for me?" I ask directly.

"Do you want me to wait for you?"

"With all my heart! Don't you want to wait for me?" I ask.

"Yes, I do. I will."

She looks deep in my eyes and smiles, a wonderful smile and I am taken again. "Already, I cannot stand the pain of our separation," I tell her. The sun dodges back behind the clouds. Her shadow no longer follows Leila. I stand in place, watching Leila walk around to the other side of the lattice-fenced wall. I know I will visit this scene again, a premonition of things to come.

I walk slowly in a sad rain back to my hotel, the Zum Zum. Lahore, the city of Badshahi Masjid and Shalimar Gardens, claims to be the city of love, beauty, and friendly sunshine. The city was not kind to Noor Jehan, a queen, the wife of Mughal king Jahanger, who lies buried here in obscurity. Noor Jehan, the light of the world, wrote poetry during the last years of her life, while living in solitary confinement:

> *On the grave of poor me, there is*
> *no lit lamp and no freshly cut flowers,*
> *There is no moth to burn its*
> *wings and no mockingbird to sing a song.*

The city of Lahore has not been kind to me either. It continues to rain for three days; heavy thunderstorms with dark clouds that pour relentlessly. The rain will not cease. Our second cricket game never gets played. On my last night in Lahore, a puppy tied in someone's back yard yelps all night in the falling rain.

Lying in my room beside a dust-covered intercom that doesn't work, I listen to *Where Things Are Wild And Crazy,* a weekly drama series on the radio. In this episode our hero's father has a dream of becoming a doctor, but the responsibility of taking care of his widowed mother and two younger siblings keeps him from becoming one. To fulfill his dream, Aurangzeb insists that his son, Jamil, our hero, become a doctor. But our hero has his own dream: he wants to be an architect. No one will listen to Jamil. His mother is busy making bread; his sister is too busy talking to her friends on the telephone. Jamil is extremely lonely. In the meantime, in an aside, he finally declares his love to his sister's best friend, whom he has loved and worshipped quietly from a distance for over a year. He tells her how much he adores her, but the woman of his dreams tells him that while she appreciates the thought and will always be his friend, she is engaged to marry someone else. And yes, she loves him; this drama is to be continued next week.

I feel like I did not allow Leila to be herself. She was building up the courage to break up with me and I made her think and feel that she would eventually regret leaving the one person who loved her. This is a lopsided relationship. With time she will grow distant and I'll only become more needy. In the end, she may not even feel sorry for me. Does she really not love me like I love her? Does she? Does she not?

CHAPTER 10

I find good news awaiting me upon my arrival home. Oklahoma State University in Stillwater has not only accepted me to study civil engineering, they've given me a scholarship.

Conflicted with a heavy heart, I see my life like I am watching a movie in Technicolor and CinemaScope. Sometimes life is a big error, a major mistake, a full-time errand, an assignment, a mission, and you pay a price to survive it. I know that five or six years are too long to wait to see the one you love. I already miss Leila. At least now I can communicate with her from America. I have her address, and she is willing to wait for me. I'll see Leila again. I feel like I have two strikes against me, but I proceed like a good cricketer. I play each ball like it is the first ball that has been bowled to me.

I wake up early every morning. I lay in my bed with my eyes wide open in the darkness, drained of energy, wondering if there is any meaning to life. I gather my energy, and before the muezzin calls out *Salat is better than sleep*, I'm already out of bed. I'm jogging, my daily three-mile run. I walk like a man. I jog like a man. I jounce, rock, joggle, I shake and press, prod and shove, I nudge forward. With every step, I repeat over and again, like a yogi's mantra, "I am going to leave it all behind—I am going to go away." In the loneliness of a long-distance run, I tell myself, this may be my time to live in anguish but one day all will be well.

When I'm done with my jog, despite my sadness, despite my inner gloom, I am uplifted with a euphoric glow. Sweating from head to toe, I walk back to my flat in my white T-shirt, white shorts, and white canvas shoes from the Big Bata Store. I can see things before they happen. I'm at peace, body and soul in rhythm, comfortable with myself. I'm ready to face another day. The warm summer morning breeze feels good against my wet skin and life seems worth living. I daydream of things and places I've never seen before, meeting new people and having conversations in a language I do not yet speak, romancing women with blue eyes and golden hair, meeting my own Marilyn Monroe. I can't be in the Garden of Eden and not taste the forbidden fruit.

A week before my departure, after getting my visa, I go in a rickshaw with Baba to the American Express office on McLeod Road to pick up my ticket and traveler's checks. No one is A-One and no one is perfect except Almighty God. Baba does not ride rickshaws—he doesn't like the idea of a human pulling other human—but there is no direct bus to where we are going, and hiring a Victoria would cost more than three times the rickshaw. Rickshaw drivers grow old fast. It is a literally exhausting job.

I don't like riding a rickshaw either—I think it's inhuman. Our rickshaw driver, a middle-aged man with graying hair, pedals his three-wheeler efficiently, weaving in and out of traffic. He moves away from the buses and trucks cutting into his path, wiping his forehead with the tail end of his *lungi*. Today though, my mind is on my own journey ahead—from Karachi to Liverpool on *RMS Circassia*, then Liverpool to London for two days on my own, and then from Southampton to New York City on the *Queen Mary*, the world's second-largest ship. From New York, I will proceed to Stillwater, Oklahoma, on Greyhound and Trailways buses. I am dreaming again. The world out there is mine to see, to experience, to enjoy. Life still could be wonderful.

Baba is a man of few words, industrious and proud, a person with courage. He shows little emotion. Baba is proud that on an art master's meager salary he has been able to provide—*beg* or *borrow* are his words—for his son's wishes. Pride does a man good! He is proud that his son has been accepted to study civil engineering at an esteemed American University on a scholarship. Baba is a kind man. He never makes me carry his baggage, his burden. He lets me be, he lays few expectations. He gives unconditionally.

My mother has cried every day since I've gotten my tickets. She is heartbroken. I hate leaving her. My favorite memory of my mother is her sitting in the kitchen beside her wood-burning clay stove on a cool morning, preparing breakfast. There is an art to cooking on this stove. One must maintain a certain degree of heat by adjusting the burning wood, adding the next piece at just the right moment, neither too early nor too late, and at the same time rolling the dough flat, greasing the pan, and frying the *paratha* to the proper crispness without making it crunchy. My mother is an expert, an excellent cook.

I sit on the low kitchen cot now, across from my mother. She sits next to her stove. As she rolls the dough with a red-handled rolling pin, she says, "I have this feeling that once you leave for America, I'll never see you again."

"That cannot be," I protest.

"It shouldn't be," she says in a low voice, "but I know you are romantic and fanciful, and you have imagination. I fear you will meet a woman and never come back to live here."

"Amaji," I protest, "how can you say such a thing?"

"I don't know why I have such a fear," she says, pausing to carefully put perfectly round bread onto the skillet, "but I am afraid I do. One can never be sure of anything. It's all written, one's fate is in the stars." She speaks as though she is talking to herself. Then, to me, "One day I'd like to choose a woman to be your wife. A good-looking girl who can cook and clean, love and care for you and your children. Someone you can communicate with and someone who will understand you, a partner with similar values and background."

Without a word, I get up from the cot and walk to my room. I open my desk drawer, take out the Jacob's biscuit tin, and remove Leila's letters, leaving the open tin behind on my desk. I go back to my mother. She is frying a *paratha* and crying, wiping her eyes with the cotton shawl. Finally she serves me fresh bread with a dab of *alu chana*. I hand her the packet of letters. She looks at them for a moment. "I know about these," she says. "The day your matriculation results were announced, Yasmin discovered them while cleaning your desk. She read them and told me what they said. I told her that she should not have read them." Handing me the letters back, she says, "I asked her to put them back where she found them. I don't need to read them."

Wiping more tears, Amaji says, "You should save them. The day you return from America, everything will be different."

I want to believe her, but I know it is not going to be simple. It doesn't come easy. Amaji takes another ball of dough, dusts it with flour and puts it on a flat grey rolling stone. She rolls out another *paratha* quickly and efficiently and fries it in a spoonful of Dalda. I sit there eating my breakfast, breaking my bread into small morsels and neatly scooping up the right amount of *alu chana* with a pinch of mango pickle. I eat in small bites and watch my mother cook and weep. I want to comfort her, ease the pain of our separation. It is customary for parents to arrange marriage for a son before he leaves home to study abroad, especially England or America. I say, "Amaji, you know, I'd like to marry Leila. If you want, you can choose her as my bride one day."

My mother's heart is generous, soul kind, I've always known that. She dabs at her tears. "Your happiness is my pleasure. If Leila is your pick, I'll choose her as well," she says softly. "When the time is right, I'll arrange your wedding."

"If all goes according to plan," I tell her, "I'll graduate from college in four years. I'd like to work for about two years, and in six years, when I return, I'll bring you an electric stove with a baking oven, and a washing machine to do the laundry, and an automobile for Baba." She says nothing. This serves only to make her cry harder.

When we lived in the city by the River Betwa, my mother combed her long dark hair after her bath with a small palm-sized wooden comb. It had teeth on both sides, one side more finely spaced than the other. After she was done, she'd remove the long strands of hair carefully from each side of the comb, loop them around two fingers, and tie them off. Then she'd spit on the loop and bury it in the indoor courtyard. Likewise, when she cut her nails, she'd collect the crescent tips, tie them in an old rag, and bury them in the dirt. We've come a long way from that city by the River Betwa.

"Just think of it as the exile of Lord Rama," I say, "the trials and tribulations of a prince living in a hermitage!"

"But Rama had Sita to come home to," she says.

I will be sad to leave, but sitting in front of the burning fire I feel a certain excitement, a sense of freedom about going away and leaving it all behind. And I still have Leila to come home to.

CHAPTER 11

On a bright sunny day in August, a chauffeur-driven blue 1958 Chevrolet Caprice arrives at Ali Manzil. The car is ours for the day, courtesy of Doctor Zain-ul-Abidin, a former pupil of Baba's, who studied at Boston University and brought the brand-new Caprice back with him upon his return two years ago. I sit in the back seat by the window next to my mother and Yasmin. My brother Kamran sits in the front seat between the driver and Baba.

I look out the window. Everyone I know on Mission Road is out in the street to wave goodbye. Leaving home by River Betwa, my first home, has made me brave. I've learned to leave; Kazi and Rahman's deaths have taught me how to lose and continue living, and living away from Leila has trained me to carry on. Dressed in my green Muslim Science College blazer, I wave back like I am already gone, a man who was never there. My photograph has already appeared in the Daily Jang, on the front page of the Sunday supplement. The caption reads, "Mr. Ramzan Perviz Malik, leaving on Thursday, August 5, on *RMS Circassia*, to study Civil Engineering at Oklahoma State University, on scholarship."

Sitting beside me, Amaji weeps silently. I always forget that she has a mole, a beauty mark, on her chin. With a tear rolling down her cheek, she quietly begins to recite *suras* from the Quran to ward off demons and for my safe journey.

We enter the yellow stone seaport building at the west wharf. A hot day in August, a bright sun radiating heat. Our car stops. A horde of coolies attacks with offers of assistance. Baba picks a young, muscular Pathan to carry my two pieces of luggage—a medium-sized metal trunk, grayish silver, and a smaller leather suitcase. When no one was watching, I had packed the Jacob's biscuit tin with Leila's letters in the leather suitcase.

Baba had printed my name on both pieces of luggage with white oil paint. I'm carrying a blue canvas handbag over my shoulder. Baba carries a fruit basket. Kamran carries a quilt with red, blue and white flowers on a yellow background, which Amaji made for me to help me cope with American winters.

73

We are engulfed in a tide of people moving in every direction. With coolies bearing mountains of suitcases over their heads; vendors offering bananas, apples, oranges, papayas, sugar cane, watermelon, and cantaloupe. *Samosas, dalmoth, pan, bidis,* and cigarettes are all on sale. Beggars assail us from all directions. Other vendors are selling combs, sandals, bags, and purses. We hear announcements for shoe shining, ear cleaning, letter writing, and fortune-telling services. Who would want his ears cleaned at this hour and at this place? I need to have my ears plugged. I guess I'd consider having my ears cleaned if I were waiting for my ship to arrive.

There are trucks, buses, taxis, rickshaws, horse carriages, donkey carts, camel carts, and human carts. High cranes move luggage on and off the ships. The *RMS Circassia* stands dazzlingly black and white in the bright sun. A white flag with a red anchor waves high and low in the hot wind that blows towards the sea. On a neighboring wharf, the *RMS Caledonia* is docked eastbound.

A navy band dressed in white uniforms plays "God Save the Queen" and then *"Pak Sar Zameen,"* national anthems to honor a British dignitary arriving from Colombo.

We walk up to a stepladder, the contraption that connects the land to the ship. *Why are ships called* she? I wonder. *Is it because the ship desires only the brave and so sneers at the man whose heart is faint? Or is it because, like a woman, she requires paint to look pretty?* I suppose its nerves that make me think such thoughts at a time like this.

Before I board, Kamran says, "Have fun."

"Don't get into trouble," Yasmin says.

Baba gives me his Quran and tells me to read it for peace of mind. Amaji says nothing. I hold her in my arms and kiss her on the cheek, tasting the salt of her tears. I know she is hurting. She has never recovered from the death of Rahman. She just stands there, sobbing, tears pouring forth uncontrollably as she tries to smile but can't. If there were a reason not to go away, it would be her. In a whisper, she recites *Sura Ta'ha*, a chapter in the Quran, "Know that I have chosen you, and therefore listen to what should be revealed." She blesses me. She ties a white *imam-zamen* containing three silver *rupees* and seven *annas* to my arm. At the end of my safe journey, according to tradition, I am to remove the coins and give them to the poor and

74

needy. I cannot tell her that in America there are few poor, and Pakistani money will be worthless. She does not stop crying.

I walk away from my family to board *RMS Circassia*, the ship that claims to have shops, lounges, dining rooms with museum quality works of art, beauty and barber shops, cafes, card rooms, a library, a doctor, and a cinema screening movies from Hollywood. Standing on deck, I can see family, friends, and strangers waving goodbye. Red, blue, white, and purple ribbons ripple in the breeze. The ladder that connected the ship to the shore is removed. There is a roar of applause and cheers as the ship sounds its horn once, twice, and then three times. Confetti the colors of a rainbow, flies through the air. Slowly, the *Circassia* begins to inch away from the shore.

"Bon voyage!" my father cries out.

"*Khuda hafiz*," I shout, "Goodbye!"

I wave at my weeping mother. I stand on the deck waving until the ship and the shore are so far apart that the only thing I see is the growing expanse of water between me and the land.

My luggage is already in my cabin. The quilt my mother made for me lies on the bed. On a vanity table sits the fruit basket filled with apples, bananas, oranges and my favorite, sugarcane, cut into pieces about a foot long. Next to it I put down Baba's Quran, which I am still holding in my right hand, and sit down on the chair attached to the floor next to the vanity. I sit in my cabin full of sadness and self-pity. I am off to America. Where is the excitement? The joy of going to a new world! Where is the pleasure of getting away from it all? I begin to lecture myself: All people must have something to show for themselves. My mother can cook and sew. My father paints. I've little to show for myself so far. I flail like a fly caught between a windowpane and a thick curtain. Life is worth living only when one has a purpose. We all have our journey; I need to find my destiny. The accomplishments of the great were achieved by struggle and hard work into the twilight—where others flinch, I shall dare to go.

I walk out of my cabin to the upper deck. High tea is being served. Waiters in white shirts and trousers with black bow ties and short black jackets serve tea and pastries. The Southeast Asians, the Indians, and the English sit in their respective groups sipping tea.

I explore the ship, like Captain Ahab on his boat, observing and wondering with whom I should sit. I walk up and down without having a single cup of tea. The waiters are cleaning the tables and I still can't decide who shall have the pleasure of my company. The sun shines brightly and I am too warm in my woolen blazer and gabardine slacks. I never have much money to spend on clothing but I like to dress well and I think I have a style. Months ago, when I learned of my pending departure, I'd decided on what I would wear today, but I hadn't anticipated how hot it would be.

I locate the main dining room and find my lunch and dinner table assignments on the schedule posted outside the main entrance. I have first seating: the 12:30 lunch and the 6:30 dinner. Men are required to wear jackets and ties for dinner, it says on the bottom of the posted schedule. Back in my cabin, B-4, I sit back down on the chair in front of the vanity mirror. I feel empty, lost. Will I never know peace or joy again? I will definitely never be in love again.

Alone and lonely on this slow boat, I pick up Baba's Quran sitting next to the fruit basket. I've read the Quran now and again— just randomly opening the book to look at a verse or two. The Quran reads like poetry to me. If I were not going to be an engineer, I would've liked to be a poet. But who could afford to be a poet.

I open the good book randomly once again and find myself staring at *Sura Ta'ha*, the twentieth verse, which talks about the revelation of the book as a gift of mercy from God the Most Gracious. It also tells how the mother of Moses was directed by God to cast him into the river so that he could be brought up in the pharaoh's house under God's own supervision in order to preach and declare to the pharaoh the glory of God.

Finding this sura is a good omen. I read aloud:

Behold! We sent to thy mother,
by inspiration the message:
Throw him
into the chest and throw
it into the river:
The river will cast him
upon the bank and he
will be taken up by one

who is enemy to Me
and an enemy to him.
But I cast love over thee from Me
in order that
thou mayest be reared
under Mine eye.

I can't keep my eyes open. I put the Quran back on the vanity without finishing the verse and lie down on my bed. In my dream I am walking barefoot on deserted seashore on a hot summer afternoon. I impale my right foot on a large fishing hook. I try to pull the hook out, but I only make it worse. Leila walks by and offers to remove the hook. "I'm a doctor," she says. "I know what to do, but it is going to be painful."

I am hurting so badly. I say, "Go ahead." In one smooth, continuous motion she draws out the hook, tearing apart the tendons and the tiny bones of my toe. Blood gushes out, soaking the hot, dry sand.

"Don't talk about love," she says. "Just talk about the lover in me."

I wake up in the dark, sweating from my dream. I turn on a lamp and look at my foot. There is no blood. I look at my wristwatch. It is past six forty, and I am hungry. I wash my face quickly with cold water and dry it with a white towel. I put on my green blazer and comb my hair with my fingers as I walk to the dining room. Without waiting to be seated, I rush around the dining room like a blind man in a three-ring circus until I find table thirteen.

It is a table for four, and my three tablemates are busy eating. I sit awkwardly between Mrs. Harrison, an elderly lady, and Miss Bowden, a lovely young woman. Across from me sits Major Fazal, a *desi*—an Indian like me—dressed in an RAF officer's uniform. I can't tell what the stars and stripes mean, but his has three each. A waiter hands me a menu. He's wearing a uniform too, but starless.

There are plenty of *desi* waiters on the boat, but mine has to be a *gora* called Maxwell. I open the menu and look inside. Everything reads foreign to me. The few so-called English dishes that I've had at Cafe George, like mutton and roast beef sandwich, are not listed.

77

Neither are cucumber sandwiches or ladyfingers. Instead, the menu offers: *Pâté de Foie Gras, Saumon Fumé, Hors d'œuvre Variés,* and *Contre Filet de Boeuf Rôti.* I don't recognize any of them.

The waiter returns to our table. Anything will do, I am hungry, ravenous, carefree, and ready to eat. Living dangerously, I point my finger to a line on the menu, hoping for the best. After Maxwell leaves I sit up and examine the cutlery, gadgets of the western way of eating. Staring at me is a white china plate. On one side of the plate there are at least seven forks in all shapes and sizes, and on the other there are that many, if not more, spoons and knives. There is more cutlery here than all the silverware in my home. I take a sip from my glass of water and put it down. The elderly lady looks at me smiling. She has a kindly face.

My food is served, a plate of noodles with red sauce on top; I have never seen food like this. I don't know what it is called. I look at my noodles. The sauce reminds me of my mother's *keema masala,* ground beef in red curry. It could be delicious. I contemplate the tools I should use—a fork or a spoon? I reach for a large spoon hesitantly, but withdraw my hand, knowing the spoon will not work with the long noodles. Should I cut the noodles down to the size of long grain basmati rice and scoop it up with my hand into my mouth? I feel the presence of my tablemates, especially the Major, and it seems they have nothing better to do than to observe me. I want a separate table; I look at my hands, examining my fingernails like they need a good wash.

The art of eating with your hands is in not letting your fingernails get dirty. The kind of food in the dish sitting in front of me is not something I can eat with my hands, let alone with a spoon or a fork, even if I don't care that my fingernails get dirty. I wipe my dry lips and dry my wet forehead in the same motion with a beige cotton napkin, put the napkin back in its ring. There is no proper way to eat what I ordered. I get up abruptly and walk out of the dining room leaving my plate full of food untouched by human hands.

I walk to the upper deck. Laughter and joy are everywhere. People walk in couples; men and women have become companions. They are going to the movies and to a dance; they drink wine. Although on the boat, I may have missed the boat.

I miss Leila. How lovely it would be to accompany your love

on a ship. I am locked in my loneliness, a blind man walking in dark. I shake my head and leave without a word.

The Education

CHAPTER 12

It is a moonless night. I stand on the deck away from the maddening crowd, watching the shades of darkness and the vague shadow cast by the ship from its own lights on the restless sea. I wonder who got Baba's bicycle and Kamran's baby bed, which we left in our house in the city by the River Betwa. What's the voyage of this pilgrim? Never is a variable state, reincarnation is a second cup of tea with evaporated milk. An absence has its own presence. It is easier to seek forgiveness than permission. Einstein must have been entertaining his family when he thought of the name for his new theory. In the end there are only five degrees of separation between totally opposite outcomes and sometimes even less. Our thoughts and wishes have nothing to do with what happens in our lives. One of the most dangerous things in the world is moral certainty. It allows no room for doubt or ambiguity, which is part of the fabric and complexity of life. Everything comes to an end one day. You can leave places but your losses travel with you.

I return to my cabin exhausted. I hang my blazer on the chair by the vanity, take off my pants and carefully fold them flat and put them under my pillow to maintain the crease. I'm hungry and I want Amaji's *kabab paratha*. I lie down under the quilt Amaji made for me, feeling warm, and immediately fall asleep.

In the morning, I'm awakened from a dream by a knock on my cabin door. Half asleep, still dreaming, I call out in Urdu, "*Kaun hay?*"

"Your bed tea, Sir," says a courteous voice in English.

"OK," I say.

A steward in white uniform leaves a tray on the dressing table. I lie in bed, wondering if I am supposed to drink this tea now or wait until after my morning ablutions. I get up, brush my teeth, and shower. My tea is cold when I get to it. I eat two slices of toasted white bread with butter and orange marmalade and drink my glass of orange juice. I finish my cold tea. This should be enough. Now I don't have to worry about breakfast in the dining room, and the rigorous, scrupulous etiquette of dining civilities.

81

I wash the white shirt I wore when I boarded the ship with a bar of a #44 soap that I brought with me. I've brought six shirts, all white; two pairs of khaki cotton pants; one navy-blue gabardine suit with two matching ties, one blue-and-red striped, the other a blue and green paisley; and the beige gabardine pants and green blazer that I wore yesterday. All my clothes were custom-made by Rainbow Tailors except for my overcoat, which is blue worsted-wool and made in America. Baba and I bought it at Juna Market, where they sell secondhand clothes imported from America.

I change into another white shirt, the same gabardine trousers, and the green blazer. I walk out of my cabin whistling, "*I want to be a sailor, sailing out to sea,*" a song I remember from *The Thief of Baghdad.*

On the upper deck I find a swimming pool, shuffleboard, ping-pong table, a billiards room with a bar, and a large sun deck. I look into the vast distance: bright sun, blue skies, blue sea, as far as you can see.

"Would you care to play ping pong with me?" I hear someone ask. I turn around to see a plump woman dressed in a yellow blouse and matching yellow shorts that fit her tightly.

"Yes, of course," I say with a smile. I am warm in my blazer. Irma Copper is not only plump. She is pleasing too. She smiles like she means it.

The stewards are serving ten o'clock coffee, soup, and ice cream at nearby tables.

"I suggest we eat before we play," says Irma. I won't have to go to the dining room for lunch if I eat enough soup and ice cream, I say to myself. So we sit down on deck chairs beside one of the tables under a canopy. Irma and I eat soup and ice cream and drink coffee with milk and sugar. Irma is going back to Mansfield, England, after spending the summer with her uncle and aunt who live in Bombay, she tells me. She was a schoolteacher back home. We talk for a long time and then we play ping-pong. She is much better than I thought she would be. I win the first two games, but she wins the third game, when she begins to return my deadly serve with skilled accuracy.

Irma leaves for lunch. I skip it. I go to the library, which is on the second deck along with the ship's movie theaters and ballroom.

Sitting in the library, I read *A Passage to India*. At home I used to check out books from the library, and once I started reading a book, I wouldn't put it down until I was finished. I get involved in *A Passage to India*, so much so that once again, I'm late for dinner.

When I arrive at table thirteen, the other guests are already seated. I sit down across from Major Fazal who looks handsome and severe in a black tuxedo, a blinding-white formal shirt with rows of tiny vertical ruffles down the front, and a black bow tie. Mrs. Harrison sits at my right, Miss Boden to my left.

The waiter promptly hands me the menu. "The others have already ordered," Maxwell informs me.

"So did anyone see the movie last night?" Major Fazal asks, starting the small talk.

I did, I want to announce, but once again I have difficulty reading the menu.

Miss Boden gives a brief, "No." Mrs. Harrison says nothing. She puts on her black reading glasses again and leans over to my menu. "Do you read French?" she asks.

"French?" I say, puzzled. What is that supposed to mean? I take my eyes away from the menu.

"Madam, I can hardly read English—and I was born in British India—let alone French."

"Then why are you reading the French side of the menu?"

I look down again and turn the page. On the very next one there is a world of difference. Suddenly I could read! *Coupe de Pamplemousse Frappé* turns out to be a chilled grapefruit cup. Should they not have put *E*-English before *F*-French, I want to protest, but I say nothing. I'm glad to be able to read again.

Welcome home! I am surprised to see an amazing number of Indian dishes—vegetables, *dals*, and curries. I order fruit cocktail for an appetizer and *kaddu bhaji* with *puris* for my main course. I play smart; the fruit cocktail I can eat with a spoon, and I know how to eat the Indian food with my hands without getting my fingernails dirty.

Once again I examine the cutlery, the gadgets of Western eating, seven on one side and six on the other. Thank God for eating with your hands. I smile to myself.

"I've taught at Saint Patrick's High School in Karachi for

83

thirty-two years," says Mrs. Harrison, taking her napkin out of its ring. "As a matter of fact, I was the principal for the last twenty years." Spreading the white napkin over her lap, she continues, "Young man, I am probably older than your mother."

I look at her. She looks like Mrs. Moore from *A Passage to India*.

"And I've seen many young men such as yourself. As a matter of fact, I've raised one of my own. George." Without wasting time, she explains the silverware. "On both, the left and the right side of your plate," she says, "you pick up the silverware from the inside out as your food is served." She smiles and adds. "Or is it the other way around?"

"In either case," I say, smiling back, "that's not so hard to remember."

Our table is served. I am the only one who ordered Indian food. I quietly observe my table mates eat with their forks, knives, and spoons. Eating with my fingers, I thoroughly enjoy my meal, breaking my *puri*, making small cones and filling them neatly with *kuddu bhaji*. I chew quietly with my mouth closed.

Mrs. Harrison watches with admiration. Miss Glenda smiles at me occasionally, while Major Fazal frowns at me continuously. I watch Mrs. Harrison, how she puts the knife in the middle of the plate with the fork beside it, to indicate to the waiter that she was done eating. I order tutti-frutti ice cream for dessert. Once I'm done with my meal, I thank the waiter. I thank Mrs. Harrison. I nod at Miss Boden and ignore Major Fazal. Well fed, content and satisfied, I quietly thank Allah for a delicious meal. I leave the table. I walk out of the dining room, whistling, *"I want to be a sailor, sailing out to sea."* I hear my name called. I turn and see Major Fazal walking toward me. I stop. He catches up with me, takes off his glasses and puts them in his pocket. "Young man," he says, "this ship is like the United Nations. There are men and women here from many countries. Here, you represent your country."

Major Fazal takes his glasses out of his pocket and puts them on again. He looks at me most carefully. "In the future," he continues, "when you come to dinner, you should wear a tie and a suit." Major's voice has both admonition and sympathy.

I look at Major Fazal. He stands as if at attention, but his shadow is bent on the ship wall. His face is stoic. His grey handlebar mustache, neatly trimmed and waxed, points upward in a clumsy fashion.

I put my right hand into my blazer pocket. Looking as much like a hero in an Indian movie as I can, I say, "I am traveling to the USA with one blue gabardine wool suit that my father had made for me at Rainbow Tailors, and this green blazer. For years I have imagined myself walking up and down this ship wearing my college colors. I am saving my suit to wear when I arrive in Stillwater, Oklahoma."

The Major shakes his head. His eyes look pained. "Young Man, you are no longer living at home."

I think of a *desi* who once got furious at a *gora*, and in his rage said to the *gora* "Bugger you!" But saying it in English diluted his satisfaction so he added in Urdu, "And furthermore, *teri maa ki chot.*" I didn't care to say bugger you or *your mamma's pussy.* Major Fazal is not a *gora*, he is a *kala sahib.* He knows Urdu, but he prefers English. I glare at the Major in disgust and hold his eyes for as long as he looks at me. I shake my head and leave without a word.

ॐ

At the movies, they are showing a flashy remake of the 1934 classic *Imitation of Life* (1959, 124 min., Eastmancolor), starring Lana Turner, Juanita Moore, John Gavin, and Sandra Dee. I go and see the movie.

CHAPTER 13

The next morning I wake up hungry, wondering where I am and how far away have I sailed, when the steward knocks on my cabin door to announce bed tea. "Come in," I say in English. I even say, "Thank you," as he leaves. I brush my teeth with the tooth powder my mother made, charring almond shells and grinding them in a mortar with roasted clove and other herbs and spices. I take a pinch of the powder, balance it on my index finger, rub it over my teeth and gums, and rinse my mouth. Then I make my tea with two spoons full of sugar and just the right touch of milk. I take the cup back to bed, and sipping my tea, I say to myself, it is essential that I ace what lies ahead. Major Fazal is right. I am no longer living at home. I'm required to grow up. I have to move on. I am at a turning point in my life. I shower, shave, and go out for breakfast in the dining room.

Another warm blue-bright day with a pleasant wind blowing, I go to the top deck recreation room, hoping to find Irma Copper. She is playing doubles with three *desis*. I watch them for a while.

Another *desi*, a handsome Indian or Pakistani young man about my age, another hero material, walks by. He stops and introduces himself. Hanif Qureshi is fair complexioned with a flat, dark mustache. He is going to England to live in London with his older brother and sister-in-law and help them run a grocery store in South Hall.

"Are you planning to get off the ship at Aden to sight-see?" he asks.

"I hadn't thought of it," I answer.

"When were you planning to think about it?" he asks, smiling. "We'll be there in a few hours."

"I'd like to go," I say. "I just don't want to spend my money on sight-seeing. I should stay on board and write a letter to my mother."

"An Uncle of mine lives in Aden," volunteers Hanif. "He is going to meet me and give me a tour of the city. By the way, it is too late to write a letter as they've already collected the mail." I'm annoyed with my lack of awareness of my environment.

I eat a quick lunch before the *RMS Circassia* docks in the Gulf of Aden at one thirty. For three shillings and two pence per person, a fee that I resent paying, a small motorboat carries me to shore along with Hanif, Irma, George Frazer, who is an Anglo-Indian, and Satish Gupta, an Indian. Wearing a white *kurta* pajama and grey and white headgear like a sheikh of Arabia, Hanif's uncle Mumtaz is waiting for us with his yellow Austin Minor. Irma and George sit in the front seat with Uncle Mumtaz. Hanif, Satish, and I sit in the back. Uncle Mumtaz, a tailor, first drives us to his store; he lives in the back of the store with his wife and daughter Zarina. Hanif has told me he is engaged to Zarina. I guess no Indian or Pakistani man can go to England or America unless he is betrothed or has promised to marry the choosing of his mother. Hanif enters the women's domain behind a white curtain to visit his aunt and cousin.

Satish and George sit on a blue-and-red *dhurrie* on the floor. Irma sits on the only chair, a teakwood chair with arms. I sit on a stool in front of a Singer sewing machine. We drink hot tea with milk and sugar, promptly served in small clear glasses along with a plate of biscuits.

Afterwards, Uncle Mumtaz drives us around the entire town. Aden, the capital city of Yemen is old, full of oil wells and gray, barren hills.

The city has been a trade center for ages and is mentioned in the Bible. Noah's Ark landed here, but the land was too barren for them to stay. In the sixteenth century it came under Ottoman control. In 1802, the British established themselves by treaty. Now there is an oil refinery on the west shore. It's the refueling stop for all the ocean liners. Before that, in the days of steamships, it was a coaling station. There is an old commercial section called Crater, the Tawahi business section, and Ma'allah, the native harbor. "The days are hot and the nights are cold," Uncle Mumtaz informs. "We get sandstorms all year round. Goggles and hats are a must even though they don't offer much protection. Sand and more sand and sand everywhere, inside our houses, inside our stores. It is a total mess. I've lived here for about ten years now. It has rained exactly once. The sky is always blue, the sun is always bright, and it never rains. I remember how happy we all were when it rained that one year."

Aden is a free port. Liquor is inexpensive, so are cigars, cigarettes, and transistor radios. Grains, fruits, and vegetables, however, are expensive. Hanif buys a short-wave transistor radio. Irma buys Chanel No. 5 perfume, and Satish some flip-flop sandals. George buys tins of 555 cigarettes, and I buy myself a silk scarf.

On the way back to the harbor, I sit in the front seat next to Hanif while Irma, George, and Satish sit in the back seat laughing, chatting, and singing songs from Indian movies like old friends. "I think I liked *East of Eden* best," says George, laughing.

East of Eden, US, 1955, 115 minutes, Warnercolor, Cinema Scope.

Our ship sails away from Aden. After dinner, Hanif, Irma, and I carry the fruit basket my mother packed for me to the top deck. It is late at night and we find an isolated corner off the sun deck. There is a bright quarter moon showing. We listen to Indian movie songs on the short-wave transistor radio and pounce on the sugar cane stalks, sucking the juice, tossing the husks into the ocean.

CHAPTER 14

In the dining room, one thing goes wrong and the whole house of cards collapses. Major Fazal no longer sits at table thirteen. A mysterious round of musical chairs, initiated by a party or parties unknown, has replaced him with Hanif. I have started wearing ties to dinner. I am proud of myself for remembering how to tie a knot. Baba taught me, and I got it right on my first attempt. It looks pretty good. I only have two ties, so I alternate them. Hanif always wears the same tie to dinner. Every night he removes it without undoing the knot and hangs it on a hook. He slips it over his head again the following evening and tightens it up properly. "Christians tie a knot around their necks to symbolize the crucifixion of Jesus. Why do I have to do it?"

We need to be proper, good ambassadors for our country, I tell Mrs. Harrison one evening.

The ship sails on.

After one dinner, when our waiter brings the cheese tray, Mrs. Harrison suggests that Hanif and I try some cheese. Other than reading the story of the fox that jumped into the well after seeing the shadow of the full moon and taking it for cheese, I am not familiar with this food.

"Indians don't eat cheese," I say, "and I am very careful about what I put in my mouth." Hanif, on the other hand, is a bold soul. Not only is he ready to try it, but unlike Mrs. Harrison who asks the waiter to serve a small sample of this or that variety, Hanif reaches out with his fork, stabs a large slab of a yellow-green piece filled with blue and grey speckles, and drops it on his plate. "It reminds me vaguely of *habshi halva*, one of my favorite sweetmeats, except this cheese is green," he says, picking up a knife. Max looks amazed and so does Mrs. Harrison, who opens her mouth, but says nothing. Glenda Boden watches, also with an open mouth.

With obvious anticipation, Hanif cuts a large slice and pops it into his mouth. He chews it once, then maybe once again. His eyes roll wide open. He seems to be in a great deal of pain. He closes his mouth tightly and puckers his lips to keep it shut. For a moment, I think he is going to throw up on the table. Instead, without a word, he

89

gets up and runs out of the dining room as fast as he can.

I excuse myself from the table and go looking for Hanif. I find him standing on a quiet part of the deck. He has thrown up a bellyful. He looks up and says, "That tasted like *gobar.*"

"I wouldn't know," I smile. "I've never tasted cow dung."

As our ship moves at a snail's pace through Suez Canal, a package deal is offered to all passengers, an excursion to the Nile Valley. For six pounds, we can take local transportation to Cairo and see the pyramids, travel to the ruins at Alexandria, then catch up with the slow moving *RMS Circassia* before it docks at Port Suez.

"I am traveling on a student budget with only two-hundred and ninety American dollars in American Express traveler's checks and less than ten dollars in cash. Six pounds is ninety rupees. Money is always a concern," I say.

"How often will you have a chance like this?" asks Hanif.

"I don't know. I can do it on my way back from the States."

"Well, have a good life!" he says sarcastically. "Blessed are those who can make peace with their surroundings and are at home anywhere. Then there are those, like me, who, under the disguise of seeing the world, are running away from the pain and sorrow at home."

"I don't run away from the pain," I say. "I'm planning to come back, to return home and build bridges. I'm a traveler, not a tourist. I'll pass this way again."

At Suez, Satish, George, Irma, and Hanif get off, along with hundreds of other passengers, for the excursion to the Nile Valley. I do not go. I have a goal, I repeat to myself. I am committed to a purpose. I am not on vacation. I sit in the library and write a long letter home, to be mailed from Port Said.

> *Dear Amaji dear, Baba, Dear Yasmin and Dear Kamran:*
>
> *We arrived at Suez this morning. Tonight we stop at Port Said and sail from there sometime next day. For six pounds I could have gotten off our boat at Suez and taken a tour of the Nile Valley, Cairo, and Alexandria, and seen the mummified kings and queens, the Pharaohs, and the pyramids, the wonders of the world.*

I wanted to go. I always wanted to see the mummies, the deceased men and women of centuries ago preserved for our viewing, but I decided against it. Six pounds is more than fifteen dollars. I can do this tour on my way back; at present I am traveling with a purpose.

I am in the first sitting for meals—12:30 lunch and 6:30 dinner. My tablemates are two memsahibs, *one elderly Mrs. Harrison, whom I think of as Mrs. Moore in* A Passage to India. *The other is lovely Miss Boden, young like Adela.*

I've washed the white shirt I wore when I boarded with the bar of washing soap, in the sink in my room. There is a laundry on the ship, but I don't want to add any extra pence to my travels.

In eleven more days we'll be in Liverpool.

I've already made a few friends, including Hanif Qureshi from Lahore. Hanif is going to live and work with his brother in London, where his brother runs a grocery store. Since I have a two day layover in England, I was planning to stay at a YMCA in London and spend two days sight-seeing and then take a train to Southampton, but Hanif is insisting that I stay with him and his brother.

I am looking forward to seeing the London underground train system. I also want to see King James Park, Westminster Abbey, Big Ben and Buckingham Palace. I can't believe that I am really going to be in London. I want to go to Oval and Lord's Cricket fields, not to mention Hyde Park and Piccadilly Circus, Regent Street and Oxford Street.

My first meal was disastrous. I didn't know what I had ordered or how I should have eaten it. There are times when this journey seems like a dream; us Indians and Pakistanis are rude and talkative. We will not hold doors open for ladies, we walk onto elevators ahead of everyone else, but I am learning and I am glad that I have seen English movies. It's just like An Affair to Remember.

I wish we could all have been on this trip together. I've been thinking a lot about our boat ride from Bombay to Karachi, where we all lived and slept on the deck. Did we have the deck seat or did we just get loaded like luggage with no assigned space? Does anyone else ever think of that voyage? There are times I dream of our house, across the street from the temple. If I were not

91

going to study engineering, I would definitely want to be a sailor. It sounds romantic.

The ship is large, like the Boulton Market, layer after layer of exciting things to see and do, including shuffleboard, ping-pong, billiards and swimming pools, ballrooms, movie theaters, and a library. I see myself sitting by myself, wondering at my own world as it all changes. One day I'll be back. Soon!

We finally finished all the fruits. Today is Saturday. It has been eight days since I've left you. There are times when it feels like it has been ages, and then I say to myself, with a blink of my eyes it will all be done and I'll be back where I belong. I am enjoying myself. This voyage is wonderfully educational. I am sad most of the time, but I am happy just the same to have this opportunity, this chance of a lifetime. Dreams are made for young men and I have dreams.

I am reading E. M. Forster's A Passage to India, *and I wish I could be as proficient in English as Mr. Forster was in Urdu. Maybe I will be by the time I am an America-returned.*

Last night I went to the ballroom, but I only watched. Most desis *do. They don't know how to dance, how to hold hands with a lovely lady. We Indians don't dance like Fred Astaire—or Ginger Rogers.*

I miss you all terribly.

Yours,

Rama

Saturday, August 20, 1960

CHAPTER 15

Eighteen days after I boarded *RMS Circassia*, one day ahead of schedule, we anchored at the famed Port of Liverpool, which gained prominence in the eighteenth century because of the sugar, tobacco, and spices trade with America. It is eleven o'clock in the morning, a cool but sunny Sunday in August. Before leaving the boat, I eat lunch on the deck to save a few pence. During the customs check, I proudly tell the immigration officer that I am traveling on a student visa and that I am on my way to America to study civil engineering.

Hanif and I collect our luggage hurriedly, my ticket to London costs one pound and sixteen shillings. I have to pay four shillings to a porter to carry my luggage and another twelve shillings to book my luggage in the freight compartment. When we are finally on the train, I realize with dismay that in the madness of leaving the boat and rushing through customs, I didn't get a chance to say goodbye to Mrs. Harrison. I'll always remember her kindness, the woman who made me feel at home eating with knives and forks.

Hanif and I are sitting in the second-class compartment of a London-bound train, a boat train from Port of Liverpool to London City. People appear happy and jolly to be arriving home. I'm apprehensive, and say, "I crave for an English toffee."

"An English toffee was Irma Copper," Hanif says with a grin, "to a few chosen men on the boat."

"It is too late now," I say. "My ship has already arrived at its port of call."

"It's the ones who get away that you remember most," sighs Hanif. We ride quietly for a while looking out the moving train.

"Are you happy to be in England?" I ask.

"I'm excited over a new beginning," he says, looking very serious. "I want to help my brother the best I can, but I also want to study literature in England. It's something I always wanted to do. I know I'm going to marry my cousin Zarina, whom I love. I also know that I'm not going back to Pakistan. God willing, one day I want to write about it."

I look at him; he looks contemplative and makes me think of

Kazi, who used to say the only way he understood things was by writing them down. He used to keep a dairy. "I'm sure you will make a good writer," I tell Hanif.

"Maybe," he says, lost in his thoughts, "but I want to write one day to understand my journey."

Sitting beside Hanif, I wonder how he knows that he won't be going back home. There is something about the way he spoke that I admire like a real hero in a cowboy movie, claiming his homestead. Maybe there is something about life he knows that I don't. I'm already counting the days to when I get back home.

Our train arrives in London, Victoria Station, late on a cloudy afternoon. Hanif and I manage to fit our entire luggage onto one cart and roll it out of the station. It looks like it is going to rain. We take a taxi to South Hall where Hanif's brother Nazir lives above his grocery store. The least I can do, I say to myself, is pay for our taxi ride. Nazir is right there when our taxi pulls up in front of Pak Land Grocer and pays the cab driver before I can take my money out of my pocket. Nazir is a generous man. For the next two days, he feeds me breakfast, lunch, and dinner. Before leaving London, I go back to Victoria Station and take a three-hour long tour of the West End, stopping at Westminster Abbey, the House of Parliament, Horse Guards, Piccadilly Circus, Trafalgar Square, and St. James Church. I watch the changing of the guard. On my own I go to the Royal Academy of Arts and walk around Hyde Park. On the day of my departure, Hanif comes to see me off at Victoria Station where I board a boat train to Southampton to sail away to New York on *Queen Mary.*

It is only after we've left the dock at Southampton that I realize I had left the quilt Amaji made for me in Nazir's apartment. I can never tell Amaji of this loss: the quilt was meant to keep me warm during the brutal American winters. At least, I think with a sigh, it will keep a fellow countryman warm in the stranger English winter.

CHAPTER 16

On Friday, September 2, after three days and four nights of voyage from Southampton, the *Queen Mary* arrives at New York harbor. Ellis Island and the Statue of Liberty come into view. The choppy blue ocean seems merry and passionate. A jubilant crowd stands on the decks and gazes at the distant Manhattan skyline. As we get close to the Statue of Liberty, my fellow passengers celebrate our arrival, but for the first time in my voyage, I get seasick. This pilgrim has to run to his cabin, throw up in the sink, and lay down. By the time I feel well enough to get up from the bed, the ship has docked. A strong breeze blows from the sea; an American flag pulsates wildly on a flagpole. I pray to God that my ill-timed seasickness is not a bad omen.

The most painful part of being in New York was not being able to stay there for a few days and see a play on Broadway, visit Macy's, the Empire State Building, Times Square, Radio City Music Hall, and the Rockettes. I would have loved to go to a Yankees game, but there was no way I could have afforded to stay. In *An Affair to Remember*, it was the top of Empire State Building where the star-crossed lovers Cary Grant and Deborah Kerr could not meet. My cab ride from New York Harbor to the Port Authority Bus Terminal on 42nd Street cost me over four dollars. "Transport Workers Union President Milne Quill joined Pennsylvania Railroad Strikers in New York. Pennsylvania Railway, the nation's busiest railway, lies idle," reads a newspaper headline. I was glad to be traveling on a Greyhound Bus. I am fascinated with the quick glimpse of New York, and I promise myself to return one day soon.

Long and winding roads take me away from New York and its postcard perfect skyline toward Stillwater, Oklahoma. I am amazed by the vast boundlessness of the American horizon— green, open, and unlimited. I cannot read books while riding the bus. Reading in that motion gives me a headache. I could fall asleep in that motion, but I am wide-eyed.

Are your whiskers?
When you wake

Tougher than a two-bit steak?
Try Burma Shave

I read hundreds, maybe thousands, of Burma Shave signs.
Counting keeps me engaged, interactive.
    I try memorizing them as they fly past and then scribbling
them down before I forget them.

Grandpa's whiskers
old and gray
often get in
Grandma's way

Once she chewed them
in her sleep
Thinking they were shredded wheat.

Some I understand, others I don't.
After a few more miles:

Ben met Anna
Made a hit
Ben wouldn't shave
Ben-Anna split.

    I puzzle over that one for a few moments. The flat landscape
gets monotonous, but I jerk my attention back to the window before I
miss the next series:

When passing school
Please go-slow
let our little
Shavers grow.

I especially like:

Don't lose your head
To gain a minute

96

You need your head
Your brains are in it.

Some are silly, some surprisingly thoughtful . . .

A fellow who passes
On hills and curves
Is not a fellow
With lots of nerves—He's crazy!

. . . And I am ready to buy the product:

He tried to cross
A fast train appeared
Death didn't draft him
He volunteered.

My favorite:

Beneath this stone
Lies Elmer Gush
Tickled to death
By his shaving brush

At a dinner stop somewhere between Saint Louis, Missouri, and Tulsa, Oklahoma, this curious pilgrim steps off the bus. I've run out of the biscuits I took from the ship, and I am hungry. I stand in front of the counter, staring at the food display. Chicken is too expensive. I don't like the name *hot dog*; maybe it's made with pork. Even though ham is pork, I know that hamburger is supposed to be ground beef. I don't want to spend too much money on food. I've already paid for tea, coffee, and Coca-Cola from New York to Saint Louis. On the bus, the jar of pickled mangoes in mustard oil that my mother had sealed with melted wax is sitting in a bag above my seat.

I suddenly feel an uncontrollable desire to eat pickled mango, the way some pregnant women crave for white Multani clay. All I need is a few slices of bread and I can make myself a pickled mango sandwich.

97

Shining black in an all-white uniform with a white cap, a Negro man is standing behind the counter. I walk up and ask, "May I have two slices of bread, please?"

"What kind of meat you want on your bread, young man?"

"No meat, please," I answer. "Two slices of bread only."

He looks at me, shrugs, his large eyes wide, then from inside a yellow cellophane pack of white Holsum Bread, he takes out two slices and hands them to me. When I take out my change to pay, he waves me away with a smile.

I hurry back to the bus. It's empty except for an obese white woman sleeping in the seat behind the driver and an elderly Negro couple in the back seat. My seat is in the middle of the bus, a window seat, and no one has sat next to me since we stopped at St. Louis. I take my white cotton handkerchief out of my pants pocket and spread it out on the seat next to me. I first put the pieces of bread down on the handkerchief then take my bag from the overhead rack. Removing the melted wax from the top of the jar is more of a chore than I expected, but I manage. Salivating in anticipation, I pull out the mango slices carefully so the oil drips only on the bread. I quickly make my sandwich.

I look from my window towards the setting sun. Over a distant sphere, I eat slowly, savoring each bite. I suddenly miss my mother.

When I am finished eating, my fingers are greasy with mustard oil, the nails yellow from turmeric in the pickle, and my face wet with tears of joy. Well-fed and satisfied, I pick up my white handkerchief carefully, so as not to spill breadcrumbs. I walk off the bus, shake off the handkerchief, and wipe my hands. Putting the handkerchief back in my pocket, I wash my hands and face and get a drink of water.

When I return, all I can smell is the pungent odor of fermented mango and mustard oil. The aroma permeates the entire bus and travels with us until Tulsa, where I switch from the Greyhound to the Trailways that will take me to Stillwater.

After long days and nights on unending highways, after counting a total of 9,786 Burma Shave signs, I get off the Trailways bus in Stillwater on a hot sunny day. It's eerily quiet. I had anticipated the circus of noise, color, movement, and confusion that characterizes the train stations of Karachi, not to mention the bus terminal in New York City, and I feel mildly shocked by the dead silence, which gives the impression that I've arrived at a village in the immediate aftermath of a plague epidemic.

During the short taxi ride from the bus station to my destination, I notice that all the stores are closed. I ask the driver where all the people are. "It's Labor Day," he answers, as if this explains something. I have heard of May Day, but all I know of Labor Day is from the movie *Picnic* (US, 1955, 113min., Technicolor, Cinemascope). Mr. William Holden, another of my favorite leading men, plays a wanderer who arrives in small-town America on Labor Day, a holiday when no one labors. I can appreciate such a holiday, but unlike the movie, which I liked a lot and saw twice, I see no parks and no picnics in progress. There are signs, however. "Re-elect Senator Robert Kerr" says one sign. "Vote Democratic, Vote KENNEDY For President" says another. Red dust blows with the wind. Certainly, this is not the city on the river Betwa. *I'm in America, the beautiful.* I'm in *the land of the free and the home of the brave.* I left Karachi with two hundred and ninety dollars in traveler's checks and ten dollars in cash. I arrive in Stillwater with two hundred and forty dollars in American Express traveler's checks, six dollars in cash, and sixty-seven cents in loose change. Welcome to America, Pilgrim, welcome to America indeed!

After living in Karachi and traveling through London and New York, this feels pretty anticlimactic. Stillwater does not feel like an exciting city. The driver drops me off at an address provided courtesy of the foreign student advising office: 424 Knoblock Street, the home of Vilayat Jan and Latif Shah, fellow Pakistani students. It's a small two-story house, painted green, with a front porch. Inside, on the first floor, there are two adjoining kitchenette apartments with a single bathroom under the stairs; on the second floor, there is a one-bedroom apartment with a living room, kitchen, and bathroom. The strong aroma of curry fills the vestibule that leads me upstairs. I climb the stairs feeling uncertain.

I put down my luggage in a corner and take a seat at the grey Formica kitchen table, where V.J. and Latif are sitting in matching chairs. They offer me hot black tea, thick with sugar and Carnation condensed milk. V.J. is squatting on the kitchen chair, his feet on the seat, his stomach pressing against his thighs, wearing a white cotton *kurta*, drawstring pants, and a thin white gauze cap. His long, dark beard gives his face a double shadow. His flip-flops sit under his chair. It is an odd sight. Latif wears khaki cotton pants and a light-blue shirt. The first thing V.J. and Latif advise me, the new foreign student, is that I shall not stay at the college dormitory, even though all new students are required to. They provide a ready excuse: Islamic dietary laws do not permit me to eat pork, nor can I eat food prepared in lard. Most important, the kitchen at the dormitory isn't kosher.

"It's much cheaper to rent your own place and prepare your own meals," says V.J. "More to your own taste, as well."

"This cup of tea would cost a nickel at the cafeteria," says Latif, raising his white teacup, "and taste like water."

"Americans don't know how to make tea," adds V.J.

"Most foreign students work at different dormitory dining halls or at the cafeteria in the Student Union," Latif informs me. "The good part of the job is that you can eat all the leftover food for free."

Why live in a dormitory and pay for room and board when I can live cheaper in an apartment and eat free by working in the cafeteria? It all makes sense, these pieces of advice.

It is decided. I will stay in their one-bedroom apartment as the third mate. Latif and V.J. will sleep in the bedroom on a wooden bunk bed, and I will sleep on the living room couch that's covered with dust-colored velvet. We'll pay fifteen dollars each for rent and probably spend another five dollars a week on groceries. We'll share the cooking—V.J. is a good cook, Latif is acceptable, and I'm to learn fast.

"There are twenty-nine Pakistani students, fourteen *desi* females, and fifteen *desi* males," Latif informs me. "If you want to continue to play an Indian hero here on an American campus, your chances are good. And, of course, you could always meet *goris*. They like us brown-skinned boys."

I fail to repress a smile.

CHAPTER 17

What a difference a month makes! I'm all settled living with V.J. and Latif, registered for school, and I already have a job serving dinner and helping with clean up from 5:00 p.m. to 7:00 p.m. at the Scott Hall dining room for 75 cents per hour. On a cloudy fall afternoon, sitting in the music room upstairs in the Union building, I write my weekly letter home while listening to the Brothers Four sing, "Once there were green fields, kissed by the sun."

I've certainly arrived a long way from green fields and our home by the River Betwa. In my letters home, I am never worried, depressed, sick, or sad. I write about how hard I am studying in the land of joy, how wonderful life is in America. I'm already counting the days until I graduate; I still plan on staying in the U.S. for a few years after graduation to get American work experience and to earn a lot of money so that I can bring all the luxuries of easy living to my family. Occasionally, I digress and give them a glimpse of America, but I've been here for only five weeks, what do I know of this land.

> *Everything is available here—many different brands of soaps, shampoos, toothpastes, razor blades. There is no ration on sugar or flour. All brands of cigarettes cost the same, and in the movie theaters there is only one class, you pay the same price no matter where you sit, including the balcony. Safeway, the grocery store, is unreal. You can buy everything you need— meats, milk, bread, butter, and vegetables—in one store. Amaji should see it—long-grain and short-grain rice, cleaned and ready to cook. Spices whole or ground, curry powder already mixed.*
>
> *And every fruit and vegetable! What they may not have fresh you can buy frozen or canned. What's amazing to watch is not what Americans consume, but how much they throw away—food cooked and uncooked, tin cans, glass bottles, newspapers, the list goes on.*
>
> *Stillwater is a small town, smaller than Lalukhet in Karachi, but anything you can buy in New York or Chicago you can buy in Stillwater. There are only two cinemas, but*

101

thank God, they show movies in the Student Union. People are nice and hardworking. Negroes are poor and separate and native Indians have a difficult life. All is well for me. I go to sleep happy and wake up hungry.

The American presidential election campaign is in progress now. The second debate between Kennedy and Nixon is scheduled for 8 p.m. tonight. I plan to watch it. We don't have a TV at our apartment, but we can watch it at Student Union. On Monday, September 26, sitting in the Student Union with my fellow students, we watched the first of the three scheduled nationwide television debates between Vice President Richard M. Nixon and U.S. Senator John F. Kennedy. They all said that Mr. Nixon's five o'clock shadow got there before he did. I felt bad for Mr. Nixon. I remember seeing him in Karachi, during his visit to Pakistan, waving from his motorcade.

There are twenty-nine Pakistani students. To promote better understanding between Pakistanis and Americans, there is a Pakistani student association on campus. Cultural activities are planned to provide a closer contact between fellow Pakistani students and the community at large. I've already made a few good friends. I am taking thirteen semester hours of schoolwork, as follows:

Sem.	Hrs.	Mon.	Tues.	Wed.	Thurs.	Fri.
Ge107	3	8-10		8-10		8-10
CE181	3	10-12		10-12		10-12
Rhet101	3	1		1		1
PEM	1		8-10		8-10	
Cal301	3	2		2		2

This amounts to courses in Mechanical Drawing, Survey, Calculus, and English for Foreign Students, and Physical Education. I'm taking Fencing. I love it.

Otherwise, all is well. I'll write you next week.

Yours,

Rama

Friday, October 7, 1960

I also write to Leila:

102

Dear Leila,

I'm here. You're over there, different cities, different countries and time zones. The America of our movies and America for real is not one and the same. In some ways I liked the America of our movies better than the America I live in. Don't get me wrong. I like it here, almost free and almost equal for all. I like what I see except for how they treat their Negroes and Native Americans, not fair nor equal, but they don't mind foreign students. I can't believe that when I was living in Pakistan, I didn't know that some of the American schools were segregated. Maybe we just didn't see the right movies. It is hard to live with that kind of prejudice in the community, prejudice based on the color of one's skin. I'm working hard and studying even harder and I'm enjoying myself. They show new and old movies at the Student Union and there is Campus Theatre near the university and there are movies on the TV, free. I see at least two movies a week. I'm in a movies heaven. I wish you were here so we could share this American experience together that would have been a source of joy. I'm lost in love. Love my girl back home. Devoid of feelings and dreams, I can't wait to be with you again.

With all my love,
Yours truly,
Rama
Saturday, October 8, 1960

Latif is a happy soul, fun-loving, debonair, with dark hair and dark eyes. He wakes up singing, "Oh what a beautiful morning, oh what a beautiful day." V.J. is dark like Latif, but not as debonair. He has a thick beard, and his eyebrows grow together across his brow, giving him a frowning, simian look. V.J. is always up before Latif, and like a *muezzin*, he calls out for the *Fajr* prayers every morning:

"Prayer is better than sleep. Prayer is better than sleep."

Latif and I join him in the morning prayers. It's not so much that I want to, but I feel obligated in a way I never did at home. Peer pressure, I guess, or maybe everyone becomes religious when living in exile. V.J. loves to preach. Today he says, "Worship of Allah is the pillar of Islam. The Quran speaks of it more than a hundred times: *salat, dua, zikr, tasbih,* et cetera. In order to create the sovereignty of Allah on earth, Islam has prescribed five periods of daily worship. With worship comes divine transfiguration, which transports your soul to the threshold of Allah. I'm told it is all in letting go, parting with worldly concerns, embracing, what is everlasting. What makes a person Muslim begins with belief in the one and only God and Mohammad as His last messenger."

V.J. is our *imam.* He leads worship for the Friday prayers held at the University Chapel. The university has very generously allowed Muslim students to use the chapel on Fridays.

I watch as he gets into his preaching mode. "A Muslim must pray the five obligatory prayers every day, must give a portion of his wealth each year to the needy, must fast during the month of Ramzan, and fifth and finally, he must make the pilgrimage to Mecca if he is financially and physically able.

"The Quran is the truth—unfortunately there are many Muslims who don't study the message and take Islam as a cultural and religious identity, not as an educated choice."

I hate being lectured, but I'm in no mood to argue or discuss. I don't like talking religion. I think it is something between men and their God. So I sit quietly and listen to V.J. Many Muslims do not fulfill the five pillars of Islam, and very few consider inviting others to Islam. This to me is a very important consideration because if the people of the book—Jews and Christians—become Muslims, by the grace of God, they'd receive twice as much reward, and the message of one God would resonate in our souls. V.J. and his lectures and sermons are with us constantly, both at home and at the chapel after Friday afternoon prayers.

After the morning prayers, V.J. sits on his prayer rug in our apartment, and like a *hafiz,* he recites the Quran in a loud, audibly laconic voice while I make a pot of tea for everyone. We now buy Milnot. "If cows could, they'd give Milnot," says the commercial. It certainly is cheaper. And we the Muslim students are ready to save every penny we can, as long as V.J., the campus priest, declares it kosher. Other than pork and wine all is *halal* to me. Latif would even drink, but he does not flaunt it, especially not to the campus holy man. On school days we drink our strong tea with Milnot and three spoons of sugar. We eat toasted Wonder bread with grade AA butter and Dundee orange marmalade before going off to our classes.

Latif dates anybody and seeks the proverbial hole-in-one with every date. "American white boys are nice to you and your buddies," he says one day, "as long as you don't eye their girls."

V.J. thinks it is a sin to even eye a woman. And since Islam attaches great importance to morality, V.J. says that promiscuity must be suppressed at all costs to protect women from the wickedness of men. He believes that the motive for love among men is a fleeting fantasy: her sweet voice and delicious smile, the color of her eyes, her hair, and the subtle gestures she displays—these start the drama.

Latif says that one should not deny any God-given trollop and that all western women are sluts. I believe in the difficult separation of love and lust. Between Latif being so all knowing about American Women and V.J. so all knowing of Islam, I feel like an outsider.

V.J. works at the chemistry lab. Thanks to Latif, I work with him at Scott Hall, a women's dormitory. The dining room serves dinner from five to six thirty Sunday through Friday. Other than the cook and the manager Mrs. Dobson, most of the dining room employees are foreign students. We are permitted to eat the leftovers. Some of the foreign students complain about how awful American food tastes; others eat with pleasure, the turkey à la king, meatloaf with gravy, roast beef with mashed potatoes, the Cornish game hens and prime rib for special dinners. And, of course, pork roast and pork chops, which Latif and I will not eat. Best is dessert. My favorite is pecan pie. Latif loves the banana cream. On Fridays the coeds arrive for dinner with their hair in curlers, wearing their bathrobes. They eat little in anticipation of their dates. Some of them don't show up at all, either because they have dinner dates, or because they've gone home for the weekend. Friday evenings are great for leftovers.

We don't have a TV in our apartment, and we only have one desk, so we all study in the library and watch TV at the Student Union. On Thursday, October 13, sitting in the Student Union, I watch as Bill Mazeroski's ninth-inning homerun defeats the N.Y. Yankees in the seventh game of the World Series, lifting the Pittsburgh Pirates to their first championship in 35 years. On October 21, I

105

watch the final Presidential campaign debate where Vice President Nixon and Senator Kennedy clash on national television over U.S. policy toward Cuba. On October 26, the US announces its determination to defend Guantanamo Naval Base if Cuba tries to abrogate the 1903 base treaty. On November 8, Senator Kennedy, a democrat from Massachusetts, wins the 1960 Presidential election over Vice President Nixon by an astonishingly close vote. Though Oklahoma gave 533,039 votes to Nixon and 370,111 votes to Senator Kennedy, if I could have voted, I too would have voted for Kennedy.

⁂

During the Thanksgiving holidays, the foreign student office finds host families for us foreign students to visit for a taste of American hospitality.

On Thanksgiving Day, I take a bus to Ponca City on my way to Tonkawa to attend a Thanksgiving dinner at Reverend Freeman's house. The good Reverend had intended to pick me up, but was called to a deathbed at the last moment. Mrs. Walsh, the foreign student advisor, came in person to my apartment, since I don't have a phone. She waits while I got dressed, then drives me to the bus stop, buys my ticket, and sees me onto the bus. Americans are nice people, I must say.

Riding on the Trailways bus, I stare out onto the rainy landscape and think of when I was a little boy and lived in the city by the River Betwa. On rainy days, my mother made paper boats for me to sail in the stream created by the cascade of water that poured from the open terrace above our veranda. Nostalgia grips me fleetingly.

I get off at the Ponca City terminal to switch to the bus to Tonkawa. There aren't many people around, just an American Indian, a couple of Negro folks, and me, a foreigner. Waiting, I sit on a dark mahogany bench looking down at the green-speckled concrete floor. I hear a drunken voice say, "Don't look down, Son. You are as good as them."

"Yes, I am," I say softly, not believing what I've said. I look up and see an American Indian standing in front of me. His dark hair is styled in a crew cut. I wonder if he thinks I'm one of his own people.

106

"I am not from around here," I tell him.

"I am," the native says. He sits down beside me.

"I am Pakistani and Indian," I continue. "I was born in India."

"I am an Indian," the native says with a smile, "and I was born here." He has a pleasant face; his nose reminds me of my Uncle Aftab.

"What is your tribe of origin?" I ask, showing a tourist's interest in a national monument, in one of the last of a dying breed. He looks at me like he does not know what I am asking. Looking away from me, he says, "We're the children of a trail of tears and broken treaties." He pulls a pack of Lucky Strikes from the brown plaid cowboy shirt he wears under a denim jacket. He takes out a couple of cigarettes and offers one to me. I decline.

"In Oklahoma, we are Cherokee, Choctaw, Chickasaw, and Seminole."

I forget each name as soon as I hear it, except Cherokee. The native puts the pack of cigarettes back in his shirt pocket.

"But what tribe did your forefathers come from?" I insist.

The native takes the unlit cigarette out from between his lips and lets out a deep sigh. He stares at me absently, his eyes haunted. I look away.

"Can I buy you a drink?" he asks.

"I don't drink," I explain. "I am a Muslim."

The native feels for a match in his pocket. "I pity the white man for having no pity for us. For me to survive, I have to adopt the law, the religion, and the customs of the aliens."

"I feel like an alien all the time," I say.

"I don't mind feeling like an alien," the native says, smiling sadly. "What I can't accept is being treated like an outsider in my own land." He pulls a matchbox from his jeans. A nickel falls out of his pocket and rolls over the concrete floor. I reach down and pick it up for him. He lights his cigarette and takes a deep drag, holding his breath for a moment. I hand him his fallen change.

Looking at the Indian head on the nickel, he exhales the smoke through his nose and says, "In times to come there will be no more Indians or buffalo on this land."

107

"Maybe we Indians should start a rebellion in the United States," I say in all seriousness.

Shaking his head, the native says, "It has been tried, but the oppressor won. They slaughtered most of us and put the rest of us in concentration camps."

I want to say something, but he's right, there is nothing to do. I hear my bus announced. The native asks me where I am going. I tell him I am on my way to Tonkawa for a Thanksgiving dinner at the Reverend Freeman's house, arranged by the foreign student advisor's office. I get up to walk to my bus.

"Do you celebrate Thanksgiving?" I ask him.

"I am an Indian with little to give thanks for," he says, rising from the bench. "It's just another Thursday in November."

We stand quietly for a moment. I want to embrace him, but I awkwardly shake his hand instead. "Goodbye, Indian," I say.

The native puts his hand over my head and rubs it gently. "Good luck, Indian," he says.

Sitting in the moving bus, I look out as a gentle rain continues to fall silently.

CHAPTER 18

On Monday, April 17, I sit in the Student Union TV room, in the first row, excited, to watch my first-ever live televised presentation of the Oscars. Not only is it my first time, it is *the* first. On ABC, Bob Hope hosts the event from the Santa Monica Civic Auditorium. I come totally prepared having seen all five of the movies nominated for the Best Picture: *The Alamo* (1960, 193min., Technicolor) directed by John Wayne, *The Apartment* (1960, 125min., bw) directed by Billy Wilder, *Elmer Gantry* (1960, 146min., Eastmancolor) directed by Richard Brooks, *Sons and Lovers* (1960, 103min., bw) directed by Jack Cardiff, and *The Sundowners* (1960, 133min., Technicolor) directed by Fred Zinnemann.

The thing I find quite confusing is that while *The Alamo* and *Elmer Gantry* are both nominated for Best Picture, neither John Wayne nor Richard Brooks are nominated for Best Director. On the other hand, Jules Dassin and Alfred Hitchcock are nominated directing *Never on a Sunday* and *Psycho*, but neither movie is nominated for Best Picture.

As the winners are announced, I agree and disagree, approve and disapprove. For the best song I had difficulty picking between "The Green Leaves of Summer" and "Never on a Sunday," which wins. Peter Ustinov, whom I was rooting for, is gracious in his acceptance speech for his supporting role in *Spartacus*: "Having been educated in English schools, we were taught for at least fifteen years of our lives how to lose gracefully, and I was preparing myself for that all afternoon. Now I don't know what to say."

For Best Actor, I wanted Spencer Tracy in *Inherit the Wind* to win, but Burt Lancaster wins for *Elmer Gantry*. I also enjoy Mr. Lancaster's acceptance speech: "I want to thank all who expressed this kind of confidence by voting for me. And right now I am so happy, I want to thank all the members who didn't vote for me!"

For Best Picture, I liked *The Sundowners* the best, but *The Apartment* wins. And, yes, Elizabeth Taylor wins the Best Actress Award for *Butterfield 8*. She flew in directly from a hospital in London after miraculously surviving a near fatal bout of pneumonia. Walking

109

into the Santa Monica Civic Auditorium with her new husband Eddie Fisher, she displayed a jagged tracheotomy scar above her ample cleavage. Everyone knew she was going to win, and in fact, none of the other nominees for Best Actress, except Greer Garson, even bother to attend the ceremony. Yul Brynner announces Elizabeth Taylor the winner for her portrayal of a call girl. Shirley Jones also wins the Best Supporting Actress award for playing a hooker. This year, four of the female nominees played women of easy virtue. In the end, everyone, especially me, has a good time. And by the way, director Billy Wilder says something I have been saying all along: "Some actors are not handsome enough to play leading man roles." Mr. Wilder told Billy Bob Thornton that he's too ugly to be an actor.

By the end of the academic year, I have accumulated thirty-two semester hours and a grade point average of 3.6. Since my scholarship pays my college tuition, summer is when I need to work full time to supplement the payment of my room and board.

In June, I travel with V.J. and Latif on a Greyhound bus to Chicago for the summer. V.J. and Latif are veterans of previous summers in Chicago and know exactly what to do. I've been told that Chicago is the second largest American city, and jobs there are plentiful. Our bus from Tulsa arrives in Chicago at 11:00 a.m. on a Sunday. We put our luggage in the lockers at the bus terminal.

From a bookstall, V.J. picks up a copy of *The Chicago Tribune* and begins making phone calls for furnished apartments ready for immediate occupancy. This is my first encounter with a large American city. "There is nothing to it," says V.J. "Chicago is a civilized city, the streets run straight, north and south, east and west, and all the streets run parallel—named and numbered. State and Madison are the zero point. There is a train that loops around downtown, and a subway that goes in more than two directions." I am impressed with the knowledge of the city my friends have. We find a one-bedroom apartment in Uptown on North Kenmore Avenue off Irving Park. We walk out of the bus terminal to the subway to check out the apartment. Within the two blocks, from the bus station to the subway, from Clark to State Street, I count five cinema houses: the Woods is showing *The Misfits*, starring Clark Gable, Marilyn Monroe, and

110

Montgomery Clift; the United Artists is showing *The Hustler*, starring Paul Newman, Jackie Gleason, and George C. Scott; the Oriental, *Breakfast at Tiffany's*, with Audrey Hepburn and George Peppard; the State and Lake, *Town Without Pity* with Kirk Douglas and E.G. Marshall; the Chicago, *West Side* Story, with Natalie Wood, Richard Beymer and Rita Moreno; and the Loop Theater, *Two Women*, with Sophia Loren and Jean-Paul Belmondo. They are all first-run new-releases. I love the thought of all the movies to see and the entire summer ahead. The big city life is the life to live, I believe.

We decide to rent the apartment on Kenmore Avenue. After picking up our luggage from the bus station, we go out to supermarket under the Montrose Avenue Station to buy groceries: chicken, Mahatma brand rice, Wonder bread, a large tin of A&P curry powder, onions, potatoes, vegetable oil, vegetables, salt, and sugar.

Over a large dinner of curried chicken and steamed rice, we strategize the job hunt. We'll get up early at 5:30 a.m. and walk over to Manpower on Broadway to look for temporary factory jobs. If the job manager at Manpower cannot place us, we'll take the train downtown and go to employment agencies, then walk from restaurant to restaurant and hotel to hotel to see if they need any help.

We go to bed early. I sleep on a large brown couch in the living room, while Latif and V.J. sleep on two single beds in the bedroom. Early the next morning, after V.J. leads the *Fajr* prayers that even I join with hope, we eat a quick breakfast of tea and toasted Wonder bread with butter. The three of us leave our apartment in a hurry. A cool breeze is blowing from the lake when we arrive at the Manpower office on Broadway. Inside a large storefront sit scores of men dressed in blue and gray work clothes and brown work shoes. Some show the hardship of their lives, unshaven, eyes red, hung-over. Sitting on a wooden bench, dressed in beige jeans, long-sleeved white shirts, and black dress shoes, the three of us look out of place.

A young man in a white short-sleeved shirt with a red-and-blue striped tie and grey flannel pants walks out of a glass booth, looks around, and picks this man and that in some random order, giving them instructions with a voucher. He tells them to get on a Manpower bus. Others are instructed to take public transportation to a certain address. At 6:55, when most of the others have already been sent to

111

different locations, the man gives me a voucher and directs me to an address on California Avenue just north of Devon. He tells me to see Mr. Conroy at Glo-Brite, a manufacturer of polyfoam packing.

At Glo-Brite, I roll up my sleeves and work hard. I am everyone's helper, going from one station to another, making packing material for industries. I work all day, my leather-soled shoes make a lot of noise as I carry planks of polyfoam from one worker to another, who measure and cut them into different shapes and sizes with a table-saw. Others work on steam-molding machines that melt granulated polyfoam, white like milk, soft as snow, into egg boxes and other shapes. Workers at Glo-Brite work long hours, from seven in the morning to six at night, with three hours of overtime at time-and-a-half pay. Besides being everyone's errand boy, I also pack the finished materials to be shipped to different clients. Only in America do they have factories that make products that they use to pack other products. I keep wondering if Latif and V.J. were sent to work as well.

At the end of the day, Mr. Conroy, the shop manager, a tall man with a freckled face and crew cut red hair, tells me he is happy with my performance and wants me to come back tomorrow. To my joy, he thinks he can use me for the entire summer.

Exhausted and covered in fine white polyfoam dust, I return to our apartment after taking two buses and smell the strong aroma of curry in the stairway. I walk upstairs.

V.J. squats on the kitchen chair, scooping rice and chicken curry into his mouth. V.J. always eats squatting. He says that's how Prophet Mohammed, peace be upon him, used to eat. Eating this way with your legs pushing into your stomach prevents one from overeating. At the same table, Latif sits next to him like a proper gentleman. He scoops chicken and boiled rice with a spoon and a knife. The good part of eating with forks and knives, he claims, is that you can eat without washing your hands.

I wash my hands and face at the kitchen sink and serve myself a large heap of rice, a chicken wing, and a thigh with plenty of sauce before sitting down across from V. J.

Latif immediately says to V.J., "Do you know why RPM was sent to a job and not you or me?" He fills his spoon with rice, and waits. V.J. says nothing. He does not like talking while eating. Latif continues, "It's because among the three of us, Rama matched best with that skewbald crowd, the damned and the misfits seeking temporary employment."

I smile. "I can't help it if I look like Gregory Peck," I say.

In less than a week, V.J. finds a job selling encyclopedias. He has to work evenings and Saturdays. Along with four other men, he is driven to areas like Skokie and Lincolnwood. They go door-to-door selling encyclopedias. "Some wives treat me worse than their hounds or their husbands," he says.

Latif finds a job as a bellboy at the Sherman House. He has to work every Saturday and every other Sunday. He says that he likes working Sunday evenings because that's when folks feel the loneliest. This provides him plenty of opportunities to meet women.

I continue to work six days a week at Glo-Brite. At work I learn all the great American phrases like "even God rested on the seventh day," and "no kidding," and "you know." Soon I am shrugging my shoulders like the "natives" without even knowing it.

CHAPTER 19

On Friday evenings, no matter how tired I am, no matter how late it is, I go to movies, often alone. Latif either works on Friday evenings or goes out on a date. V.J. does not go to movies at all. I've not seen as many movies downtown as I thought I would; they're too expensive, $1.25 for the early show and $1.50 thereafter for a first-run movie. I go to the uptown theaters in walking distance, Rivera and Uptown, where for 75 cents I can see double features. I have already seen *Lover Come Back* and *Splendor in the Grass* as well as *The Absent Minded Professor* and *One, Two, Three*. On Sundays we sleep until ten thirty or eleven. Even V.J. will say the *Fajr* prayers late. I get up first, shower, and then make a large omelet of six or eight eggs with chopped green peppers, red chili powder, and onions—no cilantro. After mistakenly buying parsley more then once thinking it was cilantro, we stopped buying it. We sit at the kitchen table until noon, drinking tea, eating our omelets with slice after slice of Wonder bread, the bread that "builds strong bodies twelve ways."

After our brunch the three of us will put on our white full-sleeved shirts, dark pants, and black leather shoes and walk down to the Montrose Avenue Beach. Until dusk we'll sit there watching beautiful women sunbathe in their swimsuits. Actually, I am very discreet about it. I never look at them when they're watching me. I won't even accidentally meet their eyes.

I look as Latif observes each new woman, each beautiful face, and every *body* that walks by on the beach. He pays attention to each lovely as she carefully unbuttons her skirt and blouse, one button at a time, before gently folding them to place beside her beach bag—every woman who moments ago was pulling her skirt down over her legs against the warm summer breeze would disrobe and stretch her swimsuit over her crotch, right in front of you. Most women take their bottoms off first, then their tops. According to Latif's unscientific survey, it is because women are used to men helping unsnap the bra.

"These swimsuits leave little to the imagination," comments Latif. "If you look close enough, you can see their pubic hair."

I smile and say nothing. I have a preference for redheads, but

I won't admit it if asked. Latif believes that gentlemen prefer blondes —statuesque, buxom, bombshell, silver-haired, Marilyn Monroe, Jane Russell blondes. V.J., on the other hand, sits on the beach looking down. Like a good Muslim, he truly doesn't look up and eye women. Latif thinks naked women have no faces, only bodies. I have to be attracted to the face to look at the body.

Sitting on a bench shaded by an old oak tree, watching beautiful American women—blondes, brunettes, redheads, all almost naked—we the pilgrims in a fool's paradise exchange stories of amour. I tell Latif about Leila, the woman of my dreams and the one I plan to marry.

"I'm talking amour like making love," says Latif.

"You mean Latif's exploits."

"When I was sixteen, living in Multan," starts Latif, "I asked the young washerwoman to come and collect the laundry on a certain day when I knew no one was going to be home. She came at the appointed time, dressed in a white cotton sari and a short white blouse that exposed her belly button. She wore no shoes. I unbutton her blouse; under it, she didn't wear a bra. Her sizeable breasts, well built, her nipples stiff and erect, with great anticipation I unfolded her sari, under which she wore a petticoat. Under her petticoat she was bare— smooth and silky." Latif takes out a cigarette from his pack of Pall Malls and lights one. He takes a puff and looks in the direction of a woman disrobing to her swimsuit. "American women shave their legs and under arms but not the pubic hair," he informs. "Indian and Pakistani men and women traditionally remove their pubic hair. The washerwoman's *yoni* was beardless. She smelled clean, spick-and-span. We did things that were divine and heavenly. Afterward, she picked up the soiled sheets and made the bed. Gratified beyond words, I emptied all my savings from a Player's Navy Cut cigarette tin into my wet palm, it amounted to ten silver *annas* and two copper *paisas*, to give it all to her. She held on to my hand, rubbed my palm with her index finger between two silver coins. Her fingertips were wrinkled from the washing of clothes. She closed my palm and withdrew her hand, leaving the money. She held me to her bosom and said, '*Muna Babu*, I came here because I wanted to. I didn't come for your money.'" Latif looks up smiling, takes another long puff off his cigarette and adds,

"So, at age sixteen I lost my virginity—and I still have not found it."
He grins. "Love in the afternoon is most delightful."

I think of that warm summer afternoon when everyone in my family was gone, attending a wedding. In those days, I used to believe in magical thinking, that if you think of someone long and hard, and if she loves or cares for you, she will know that you are thinking of her. On that day, I wished and I wished, I prayed, I waited and waited and prayed again for Tara to come by. When the sunny afternoon turned into grey evening, my prayers were answered. Tara did show up. I didn't know what to say or what to do. We didn't know what to do, so we did what came naturally. We got undressed like Adam and Eve. We looked at each other, exploring the differences. I kissed her wetness down there, and she put me in her mouth, but I didn't conclude. In the end, we were fearful, too afraid that something might go wrong, so we did not do the real thing. Afterwards, Tara went to the bathroom and rinsed her mouth. She got dressed and rushed home. We acted like it never happened.

Tara never came back to visit me again. I was fourteen. Until I left for the States at the age nineteen, I slept on that faded red cotton futon. Every night, lying down in my bed, I would smell the musky, merry, sweet smell of Tara. I still catch myself daydreaming, lying with Tara on that faded futon.

I watch Latif follow a fleeting object of desire, a gorgeous woman, a 36-28-36. V.J., who grew up an orphan, keeps his head down and says, "When you lose your father you are an orphan, and when you lose your mother, you have to grow up." He looks at his wristwatch, I check mine, it is after five, time for *Asr* prayers. "I've accumulated my share of loneliness," he says, getting up from the bench. "It's time to worship." He goes to pray under a large maple tree, facing *qiblah*. V.J. aspires to convert Christians, Jews, white, and black men to Islam. "My commitment to Islam is such that I want to share this treasure of knowledge with others. I consider this to be my calling. I want to reach out to people who have many misconceptions about Islam. Allah the Almighty can change their perception in a second if He wishes, but we shall also set a good example." As a practicing Muslim, he believes it is his calling to preach. He claims that the reward of converting someone to Islam is everlasting youth and life in Paradise, where there are virgin *houris* and rivers of red wine. Latif thinks he is already in Paradise. "A fool's paradise," says V.J.

Every time V.J. prays in public, he hopes to be discovered by someone in the act of praying. A curious onlooker will ask V.J. a question regarding his method of praying, which allows him to explaining the Islamic ways and what a good Muslim is supposed to be. This leads to further discussion on religion.

A pleasant breeze is blowing off the lake, and today is his lucky day. A pleasantly plump platinum blonde, a citizen or maybe an accidental tourist, encounters the purposeful pilgrim. Latif gets up and walks over to see if he can meet someone as well. I have nothing better to do, so from a safe distance I watch and listen to V.J. in action. With his eyes down and away, without ever looking at her face or making eye contact, V.J. explains, "Islam means to submit. I am a Muslim. I've submitted. Let's examine the nature of Muslim worship for a moment." His accidental tourist seems to have nothing better to do either. She listens to V.J. explain the *Al-Salat*. "To begin with, there are no empty words. The Muslim worshipper stands up, raises his hand, and proclaims, 'God alone is great.' Then he recalls the merits of God. He is so humble that he bends a little, his hands on his knees, proclaiming, 'Glory to my Lord, who alone is majestic. Then he stands up, thanking God for guiding him onto the right path. He is so impressed with the greatness of God that he goes into prostration He prostrates in all humility, declaring, 'Glory to my Lord who alone is high.'"

I wonder if it is human curiosity or courtesy that is keeping the tourist there. She stands like she has turned into stone. Not only does V.J. tell her all about Islamic worship, he also demonstrates. The Blonde stays, and he continues, "Besides an enormous spiritual reward for the Islamic way of worship, there are physical benefits in the performance of *salat*." His eyes now have that distant look, his speech the tone of an *imam*, and he is delivering his sermon: "Every day in our life we are pounded with too many electrostatic charges from the atmosphere. These charges precipitate within our central nervous system and supersaturate it. One has to get rid of these extra charges, or else one will suffer headaches, neck aches, and muscle spasms."

Here he gets graphic, full of details like the street doctors who

117

sell tonics on the byways of Karachi to cure erectile dysfunction. "After you apply my tonic upon your member," the good doctor will proclaim, "you'll have no problem getting it hard and keeping it rigid, durable, and inflexible for long. You can hit it on a rock or hit it with a rock; the rock will break in each case. My tonic will keep you in joy all night long. Satisfaction guaranteed!"

V.J. has his own pitch, "The health benefits of prostration are many. In this position, a person has to support her body on the forehead, hands, and knees. It helps one drain maximum dissipation of extra electrostatic charges from the brain and the central nervous system into the ground. This posture has healthy effects on the joints. This helps eliminate cervical and other spinal diseases. During prostration a person either elevates his buttocks in the air or keeps them pressed against his calf and ankle muscles, which assists maintaining control of the genital region against the passage of any gaseous, solid, or liquid matter, which hinders the spread of hemorrhoids. During prostration, abdominal viscera may press against the diaphragm to exhale more air, thereby allowing more fresh air to be inhaled. Also, the blood supply to the brain and neck is promoted." V.J. looks hopeful, maybe he's found his first convert-to-be. "Islam means to submit," he says.

"Regular prostration during five prayers a day—and mind you that in each prayer one prostrates several times—can help drain para-nasal sinuses and bronchial trees. So, my dear brothers and sisters, let's perform the ablution before prayer and prostrate for peace, concord, harmony of body and soul, and thank Allah for the extra benefits He has granted us. And this, my friends, is the way to heaven."

To us are our deeds and to you are yours, and to Him we are sincere, I say to myself. I've accumulated my share of loneliness. I walk back to our apartment alone.

118

CHAPTER 20

I have a blind date tonight. Actually, Latif asked me to take out his blind date. He has a sure thing coming his way.

I have nothing to do, and besides, I am curious to see how it feels to meet a stranger. That's how the Americans do it. Boys, if they feel an attraction, ask girls to go out, and if the draw is mutual and the chemistry is right, they hold hands, they kiss, and much more. Or so I've been told. And as I've said before, at this point in my life, I can separate the love from the lust. I think most boys think that way. You are what you think, what you do, what you say, what you believe. I'm committed to Leila in my thoughts, in my heart, in my love. I remember the times we laughed and cared. I think about Leila more than anyone else. And even though I have agreed to let my mother one day choose Leila as my wife, today I am a single man living in America, and when in Rome, you do what the Romans do: enjoy what may come naturally. One can lust anybody, so can I, but I'm not that kind of person. Love is a mirror. It reflects one's essence. I'll have to love someone first, and lust afterwards, to marry her. My love is in check. It is for Leila only. I'm inquisitive, eager to learn. I'm ready to chance my lust.

After a long shower, I put on a dab of Bryle cream and comb my hair neatly. I knot a red-and-blue striped tie over a white shirt, and I wear a blue blazer, the one I bought on sale at Wieboldt's. I look at myself in the mirror. I look just right, my old fast-bowler self—tall, slim, and dark. I take a train downtown. Steak for dinner tonight! Who said "America is great, because America is good?" I wonder.

I walk up the stairs of the subway station to the corner of State and Washington. Alice is already there, standing under the Marshall Field's clock, 7:05 p.m. Dressed in a bright yellow crepe silk dress, she looks radiant in the setting August sun. She has brownish-blond hair, large pale-blue eyes, and thin lips, like Leila's. She is attractive, tall, with a narrow waist that flairs into full hips and a full bosom. I like her immediately.

It will not work, I know. I already like her a little too much.

She is friendly; she smiles and says hello. She holds my hand.

119

Her hands are cold. I do not say my name, on Latif's advice. "We Indians, we all look alike to them white folks," he told me.

"What shall we do?" I ask.

"Are you hungry?" she asks.

"I am starving, I haven't eaten in days! Do you have a place in mind?" I ask with a smile, looking across the street to Ted's, steak dinner for $1.99 with salad, baked potatoes, and garlic bread. Latif and I have indulged in a steak dinner there at that price. But even the well-done meat was not cooked enough for us.

She suggests a Hungarian place, the Budapest Inn on Wabash Avenue. We walk to where the train tracks bend to form the Loop. At the Budapest Inn, everything is a red—red carpet, red wallpaper, red tablecloths, and red napkins. Reading a handsomely printed menu bound in red leather, I wonder if I have enough cash while fidgeting in my pocket. After careful consideration of time, place, and money, I order the most inexpensive item—a goulash. Alice orders a glass of house red wine and no dinner. She says she is not hungry.

My goulash arrives. It is red. Sipping her wine, Alice says she teaches English to seventh graders at a Catholic school in Lansing, Illinois. Her parents are Lithuanian, and she grew up in Berwyn, Illinois.

Alice is beautiful, sometimes hauntingly so. I can hardly look her in the eyes. I know she likes me, and I want her. I can tell she'd be kind to me, but women with thin lips I can't trust, and I cannot lust after someone I can fall in love with.

"How does someone decide to study metallurgical engineering?" asks Alice.

I am Rama, not Latif, I want to say. *I am studying civil engineering. I am learning to build bridges.* I shrug my shoulders. I pick at my goulash playfully with my fork, a sterling silver tool, beautifully carved. I admire the fancy gadgets mankind has invented to eat their meals. I think of Mrs. Harrison with fondness. To eat with your hand and not get your fingernails dirty is an art. *I haven't used my deodorant today—I don't need it. I may perspire, but I won't let them see me sweat.*

She takes another sip of her wine and asks if I am enjoying my goulash.

"Yeah, it's fine," I say, avoiding her eyes.

She asks me if I read poetry. I want to tell her how I used to read the poetry of Ghalib and Iqbal every day when I was living back home. My mind wanders. "There are other galaxies beyond the stars," Iqbal had said. And Ghalib had written, "I am in that state of oblivion, from where I learn no news regarding myself." But why bother her with details!

"Not much now," I say.

She says she loves poetry. In fact, it is one of her passions. There is a gleam in her eyes, like the sparkle on the teeth of beautiful women in toothpaste commercials.

"There are nights," she says, "I forget to fall asleep, reading poems."

"Do you have a favorite poet?" I ask to carry on the conversation.

"Too many," she says, smiling. She has a lovely smile. "It's the poem, not the poet. It's the thought, the expression, the feeling. And the imagery." Picking her wine glass, she asks, "What poems do you know by heart?"

I could recite hundreds of Urdu poems, plus all the songs from the Indian movies, but I will spare her, I tell myself. "Not many. One or two," I put my fork down.

"Which one?" she asks.

I momentarily look at her. Our eyes meet. Hers are sad; I look away.

"A thing of beauty is a joy forever," I reply. "What lips my lips have kissed."

The waiter walks to our table and fills my empty glass with water. Alice doesn't order another glass of wine.

I pay our check. We walk out of the restaurant toward Lake Michigan, holding hands. Her hands are still cold. There's a chill in the August wind. She shivers walking beside me. I offer her my jacket. She declines. When I insist, she says that if she takes the jacket, I'll be cold.

"That may be true, but men are supposed to offer their jackets to their dates," I say taking off my jacket. "I've seen it in many movies."

She smiles and accepts my offer. The yellow hue of her dress

121

changes into a shade of green under my blue blazer. She reaches out for my hand.

"Name three of your all-time favorite movies," she says.

"*Love Is a Many Splendored Thing, A Streetcar Named Desire*, and *From Here to Eternity*," I reply, one, two, three.

She stops with my hand in her hand. She turns to me and looks at me, smiling. "*Love Is a Many Splendored Thing*," she repeats.

"Yes," I say feeling sad, "and *From Here to Eternity*."

She squeezes my hand for a moment. I was supposed to kiss her, I think, and I want to. I long to touch her. I want to hold her in my arms and kiss her like Burt kissed Deborah on the beach in *From Here to Eternity*. But if I kiss her once, I will want to kiss her again. If I kiss her again, I will want to see her again, and I will want more, and she may be kind to me, but she will want more, and I will not be able to give.

Summer is almost over. In less than two weeks, I'll be on my way back to school. She is the serious kind, with thin lips. I want to kiss her. I should kiss her, but I don't, I wait too long, she lets my hand go.

We walk silently down Michigan Avenue by Adams. She stops in front of the Art Institute. From her black leather handbag she takes out a worn South Shore Railroad schedule. Unfolding it, she squints at the small print.

"If we walk briskly," she says, "I can make the next train to Hammond."

"You are leaving me already," I say.

"Love 'em and leave 'em," she says with a smile.

At the train station, the 9:50 is ready to pull out. She takes off my jacket, holds it in her hands, and helps me put it on. She gives me a fleeting hug, holding me gently for a moment. "I know you're not going to call me again, but I had a nice evening." She says softly.

She kisses me lightly on the lips and gets on her train. I stand on the platform until the two yellow lights on the last coach of the departed train turn into one dim, yellow blur, like the color of her silk dress. Smelling an unfamiliar fragrance on my jacket, I think of Alice. I didn't even tell her my name.

CHAPTER 21

In the fall, as chance would have it, appears Lisa McCormick, a Ponca City woman, my Marilyn Monroe, my American *Madhubala*. She lives in Scott Hall, and the entire previous school year, I watched her while serving food in the dining room.

This semester Lisa McCormick, with golden hair and large deep-green eyes, walks into my American History class and sits down next to me. Until I met her, I had never seen green eyes. I sit next to her in class, and look into the distance, and write love letters to her that I never give her. She is pinned to Max Reagan, a senior, who plays football for the OSU Cowboys and lives in a fraternity house. I am still writing love letters to Leila, but not as frequently. I guess you can really love someone without really knowing her. Yes. No. Maybe. I don't even write to my mother every week any more.

"They are your friends until you start eyeing their women," reminds Latif.

I don't like Max much. He is big, muscular, blond, and beautiful, with a crew cut. He looks like a football player. Max treats me courteously, and I treat him likewise. Max doesn't understand my relationship with Lisa. I don't understand my relationship with Lisa. Having committed to marrying a woman of my mother's choosing, I'm not entitled to expressing my attraction for any other woman.

Lisa works at the university library from seven in the evening until midnight, the closing time, on Mondays and Thursdays. Just by chance, I always manage to run into her during her coffee breaks, and we have coffee together. Drinking my coffee with milk and sugar, I tell her about my life back home in Karachi and how I am studying civil engineering so I can go back and build bridges. Lisa is not just lovely; she is kind. She volunteers to help me with lots of things, like my English, offering to edit or even type my term papers. She listens to everything I say with fascination and tells me about American customs, and how she wants to be a writer and have many children.

I put a quarter in the jukebox and play Joe Dowell, "Wooden Heart," and Peter Paul and Mary's "Lemon Tree." Lisa presses L-23, and the Shirelles sing "Soldier Boy."

123

As if by chance, at the closing of the library, I'd fake running into her by chance at the front gate or by the lamppost and walk her to Scott Hall. Once when Max was away playing football, Lisa and I went to see *No Exit* at the University Cinema. I didn't like the movie. During one of our coffee breaks before the Christmas holidays, Lisa tells me out of the blue that she'll throw Max's pin in his face if I marry her. It is not practical, I think. One does not marry an American blonde if one is planning to build bridges in Pakistan.

I say nothing. I sit there, adding more sugar and cream to my bitter coffee.

It is a cool night, with a gray mist in the air. Walking past Theta Pond from the library to Scott Hall, Lisa holds my hand and kisses me. With much hesitation and great anticipation, I kiss her back. Yes, I kiss her full lips, her open mouth. But I don't tell her how much I adore her.

❧

At the end of the spring semester, everyone leaves me at the same time. V.J. and Latif are graduating, and Lisa, who has been talking about quitting school for a while, tells me during a coffee break on a cool evening in May that she is going to Kansas City to work at Hallmark.

"I sat next to you an entire semester, learning American History," she says, looking at me, "wanting to lie down beside you."

I stare down into my coffee.

She continues, "What I sensed from you is that you wanted to do exactly what I wanted." She shakes her head in disbelief. The curls of her golden hair bounce. "But you never let me in on what's on your mind or what you have been thinking. The lesson I've learned is to never get involved with foreign students."

There is a pause. I say nothing. She continues, "I've decided to go to Kansas City and live with Max. Max is graduating, and he already has a job with Kemper. I think we'll get married, and I'll finish college at night school." She stares at me, her green eyes wide.

I want to scream, "I love you!" but I don't. I'm not sure.

"I never know what you're thinking. I never know what's on

your mind," she repeats. "Are you seeing someone? Do you date?"

I glance her way, looking past her. *I am afraid of love because I'm lost in love* is what I want to say. Can't you see? I'm so much in love with you, but my heart is taken. If all were equal, I would be yours forever and would for wish you to be mine and mine only. But I'm not from here, I'm not allowed to fall in love or leave the tribe of my origin, I can't be yours or let you be mine. Yes, dear sweetheart, I'd love to lie down beside you, hold you in my arms, feel that precious inside of you, and contemplate, meditate, concentrate, manipulate, ejaculate. I'm bound by honor, and if I expect my wife to be pure, spotless, immaculate, how could I be tainted, stained, and adulterated. I've allowed myself to look but not touch. Without introduction, without blinking my eyes, sitting in the same position, I recite, "Of my brief life, half is gone to longing, and the other half is gone to biding my time."

Lisa stares at me. A tear rolls down her cheek. "It is not too late, you know," she says with a sad smile. "I can stay."

She is right, I think, but instead I explain, "The verse I just recited was loosely translated from a poem by Zafar, the last Mughal king of India. Zafar died in exile in Rangoon, where the British imprisoned him." I look at her, her waiting eyes. Taking pleasure in being sad, being incomplete, I continue, "Personally, I don't mind living in exile, but I would like to die at home."

Lisa with her sad smile looks so beautiful sitting across from me, wearing a red OSU Cowboy jersey. I put a quarter in the jukebox. I punch in A-17, Marty Robbins' "Devil Woman." I punch C-12, and the Everly Brothers sing "Crying in the Rain."

"Why aren't we playing our songs?" Lisa asks.

"In November 1889, the first jukebox made its debut in San Francisco at the Palais Royale," I inform. "It's not the song you play on the jukebox, it's the music you hear in your head that matters. It's your turn."

Lisa looks at me. This romance is over. She has that far away look in her eyes. She presses B-12, Nat King Cole, "Lazy Hazy Crazy Days of Summer." We finish our coffee in silence and walk out of the cafeteria. A silver crescent like a broken glass bangle follows us.

I walk Lisa back to Scott Hall. A cool wind blows silently; I

125

think how sad the spring is. We climb up the steps leading to her dormitory. Lisa reaches out and holds my hand as we arrive at the last step; there is nowhere further to go. Heroic, showing courage in the face of loss, pain, and difficulty, I hold her in my arms firmly and kiss her with desire. We both knew that we would not see or meet again. I kiss her for the last time. I hold her hand, the lights at the entrance flash, announcing curfew, and it's time to walk in the dorm. We kiss for the last time, with our mouths closed. She walks in, and I walk away.

At home I find a letter from Leila, but I do not open it.

Another summer passes, then comes fall. Like the pages of a calendar in a movie, blown by the wind to show the passage of time, I am still on the task—at another summer job, back at school again, studying fluid mechanics, thermodynamics, statistics, relating to bodies at rest and forces in equilibrium, and examining the dynamics of forces in relation to motion. The year Lisa left they raised the price of coffee with cream and sugar to seven cents at the OSU cafeteria. Black coffee is still a nickel. I start drinking my coffee black to save a few pennies, missing Lisa. I'm still lonely, still lost, and summer comes again, another fall, and at the end of a new spring, I graduate with honors, and with honor bestowed, my self-esteem is high. This year they've raised the price of coffee to a dime, with or without cream and sugar. I continue to drink my coffee black. This is how I'll always remember Lisa: coffee was a nickel, with or without cream, when I knew her.

Two days before I'm supposed to leave for Chicago to seek employment in my vocation, civil engineering, I receive a letter from my sister Yasmin. Enclosed is a photograph of Leila, long, dark hair combed back neatly, a wide forehead, an erect nose, and rose petal lips, her large eyes yielding away from the camera. She wears a choker around her slim long neck. Leila, the girl in the photograph, is now the woman of my mother's choosing. It is official; I'm betrothed to love of my life, my lovely, most beautiful, Leila. She is too beautiful for me. I shall be happy, I say to myself, and I think I am.

I put the photograph in my wallet, behind the other

126

photograph of Leila that I still carry along with my Social Security card and driver's license.

I leave for Chicago, where Latif is living and working in the metallurgy department of an industrial heat-treating oven and furnace manufacturer. "Your timing is perfect, thanks to an undeclared war in Indochina, there are plenty of jobs in the Chicago area for engineers," he wrote me in his note. "And now that V.J. has left to go back to Peshawar, we can share the apartment, as long as I get the bedroom."

❧

After spending the previous three summers in the Windy City, arriving in Chicago for me is like coming home, and, I must admit, I love the city by the lake. From the Greyhound bus station, I walk to the subway, take a train to Fullerton Avenue, and walk over to Latif's apartment in the Fullerton Arms.

Once again, Latif sleeps in the bedroom on a double bed, and I, as always, sleep on the large brown sleeper sofa in the living room. Without much difficulty, I find a job in the Loop at Love, Moore & Knott, Engineers. I design portable bridges and houses to be used in the Far East.

CHAPTER 22

On a hot Friday in July, I stop at Grocerland on Lincoln Avenue to pick up food for dinner on the way home from work. At home in the mailbox, I find a letter from Lisa. I bring the letter upstairs and put it on the kitchen table beside the bag of food. I unpack the groceries one item at a time: a large, cut-up chicken, a twelve-ounce container of Dean's plain yogurt, a loaf of Wonder bread, a three-pound bag of onions, a two-pound box of long-grain Riceland rice, two bulbs of garlic, a tin of McCormick's curry powder, a tin of cayenne pepper, and one quart of Wesson vegetable oil.

I wash the chicken, dice the onions and garlic, and sauté the chicken in onion and garlic and vegetable oil. After mixing the curry powder and yogurt in to a sauce, I add it to the chicken and turn down the flame to let it simmer. I put on water for tea. When it boils, I brew myself a pot of tea. I pour a cup, stirring in Carnation condensed milk and sugar. I sit down with my cup of tea and pick up Lisa's letter, a yellow envelope. Inside on two sheets of lighter yellow paper, she writes:

Dear Rama,

My plans to go to Kansas City have worked out nicely. College is just a part of my past now, something I enjoyed and will never regret, but for now I have no desire to return to school. I guess I just grew out of it. My job at Hallmark is great and Max's job at Kemper is also working out well. He's in marketing. He doesn't want to join the Army and does not want to get drafted. He wants to get married in October and plans to go to graduate school for business in the spring. I want to start having babies. After all my unhappiness at school, I guess it's about time something 'swell' came my way. I'm taking an art course at night, figure drawing (that's sketching nudes). It's been interesting and challenging, and my teacher is pleased with my progress. There's a possibility that one day I may be able to work in Hallmark's art department.

I want to thank you for being such a dear during the school years. I am eager to hear from you soon.

128

Love,
Lisa
July 12, 1964

It had to happen; I knew it. Somehow, though, I still feel low. I want Latif to return from work so I can talk to someone. I put the letter on the kitchen table and attend to my cooking. I turn the fire down lower.

Before I can finish my second cup of tea, Latif comes into the kitchen through the back door, accompanied by a young woman with bleached blonde hair. Her roots are showing. She is carrying a small green vinyl suitcase. She smiles vaguely at me and without saying a word, slips off to Latif's bedroom.

"I met Mary Lou at the Greyhound Bus Station," Latif informs me. "She lost her purse, with all her money and her ticket to Memphis, Tennessee."

That meant it's time for me to get out of the apartment. I stir the chicken one more time, it is done, I turn the flame off. I smile at Latif knowingly, pick up my keys from the kitchen table, and get out. A warm day in July, I walk east on Fullerton Avenue, turn left, and head north on Clark. I see *Lawrence of Arabia* (221 min., Technicolor, Super Panavision 70) now in popular run at the Century Theater after a long downtown run. Latif thought that Peter "Lawrence of Arabia" O'Toole, was robbed of the Oscar for Best Actor that year because the members of the Academy of Motion Pictures voted with their hearts for familiar dollops of social conscience and gave the award to Gregory "To Kill a Mocking Bird" Peck. Always a bridesmaid but never a bride, Peck, had been nominated for the best actor award four times: *The Keys of the Kingdom (1945), The Yearling (1946), Gentleman's Agreement (1947),* and *Twelve O'clock High (1949).* I thought it was about time that most handsome, most deserving, my favorite American actor won the prestigious Academy Award for Best Actor. Omar Sharif was also up for an Oscar that year for Best Actor in a Supporting Role for his performance in *Lawrence of Arabia,* but Ed Begley bagged it for *Sweet Bird of Youth.*

After three hours and forty-one minutes of adventures with Sir Lawrence and the Arabs, told through flashbacks after his

129

accidental death in the 1930s, I get out of my movie at eleven thirty.

I'm hungry. I walk home with the anticipation of heating up my chicken curry for a late dinner. I get home at midnight. The action in Latif's bedroom penetrates through the walls. I enter the kitchen to find it robbed clean, all of the chicken eaten, from wing to wing, from neck to tail, along with the entire loaf of Wonder bread. The pot has been washed. I drink a glass of milk and eat couple of stale Salerno butter cookies. I go back to the living room where my pillow and a white sheet lie on the couch. I use the bathroom, brush my teeth, and pack my ears with cotton balls. I get undressed, hanging my pants and shirt on the arm of the couch. I lie down in my Fruit-of-the-Loom briefs without unfolding the couch. I lay there for a long time, trying not to hear protesting gurgles of my empty stomach and the unabashed noises filtering from Latif's room in waves.

I wake up early in the morning. I am glad to be working on Saturday. I put water on stove for tea and take a quick shower and shave. I drink my tea quickly and leave the apartment. I work ten hours of overtime at time-and-a-half, earning one hundred and twenty dollars for a day's work. I get off at six in the evening. I eat a cold roast beef sandwich at Mr. Beef on the corner of State and Adams.

I go to see a double feature at the Clark Theater so as not to arrive home too early. The Clark is a wonderful movie experience; it shows a different double feature every day of the year. Often, the features are chosen according to a weekly or monthly theme. Once, they showed an entire series of Orson Welles pictures. The doors open at 7:30 a.m. and the last show starts at 3 a.m. Today they are showing *Hud* (112 min.), the story of an aging Texas cattleman, Melvyn Douglas, and his son, played by Paul Newman, who is an abomination and a disgrace to his country, home, and family. Melvyn won the Oscar for best supporting actor for his performance in *Lonely Are the Brave* (107 min.), which also stars, Kirk Douglas, no relation to Melvyn.

I get home after eleven through the back door. Sitting on the kitchen table leaning against the salt and pepper shakers is a pink envelope from Leila. I open it carefully; the aroma of *raat ki rani* fills the air. How little have I communicated with her, and how little I've

130

missed her of late. I have talked about her a great deal with friends and strangers. I've also shown her photograph to everyone with much pride and appreciated the compliment, "She is very pretty," with a broad smile of a lucky man. I'm delighted.

Dear Rama,
I feel your presence everywhere and I miss you all the time.
O morning breeze, go tell my Lad of dreams
That in the mornings and in the evenings, I miss him immensely,
O whisper of my heartbeat.
I sit in my room with a setting sun. I look at your letters and I see you. I want to say something to you. I want to talk to you, but you are not here, and I don't even have a photograph of you. You disappear from my sight, but not from my imagination. Without you I am empty and incomplete. When the gorgeous evening is at its peak and the shadows are their longest, I yearn for you so much. Each heartbeat cries out your name. I weep silently.
I am waiting. I am waiting! When will you come?
A thousand kisses plus one more to a special person and all his especial particular and specific...
Yours forever,
Leila
June 28, 1964

Action still continues in Latif's room. Exhausted, I lie down on my couch after packing my ears with cotton. Closing my eyes, covering my face with the white linen while imagining Leila, I fall asleep.

In the morning, I hear Latif flush the toilet, then Mary Lou, and then Latif again. I cover my head, pretending to be fast asleep. When the ten o'clock Sunday church bells ring, I hear Latif and Mary Lou leave through the rear door. I sleep late. After a breakfast of a two-egg omelet, I sit down and write a letter home.

Dear Everyone:
When I arrived in America just over four years ago, I weighed only one hundred and twenty-eight pounds, and now I weigh one hundred and forty-two. So like a camel in a

131

daffy town, I stay away from museums and zoos, fearing they may stand me up next to a stuffed orangutan or a dromedary.

It scares me to say that so far most of what I desired and wished for has been granted to me by God Almighty. And thanks to your prayers and best wishes I've had no problems, and I've not encountered any difficulties in this foreign country. I'm employed and making more than three hundred dollars a week, not counting overtime pay.

All I wish for now is to work hard, save all my money.

In the end though, the best city in the world is the one where your home is, and home is where the heart is, so like an idiot from a gathering of fools, it's only a matter of time when this native will return home.

Yours,
Rama
July 15, 1964

I write to Leila as well.

My Dear Leila:

Life is not always what one wants or desires. There are only stolen moments. But every time I think of love, I'll think of you. I desire you in more ways than I know.

To think that you love me is a reason for joy, and I am happy that your love came my way, that you love me. There is nothing more I want, just your love, your unconditional love, and your love forever is all my heart desires. This knowledge will keep the flame alive and will always bring me joy. In my life, I'll always love you...

Love,
Rama
July 15, 1964

In the evening after dinner, Latif and I are sitting in the Seminary Restaurant where Lincoln, Fullerton, and Halsted intersect. Watching a beautiful woman cross the street, Latif says, "Thirty-eight, twenty-six, thirty-eight. Watch out for those front and rear bumpers."

132

I say nothing. Latif continues, "Mary Lou was a nymph. She wanted it and wanted it. When I saw blood in my urine, I said to myself it was time to take Mary Lou back to the bus station."

I just listen.

"Mary Lou and I read Lisa's letter," Latif says, changing the subject. "I think it is for the best. You two had such a platonic love for each other. It's time you get yourself the sweets, and the good part of living in America is that you don't have to buy a cow to get the milk." He winks. "And you would never buy a pair of shoes without trying them for a fit."

I feel lost and lonely; I can't describe my emptiness. I don't know whether I believe in extramarital, premarital sexual intercourse, I only know mono-mental, handle-with-care sex. I believe in all parties concerned having a fulfilling sexual experience, and that there should be no criminal or social punishment for consensual sex between two or more consenting adults. I look into the distance. "Is that right?" I say, watching a blonde woman stand at the curb. She's waiting for the streetlight to change and pushing her skirt down to keep it from blowing up in the wind. When the wind subsides, she releases her skirt and crosses the street, smiling to herself.

"Don't ever forget one thing," says Latif. " *Gori*s are only to fuck, not to marry."

"*Gori* or *kali* is not the issue," I say. "Inside, all women look and feel the same. It is important for men to understand that women too have a right to respectful, pleasurable, satisfying sex with a partner of their choosing. She also has a right to say no to sex, and she has the right to make decisions regarding her body, including contraception, and reproduction, and protection from disease."

"Did you attend a Dykes of America or something meeting?" says Latif. "Do you realize that this is the best time of your life? Let your hair down. Enjoy." He takes a sip of his whiskey sour. "You are young and dashing and living in America, the best country in the world, where all the women are beautiful." He takes another sip of his drink and says, "Holy water is good for you. You should try it." He puckers his lips and swallows.

I don't argue. My mind is somewhere else. Latif is dashing, looking resplendent in an olive green suit that complements the color of his skin with a blue oxford shirt and striped blue-and-green tie. "You are only young once," he continues. "Like a kid in a candy store, I want to be totally self-indulgent, and I want one of everything, but I have only a dime," Latif sighs.

"I need to feel an uncontrollable desire, a yearning, a hunger beyond words before the libido will flow," I say. "I cannot be with one person while I am thinking of another."

"That is backward thinking. When you are blooming, during the tender years, there is always dew in the morning, on flowers and buds alike. These are the splendid days of rejuvenation. Let the libido flow for the one you're with."

I didn't tell Latif, or any one else for that matter, of my few escapades. During my four years of college in America, I have fooled around, slept around, once or twice, definitely not more than three times and not more than with three women, and actually, I only did it with one of them. It all happened suddenly, three women in the course of less than two semesters, my senior year.

I guess the first one was Lisa McCormick. This was after Latif and V.J. had left for Chicago and Max for Kansas City. I was walking her to her dorm on a hot day in May, a few days before she left school to moved to Kansas City, when she looked straight into me with those deep-green eyes and asked me if I desired to see her naked. I was shocked to hear what she was proposing. I was dying to see her naked. I looked at her for long time with hunger, but I said, no, that it would not be necessary.

Carrying a gray Samsonite makeup case, she arrived at my apartment that evening. She went into the bathroom and came back wearing a black silk robe and nothing more. She told me that I could ask her do anything, pose any which way, but that I could not touch her or get undressed. There was all to see, and like an ecdysiast, she got into showing her body—all the intimate spots, the spread shot, peeled open, the fanny, the twat, the slit, the slot, the tits, the rim, and the spot. We did not have sex, but when I was no longer able to contain myself, she unzipped and touched me and released my tension. I was much gratified.

Then there was Linda Long, whom I met that fall, my senior year. I was in line for a cup of coffee at the student union cafeteria,

134

when she approached me and asked if I was Arabic. I looked at her, so sensual in appearance, seemingly devoted to a luxurious corporeal life, inclined to provide physical pleasure, a certain desire was all over me.

"Arabic is a language," I say, "No, I'm not an Arab."

"Are you an Egyptian?"

"That would make me an African."

"Listen, Mr. Wise Guy," she says, "you reminded me of my boyfriend who was Arabic, Egyptian, and a great lover."

That was strike one. "Well, sweetheart," I say, retuning her smile, "I'm not Arab or Egyptian, and certainly not a great lover." It should have ended right there, but it did not. I ordered a cup of black coffee, she ordered hers with milk and sugar and slice of cherry pie. We walked to a booth in the cafeteria and sat down. She told me this story of her life, "My freshman year, I went to the American University in Beirut. A wealthy Arab from Egypt had me kidnapped and taken to a large tent in the Sahara, where I was kept as sex slave, which included sequential pulling the train. There were other slave women, and for one week, I was taught how to make love, and then I was set free. That experience made me a slave to sex." I didn't believe her This was strike two, but I stayed for one more swing of bat. We did it once, no twice, actually, three different times, counting only one for the first time, when we really did it three times. She was good, and she was good to me, but then she lost interest. I guess I was not a good enough lover.

The last one was literally a one-shot affair. I don't understand why it happened. I met BB, Barbara Burns, during my sophomore year. She ran Quick Mart right off Highway 77, open seven days a week, 365 days a year, from eight in the morning till midnight. Her store sold donuts, bread, canned foods, soda pop, beer, cigarettes, and condoms that you buy from a machine in the bathroom, which was inside the storefront. BB was from Denton, Texas. Her husband, Dick Burns ran another Quick Mart in Denton. They had a 19-year-old son, Billy, who lived at home in Denton and went to a community college. On weekends Billy worked at the Quick Mart in Denton. I used to buy day-old bread from BB, which she sold at half the price. I'd stop at her store on the way back to my apartment on Knoblock Street at night after studying at the library. She took a liking to me and started selling me bread for half price at the end of the day. Then she started giving me the day-old bread for free. I appreciated her generosity, although I did not need that much bread. Still I'd stop by her store two or three times a week on my way home just to talk with her. She was about 36, maybe 38, years old with large, sad blue-grey eyes, a round pink face, full lips, and light-red hair that drew me into her shop the first time I saw her. I'd just stand by the cash register, and we would talk and talk. When an occasional customer walked in, I'd walk away pretending to look for food in the aisles while she rang up the sale. After the customer left, we'd pick up our conversation right where we'd stopped. She was a good listener. I was happy to have her in my life after Lisa left. She helped me understand many things. Until I met her, I did not know that cowboys could be poor and cowgirls can have the blues. I'd never go to her store on the weekends. That's when Dick came with supplies and to stay with BB. She lived in the backroom that was also the storage area.

Upon graduation, after receiving my security deposit back in full from my landlord and filing a change of address at the post office effective immediately, (I bought a bouquet of flowers) I went to say goodbye to BB. It was past four on a hot Thursday afternoon in June. She looked at me more sadly than ever before. My heart melted to see her look like this. I did not know what to say or do; I was feeling lonesome on my own. Without saying anything, she locked the door to the store and flipped on a sign that said BACK IN FIFTEEN MINUTES. BB lead me to the storage area and asked me to sit on an old oak office chair that sat in front of an old oak desk filled with bills to pay. She walked into the bathroom, put a quarter into the vending machine, and cranked out a Trojan. She walked back to where I sat, unzipped my pants, and pulled me out. I was stiff. Somehow I knew what was in store for me. She tore open the Trojan and unfolded it onto my hard-on. Without getting undressed, she removes her white panties from under the sky blue dress that she wore every day to work. Dripping for it, she buried the bone. Push-pull, Push-pull, Bang, bang. Banana and cream. Thank you, Ma'am. She kissed me on the lips with passion before sending me away, all this accomplished in less than fifteen minutes.

That is the list of my sexual exploits. I think I'm slick, definitely more secretive than Latif. I should not have engaged in this much sex. I'm in love with Leila, and the fact that my mother has now arranged our wedding makes me a committed man. Other than Lisa, I was never in any serious emotional bond with the other participants, although I did like BB a lot. I don't know why Barbra Burns did what she did. I think hers was a parting gift, an act of kindness. Lisa and I did not really do it. She was just being nice, and I truly cherished it. I think men make love to forget, and women make love to remember. And Linda Long was all lust. What do I know of love or making love? Still, I'm grateful to them one and all. I probably will not tell Leila about them, there is no reason she has to know. My heart is pure. Perhaps all that I've experienced will make me a better lover, and maybe I can teach her a thing or two.

For the four years that I have known Latif, he has been a very resourceful person for finding a date. In our neighborhood there are three hospitals, and he makes a habit of having at least one dinner a week at each one of the hospital cafeterias where plenty of young student nurses also eat their dinners. Latif finishes his drink with one big gulp. I empty my cup of black coffee. Latif pays our check, and we walk out of the Seminary Restaurant, Latif to pick up his date, a nurse who works a split shift at a nearby Children's Hospital, and me to see *David and Lisa* (US, 1962, 94min., bw) the story of two troubled adolescents who meet at a special school and fall in love.

CHAPTER 23

After a leisurely breakfast on the Saturday before Labor Day, dressed in beige jeans, white canvas Converse shoes, and a light-yellow long-sleeved cotton shirt, I ride a train to downtown from Fullerton Avenue. Carson's is having its annual back-to-school sale, and I need fall clothing for the northern winters. I have to wear ties and jackets at my job. I need new clothes, and for once, I am making good money. I like dressing well, but I don't like spending a lot on clothes. I consider myself someone who dresses in style, although I'm not into fashion. It was four years ago on a labor day that I arrived in Stillwater, Oklahoma, as a foreign student. I'm not a student anymore, but I still remain a foreigner. I no longer need to translate everything from Urdu before I speak in English, but I'm not spontaneous. I don't feel fluent, especially when I'm trying to explain a complicated thought, and I still dream in Urdu. In my dreams, English is spoken only occasionally. I have had good fortune with money, and I'm careful in love. I'm not generous. I miss Leila. But I tell myself that my hardship will be over in two years when I'll be at home again, where I'll marry the woman I love. And if my wife is going to be a virgin, should I not be a virgin as well? But I'm not. I am blemished forever. Or, is it as Shakespeare says, "A little water clears us of this deed?"

I get off the train, climb the stairs to State and Madison, and exit east. In front of Wieboldt's Department Store, the screams of a totally out of control young man draw me in. "I am for peace! I am for peace!" he yells over and over again. Dressed in army fatigues and a khaki woolen overcoat on this hot day, he has short blond hair and looks about eighteen or nineteen. "Yes, piece by piece! First Vietnam, then Cambodia and Laos—piece by piece! I'm dying to go to war," he shrieks. He appears too loony to get drafted. On the other side of his rant stand seven women under a banner that reads "Women for Peace." "War is not good for children and other living things" says another sign held by a dark-haired young woman. The women for peace stand in silent vigil, watching the young man's antics from behind a folding table covered with a white tablecloth and stacked with leaflets and flyers. He paces back and forth glaring and shouting.

138

"I'm for peace! I'm for peace! But there is no peace without war." A small crowd surrounds the young man and the gathering of women. He was like of the sidewalk medical quacks on the footpaths of Karachi, who would charm snakes to attract crowds. Once an audience gathered, they'd pitch herbs, tonics, and lizard oil, and offer generous advice on how to cure impotence and erectile dysfunction.

This young man is not selling anything. He is a snake without a charmer. He rips the white tablecloth from the table with one violent shake and runs into the street, throwing it in the air. The white cotton tablecloth floats momentarily in the updraft then begins to flutter down into the traffic. Without a second thought, I run like my old fast-bowler self into the middle of the two-way traffic on State Street. I pick up the tablecloth and run back to the women for peace, who are gathering up scattered leaflets and flyers. I hand it to one of the two women still holding the banner. Without slowing my pace, I cross Madison Street and walk into Carson Pirie Scott & Co.

In the four years that I've lived in America, I've grown from a size 36 long into 38 long. Standing in the University Shop in the young men's corner, I try on a maroon blazer once, and then I try it on again. It is a 'Cricketer,' in my size, 100% virgin wool. It fits perfectly; even the sleeves are the right length. And it's been reduced twice to twenty-four dollars. I look at myself in the mirror again. I have only had blazers that were blue or green, and I am not sure if maroon is my color.

"That's your color," I hear a voice.

Before I can even turn to look for the source, the most beautiful eyes in the world appear over my left shoulder, reflected in the mirror. I am vaguely aware that all movement—traffic, trains, planes, cars, breaths, heartbeats, even the sun and the moon—have stopped. I pivot slowly, taking in her dark hair. She is tall and slim, wearing an Indian Madras dress with green leaves and yellow and blue flowers. I want to take my eyes away from her, but they will not even blink. She is my Sita, and I am totally, utterly besotted, smitten, and love-struck. Before I can even say hello, I know I want her in my life for as long as I can. She is the woman my mother worried and warned me about.

Sita, who evidently has not noticed this great cosmic event,

139

walks around me with a critical eye. "This fits you perfectly," she declares.

I look at her in the mirror again. Her magnificent eyes are dark brown. She is gallant and carefree. She has an enchanting smile. No one I have ever met smiles that way, and no one ever will, I already know. When I am gray and ancient, it is her smile I'll remember most. I look at her. "Hello, Sita, I'm Rama."

Her smile refuses to fade. She continues to smile but says nothing. She's smiling, and her eyes are upon *me*, Rama. For the first time in my life, I experience the shock of instantaneous communication without words. In the moment that our eyes lock, we exchanged something so subtle, so ineffable, so complete that all of the languages of Babel put together could not give voice to it. The intensity of it is too great to bear. I shift my gaze to her reflection in the mirror. I watch her looking at me; I swallow the delicate sweep of her eyebrows, the long, thick eyelashes. *Beautiful Sita into the mirror...* We begin a slow, intimate exploration of our reflections, first in the mirror, and then in one another's eyes, and then back to the mirror again.

"That's a beautiful fit, Sir. Like it was tailored for you."

The salesman's voice shatters our link. He's a small man, beautifully dressed, very effeminate, with a childlike eagerness in his face and voice.

"Yes," I reply, "it is perfect. I must have it."

"And you must," says my Sita.

I pay for the blazer, afterward Sita and I take the escalator to the Tartan Cafeteria. We sit down across from each other with a pot of black coffee and a pecan pie to share. My Sita tells me her life story.

"First of all," she says, combing her hair back with long, delicate fingers, "I am Sabina Dubin. I'm Jewish, and I hate being Jewish, not that there is anything wrong with being Jewish, but I hate it because everyone else hates us." She looks at me, very serious.

"I thought Jews were the chosen people," I say.

"It is a heavy load to carry," she answers.

"I can still be a child some days, but I am all brains," she volunteers. I study her; there is plenty of gorgeous body there. I let her talk and say nothing. "My father is busy teaching pathology at

Columbia, and my mother is busy being a social worker at child welfare, and I am busy being a graduate student at the University of Chicago, studying Renaissance literature, and one day I want to teach literature and write short stories." She pauses and takes a sip of her coffee. "What more can I tell you about myself? I'm twenty-four. After I graduated from Princeton, I traveled a year in Europe and lived on an experimental farm in Israel. I've seen war, and I know that life is short." There is sadness in her eyes.

A neon sign blinks garishly in my brain: *She is the one. Be warned. Run now or you will be taken.* I have tumbled over into the danger zone, stepped over the edge of the abyss. I want to be with you for the rest of my life, I wanted to say aloud, but I must be careful. I suddenly have this feeling that I'm the protagonist, and she is the leading lady, full of charm and elegance. This is a scene from a movie I always wanted to see but hadn't yet been made. I ignore all the flashing warning signs of falling masonry, radioactivity, flash floods, the third rail, and slippery rocks. I sit in frozen awe. The words of caution that my mother had uttered echo in my head. Not knowing what to say, I take out the photographs of Leila from my wallet and show them to Sabina.

"My fiancé," I say with an awkward grin. "This is the woman my mother wishes me to marry, and I've consented to it." I was falling for Sabina and I was afraid of complications, love complications. I lie. I don't tell her Leila is the woman I loved, I chose.

"A lady killer," she says, "equipped with both love possessed and love kept."

"It is the love lost that matters," I say solemnly.

"I suppose you know the meaning of life?"

I smile knowingly, but say nothing.

"So, is life a multiple-choice test or is it a true-or-false test?" she asks, looking directly at me.

"Actually," I say immediately, "life is a one-page essay."

We sit smiling at each other. When you have to think about what to say, it is hard to be natural.

"I can tell you like me," says Sabina, her smile enchanting. "Why are you afraid?"

I want to tell her the whole story from Leila to Lisa, but

141

maybe it's too early. Besides, it makes no difference. *She is the one*, the neon sign continues to flash. I never want her to leave me. Instead of thinking right, I'm thinking wrong.

"Things happen," she says with that smile that is already breaking my heart. "You should have more faith in yourself." I needed to run away from her, fast and far.

"I can't make any promises," I say instead.

She rests her fork on her plate; she looks lost in her thoughts briefly. "I haven't asked for any," she says.

"I feel like I have already loved and lost," I say, picking up my fork.

"Who hasn't?" Sabina shrugs.

We finish our coffee and pecan pie and walk outside. It is a hot, sunny day, she squints her eyes as if the light is too bright. She takes out her sunglasses from her purse and puts them on. She looks likes some Hollywood leading lady, like Ann Bancroft in *The Miracle Worker* (US, 1962, 106min., bw). A damp wind blows off the lake. I keep my head up and my shoulders straight and walk Sabina to the train station, listening to my own September album in my head. I want to reach out and hold her hand. Instead I switch the Carson's box with my blazer into my other hand. We descend the concrete stairs to track one, "I Want to Hold Your Hand." The Illinois Central 3:05 sits poised to depart, its engine humming.

Sabina takes my hand. "Come and visit me soon."

"How about right now?" I ask hanging onto her hand.

In one quick dash, we both jump onto the train. We take the first open seat for two facing the direction in which the train will be moving; Sabina sits next to the window. Before the train slides from beneath the canopy of the platform, I see my reflection grinning at me from the windowpane.

Then the sun shining from the west falls on the window, and my reflection disappears. Sabina moves closer to me and puts her head on my shoulder. "Darling," she whispers in my ear.

"I hate fake enthusiasm," I say.

"I hate sweet people," she counters. "I think everyone should be cold. Everybody should live for themselves, everybody should love for themselves, work for themselves, make money for themselves, steal

142

for themselves, cheat for themselves, think for themselves, feel for themselves, and lie for themselves and themselves only. And I think people should be responsible for their own orgasms."

"You don't mean any of it. And no one should be responsible for his own orgasms," I counter.

"Darling! You must believe me," she says. "Man is supreme. A woman should worship no one but Herself."

"Now, you're being deliberately outrageous," I say.

The train moves on.

At the 57th Street station, we get off the train and walk down to Sabina's car, a yellow Volkswagen with orange daisies pasted onto it. There is a blue sticker on the bumper of a white dove carrying an olive branch. She gets in first and opens the passenger door for me. The car is like an oven. She reaches up and opens the sunroof. It rolls open all the way to the back seat. I like it. It's like riding in a convertible. I have finally arrived. This is the American scene, like in *Where the Boys Are* (US, 1960, 99min., Metrocolor, Cinemascope). Except, I should be driving.

Sabina lives on Dorchester Street in a one-bedroom apartment. We climb three flights of stairs to her living room. There is an old carved couch upholstered in cut velvet that she tells me she bought for thirty dollars at the Salvation Army on Clybourn. An old oak rocking chair sits in front of the fireplace. On the oak hardwood floor lies a Chinese rug, purple with a green border, that the previous tenants had left behind. On each side of the fireplace are bookshelves filled with books. I note Jane Austen, James Joyce. Above the bookshelves sits a turntable.

She walks into the kitchen. I follow. Her kitchen is clean and well organized. She fills a kettle and lights the stove. We sit down at a round mission style table. The wind seems to have shifted, blowing in gently from an open window, and it feels like home, warm and cozy.

She makes Earl Grey tea in a yellow teapot. I like that not only does she drink her tea with milk and sugar, she heats the milk. I'm on my second cup of tea when somewhere in the distance church bells start to ring. I look out the window. A bluebird sits in a maple tree with yellow leaves. Sabina gets up and walks to her bedroom. There's silence, and then I hear water running in the bathroom. Sabina

143

reappears wrapped in a lavender silk kimono. She kisses me lightly on my neck.

"Somebody needs to take charge here," she whispers in my ear. "Let's take a bath."

"There is no responsibility without consequence," I say quietly.

"I wouldn't buy a car without kicking the tire, sex is something basic and necessary, at the right time and with the right person. Some people with their sexual hang-ups and neuroses act like they are kryptonite."

She is much more complicated than I am. Should I tell her that I'm a kryptonite?

Feeling a certain tingle, I shiver. Without saying a word, I walk to the bathroom. The tub is full of steaming water. On a table in the corner, under the bright sunlight leaking in from a half-curtained window stands a lighted red candle. There is the scent of patchouli.

I hear Joan Baez singing "Daddy, You Been on My Mind." In the foggy full-length mirror hanging on the bathroom door, I see my image humbled by fog, dressed in street clothes. A white sheet of notebook paper taped to the mirror asks, "Have you taken your pill lately?" May 9, 1960, was a most liberating day for the emancipation of women. The FDA approved as safe a pill for birth control use. Without wasting a moment, I undress and jump into the tub, making a big splash. The water is hot. When Sabina walks in, I'm sitting in the tub making wishes. She puts extra towels on the windowsill behind the tub.

Before she sits down on the stool, she takes out a wrinkled cigarette and lights it from the candle. I immediately recognize the aroma. I have seen rickshaw drivers in Karachi smoking *ganja*. Sabina takes a long drag and passes the cigarette. From her hands, I'll accept hemlock.

Living in Karachi, feeling nostalgic, like a lonely hero, I have occasionally puffed on Stork brand cigarettes, but I could never learn to inhale. I take a drag, a long one, and inhale deep. I cough and exhale immediately. I pass the cigarette back to Sabina. Holding it to her lips, the smoke curling into her hair, she says, "Inhale slow, long and deeply, like this."

144

After a few exchanges, following her instructions, my eyes turn to glass and the music changes. I feel giddy. This day in September was as warm as our loins. I was young, and she was free, and we both were joyously tipsy. And there was love in the air. We have been in love all afternoon.

"Let me just look at you," I say longingly.

"You can look all you want," she says, "but what the lady needs is a good lover."

"I don't know the art of lovemaking," I say honestly, "but I'll try."

Laughing, we walk into her bedroom. She pulls me towards her, and together we tumble down to her big brass bed. A yellow oak leaf flutters from the tree. Having been in school for so long, September means a new beginning to me. We both know our relationship will not last, but neither of us particularly care—desperate, reckless, gallant, imprudent, and young—we jump in.

Sabina has almond skin and her hair below is light. Later, the afternoon sun filters through a large maple tree. Its leaves cast translucent layers of shadows that enter the room from a partially opened window. Yves Montand sings songs in a language I don't know. Lying in Sabina's brass bed, her head on my shoulder, her breasts pressing against my chest, for once I'm at peace. There are no background noises. I'm not asking any questions.

"A woman's body needs to be worshiped," I say. "It is the source of all earthly joys and heavenly miracles." I sit up with my back against a large stuffed pillow, and my legs spread wide.

Sabina opens her eyes and looks at me with a smile. Without saying a word, she puts her head on my chest and slides onto her back between my legs. She closes her eyes. I massage the top of her forehead slowly, using light strokes. I move down across her forehead, down to the bridge of her thin nose, then to her full lips, finally lower to the hollows above and under her chin. I caress her jaw, working up across her cheeks and temples. Using the same smooth strokes, I arrive at her ears. I cup my palm around her ear. I hear her breath and her heartbeat.

"I have to open my eyes to make sure I'm not dreaming," she

says smiling. Her naked body, wet with sweat and joy, against mine makes me start longing for her again.

"Let's make love again and again."

"Let's," she says and kisses my hand. "I am ravishingly hungry."

"I'll make dinner," I offer.

"I love a man who can cook."

"And I'm a good one, too," I say in all modesty.

She kisses me on the lips and slips out of the bed. I watch the back of her naked form. She has the most voluptuous foundation. She bends down and picks up her kimono from under the archway that leads into a sun porch. My mind wanders. I have to hear her story, I have to know what she likes—what flowers, what books, what movies. I have so much to tell her, I have so much to ask. What's her point of view?

"I love long summer evenings, and I love waking up in the morning before sunrise," she says, looking back at me.

When she steps out of the shower, I am standing there with a towel. I dry her soft, naked-smooth body gently with long, continuous strokes, going over the highs and lows. I have a smile on my face, but in my heart I'm fearful of what I've started. I concentrate on here and now. I allow no other thoughts; for once I control my thoughts. No one knows what is in my mind, what I am thinking.

She changes into another printed Indian cotton dress and leather sandals that she said she bought at Cecil's in Madison, Wisconsin. In her kitchen, I am impressed to find cumin, coriander, cayenne pepper, and many more spices. This is a good sign. I tell her that we Indians are seriously committed to our curries. She tells me that she loves Indian food. We walk down to the corner grocery store on 57th Street. We buy eggplant, lamb chops, and a two-pound box of long-grain Carolina rice.

I sauté the eggplant in a red curry sauce, and after marinating the lamb chops in ginger, garlic, olive oil and a touch of fresh lime juice, I grill them outdoors on a hibachi on the back stairway. I make onion, cucumber, and tomato salad with cilantro and fresh lime. Sabina watches me carefully, taking notes. She's a good helper, picking, cleaning, and chopping. She sets the table with her finest china and fresh flowers.

She enjoys her meal and is full of compliments. "That was a treat, the best Indian meal I ever had." she says.

"We forgot to get any dessert," I reply.

Sabina grins, extending her hand across the table. "What I want for dessert is right here."

CHAPTER 24

When I arrive at my apartment after midnight, a blue bulb is burning in the white-shaded lamp in the living room, an indication that Latif has company in the bedroom. I have to be anonymous and invisible. On the portable Magnavox turntable, Doris Day sings "Dream a Little Dream of Me."

I quietly walk to the living room window and open it a crack. A cool breeze ripples the curtains. Rain sweeps through the gaps of my mind, blowing out the last wispy traces of the spell cast upon me by Sabina. *What in the name of God has just happened?* I ask myself. *I'm not going to fall in love with her. In fact, I won't see her again. I have a fiancé in Pakistan that I'm in love with. I'm no longer capable of distinguishing right from wrong. I should write to Amaji and tell her to set up my wedding date. I can no longer be trusted. I shall not see Sabina again. One day, when I grow old, I'll sit by a window in front of a neem tree and write a book of love lost, dedicated to the woman who will always dwell in my heart.* But even as I lay down instructions for myself, what scares me the most is the knowledge that I will see Sabina again. I am utterly powerless to do otherwise. I lie down on the couch without making my bed. I smell Sabina on my arms and shoulders. I see cherished details of her naked body, and how she welcomed me in every possible way. Mercy. Mercy me.

I wake up early in the morning, aching for Sabina. I'm bewitched, fascinated, entranced. I lie in bed in a stupor of infatuation and desire. I'm falling in love again. This I know. *Love is a dangerous thing,* Kazi used to warn me, *the weak at heart should stay away from love.* What am I getting into? I love Leila. The first thing I want to do is move out of this flat and into a two-bedroom apartment. I no longer want to be the odd man out, the perfect roommate, going to late shows so Latif can get his date in and out of the apartment.

Before having my morning cup of tea, I walk down to the corner of Lincoln and Fullerton and pick up a copy of the *Sunday Tribune.* When I return, Latif and his date are gone. I sit in the kitchen drinking my tea, circling furnished two-bedroom apartments in our neighborhood. I still want to stay in the Lincoln Park area. It is close to the lake and Lake Shore Drive and has great public transportation: it's close to the L and to the bus lines on Lincoln, Halsted, Clark, and Fullerton. The triangle from Diversey Avenue at Clark on the north to Lincoln Avenue at Armitage on the south, and from Lincoln on the west to the intersection of Clark on the east is the heart of city.

Latif joins me in the kitchen for breakfast. When I tell him my plan, he says I am acting impulsively. "One night is all you want with any lady, especially the one who gives it to you on the first night. Don't forget, *goris* are only to fuck,"

"You know, your attitude bothers me." I say angrily. "You are condescending and shallow, and you think you know it all. Please do not tell me how I should relate to my woman."

"Excuse me," he says and stares at me for a long time.

Until now, I've contained and controlled myself. I never let Lisa get close to me; I kept her in a special place in my heart but still kept my heart shut, like reserved sign on a window table in a restaurant. The way I feel committed to Leila leaves me insecure and unavailable. I feel lost, confused, like a 16-year-old teenager, uncouth and selfish. I am not a callous man. I've got to let go and see beyond my tunnel vision. I'm too young to subscribe to sex within marriage only, sex as the reward, the "special prize," reserved for married people. I think consenting adults can have sex when their feelings are not going to get hurt. *And nobody's feelings are going to get hurt.* What Leila does not know won't hurt her. I cannot deny myself the pleasure of getting to know Sabina, the pleasure of her company, the pleasure of her body. I am in a strange state, full of joy and longing one moment and worried and unsure the next. I cannot control my thoughts of Sabina. The spread of light in the morning sky saturates my world, my humblest acts, and my most trivial reflections. *The S in sex,* I contemplate, *should be capitalized, like the G in God.*

"We're going to move to a two-bedroom flat," I tell Latif. "I already have a list of places to check out."

Latif howls like a wounded animal. "We'll share the bedroom," he insists. "You can have it on Fridays, and I get it on Saturdays."

"No way," I tell him. So we walk around the neighborhood and find a two-bedroom furnished apartment with immediate

149

occupancy on the second floor of an old Victorian on Lill Street between Halsted and Lincoln Avenue. Helen Witowski, the landlady, a widow, lives downstairs.

When I get home, I pick up the phone and dial Sabina's number. I already know it by heart. I am good with numbers.

"Hi," she says. I hear her smile. I'll miss her smile.

"Dear Sabina," I say, "if I am not here, someone else just like me will be here. And I suspect my tomorrow is only somebody's yesterday."

"That can't be true, I'm told you are one of a kind," says Sabina. "You're my *A* in a spelling test."

"I feel like I'm in an Indian movie," I say. "May I sing you my favorite Cuban song?"

"Please, do serenade me," she says, "serenade me hard."

"I'll die if I don't talk to you, all my songs are for you," I sing.

"A man makes love like he dances, and he sings the way he loves."

I can't carry a tune, and I can't dance, I wanted to reply, but instead, I say, "Since I've been away from you, I've smoked one thousand three hundred and one cigarettes, drunk seven hundred fifty-three cups of black coffee, read five books, walked twenty-seven miles, and only heaven knows what I might do tomorrow."

"My prayers are with you," she says, laughing. "You must be exhausted."

"I met you only yesterday, but I know it will take a lifetime to forget you."

"I miss you," she says.

"I miss you too. I am lonely without you." I say. "All day I sat on a wooden bench watching flowering hollyhocks. "

"Who is writing your lines?" she asks.

"It is I, can't you see? I am the cross-eyed man with hair flying wild, biting my fingernails," I say. "Today is the tomorrow I worried about yesterday."

"Is that all?" she asks.

"No. I don't know quite how to say it, I steal lines from commercials, from greeting cards, posters, whatever make me sound like I know my English, but I feel an ambiguous hurt, I feel lost and

150

disillusioned like a patient on an operating table waiting to be cut up."

"Oh, poor honey."

"I long to be alone with you, again and again, and surrender myself in all the compromising positions. Yesterday I met you, today I think of you, and tomorrow I want to be with you—I want nothing more."

"How about being with me tonight?"

"Yes, yes," I say. "I thought you'd never ask. I am happy. Isn't it wonderful?"

"Come on down, Cowboy" she says. "Don't keep me waiting."

As soon as I hang up the phone, I feel a tingle, a prickle, itching uneasiness. I should not be doing this. My wife-to-be is saving herself for me, for the marriage, for a man who is doing his thing in the dating pool.

CHAPTER 25

At work I am totally distracted. Thoughts of Sabina flood me with joy one moment; waves of reproach with regard to Leila fill me the next. *What the hell am I doing? I'm engaged; my heart is already pledged to another. I can fool around if I so choose, but I am not permitted to fall in love again.* One of life's blessings that I have always longed for is to be miserably, totally, completely in love. And now that love has happened, I must control my heart and contain my feelings. Something is wrong with love and my sentiments toward Sabina. I thought my love for Leila would be forever. I thought she had a right to my whole heart, to all of my love and affection. I seem to be separating from a certain part and place inside of me. This was the unknown that my heart craved in this foreign country. Freedom is here, and it is now.

When I get home from work, there is a letter from Leila. I force myself to open it immediately.

Dear Rama,

Sometimes, on a rainy day I dream of taking shelter in a seashore inn, where a fire glows in a fireplace and we are the only two there. We drowse in one another's arms. Our bodies and souls sing songs of love. The heavy rain falls against the roof, and a high tide crushes the rocks. I am looking at your photograph, your lovely face, your brown eyes, your soft lips. Rama, you know what I want. May there always be spring in the movie of our life.

Darling, when you're not beside me, I want to weep. My dear, being away from you is a hardship, a punishment without mercy. When I am not with you, I am nowhere. The distances, the separations and the secrets, such is life. I live for you yet I live without you. My mind suffers. My heart yearns. I'll die without you. I want to commit my soul to you. Flames surround me; I feel the intensity of the heat. The man in the flames mesmerizes me. Wisdom says that one should fly away from such heat, but I want to walk straight into your arms while the flame is blue hot.

Rama, my love, please come back to me, soon . . .

Yours,

Leila

The timing of her letter and her sentiments could not have been more off, I think to myself. I am vexed.

The phone is ringing.

"Hi," says Sabina. Her smile is audible. "This is Rhonda, a long-necked preposterous female, looking for a long-necked outlandish male."

"You have found him," I say. "Not so long-necked, mostly preposterous." *Should I remind her that I'm not an available man? The honest thing to do is not to lead her on.*

"That stolen bath oil is doing my skin a great deal of good," she informs me. "A few more baths and my skin will be as soft and silky as yours." That's the other thing we shouldn't be doing: we are shoplifting just for the fun and challenge of it. We are ripping big stores off. At Marshall Field's, I took off the sunglasses from a mannequin, walked around the store wearing them, and then walked out. This is not me that I know. My mother would not approve of my conduct.

"We are living on the wild side, having sex without marriage, smoking dope, and stealing from department stores," I say. "It is crazy."

"Nothing dramatic has happened yet. I haven't been caught," she says.

"You know what I like about you?" I ask.

"I'm different?"

"No. Everything. After you're gone, your perfume lingers on my body, on my clothes and on my thoughts. At night when I try to sleep, I smell you on my pillow. In my life, I love you most."

"If I could arrange it, I'd never leave you alone," she says. "Why do I get lonesome? Why do we have that need for a special person?"

"That is a good question." I say.

"Without you, my body feels hollow, and my soul is empty. Without you, even the eggplant loses its beauty," she replies.

"I'd like to make love to you right here and now," I respond.

"Love is wonderful, don't you think?" she sighs.

"I can't find the words to tell you, so please wait until I know how. After I write or say something, I always wonder if anyone gets my

153

point. Did you hear what I said?"

"You can tell me anything that's on your mind. You can converse with me," she says. "You can talk dirty to me."

The pendulum swings, and dark thoughts sweep over me. "It's good to be carefree," I say soberly, "but responsibilities have to be met."

"So we'll enjoy ourselves as much as possible and for as long as we can. Life can be so uncertain."

"Last night I felt low," I tell her. "I had trouble falling asleep. And then I had nightmares. This morning I feel much better, although it is still raining, and you're still not around."

Sabina laughs. "The reason you dream those terrible dreams is because you sleep with your hands on your chest. That puts pressure on your heart and affects the circulation of the blood, which in turn gives you nightmares. You need to fall asleep holding my breasts, with me curled alongside, touching all of you."

"I think men are born to love. Then there are other stories, many sorrows. Think and remember that in this wicked world someone loves you very deeply, very sincerely, for now and forever." And as I say it, I am aware that I am walking a dark passage, whistling bravely. We do play a good verbal game; at least I do.

᠅

Sabina listens to Bob Dylan, Joan Baez, and the Beatles. I listen to Nat King Cole, Doris Day, and the Beatles. She loves movies, but she hates sad endings. Movies should entertain, she says. I think— movies are like life, and life is not always like a movie, full of joy with a happy ending. I am so enjoying today, but I worry about tomorrow.

We spend our nights and days, if not in bed, at the Clark Theater, watching double features, the old classics. Wednesday is Ladies' Day; women are admitted at half price. There is a gallery for the gals only. University students with ID cards and GI's in uniform pay only fifty cents every day. I must admit I still use my OSU student card.

On Saturday night, we go to see the 1:00 a.m. showing of *Shane* (1952, 118 min.), in which a mysterious stranger helps a family of homesteaders during the pioneer days of the west. We stay to watch the second feature, *High Noon* (1953, 85 min.), a classic western with tension and excitement, struggle between good and evil. Gary Cooper won an Academy Award for Best Actor for his role in *High Noon;* Gregory Peck, my favorite American leading man, had turned down the role. We get out of the movies at four forty in the morning. The city cleaning trucks start to roll on the downtown street. We stroll to the Civic Center and sit on the steps. Sabina rolls us a smoke, and we pass the joint back and forth. There is something about an early morning high. I smoke dope to take off the edge; it does not make the problems go away, but it makes me think from a different state of mind, a mellow, melancholic point of view. Having consumed our fair share of *soma*, feeling light and light hearted, in a state of full bliss, we were ready to face our own brave new world. Sabina and I get up from the steps of the City Hall, we walk down to the Monroe Street harbor to watch the sun rise over the lake.

"You'll never know about it until I tell you," I say, watching the purple sky on the eastern horizon "In my dream last night, I'm on a bus, and when my stop arrives, the bus driver calls out, 'Home, your sweet home.' I mount a pogo stick and jump off the bus onto a cold street. From the other side of the street, joy walks over to me. I stand still on my pogo stick and look at joy. She has wavy hair that drops to her waist. Her breathing breasts move alone and in consonance, her peach lips part, and joy says to me in a most suggestive tone, 'In the name of Allah, Live. Oh! Live in joy!' And then joy walks away from me. I, in turn, hop on my pogo stick and move the other way looking for my home, sweet home."

Sabina smiles at me, puts her hand on my shoulder and together we watch a new sun rise.

It's a perfect day in October, warm, sunny. The temperature is in the high seventies. The sky is clear, bright, and blue, and everything green has begun to turn russet and gold. Despite the beauty of the day, I am angry and upset as I ride the L home. At my office—Love, Moore & Knott—they have fired Larry Brown, the young black man who was recently hired to work in the mailroom. Larry had told me he was gay, a homosexual, but he never propositioned me, unlike Bob. Bob Polito is white. He works in the supply room, and tells jokes like, "Why are there so many gays if they can't have children?" and "I'd never go to a gay urologist—I don't want him to have any pleasure for what he's getting paid to do." Bob has never told me that he is gay, but he has propositioned me on more than one occasion. "Only a man knows how to take care of a man," he said. When I told him that I was not gay, his reply was that you are not gay if you are on top.

Larry and Bob had an argument regarding the recent arrest of four white law enforcement officers in Meridian, Mississippi, by the FBI on the charge of depriving seven black men of their civil rights. After the argument, Bob went to see Al Mix, the supervisor, and Larry got fired. When I spoke to Al Mix he told me, "The Negroes are different and their racial characteristics are such that we cannot understand or trust them."

I wanted to tell him that his speculation was ludicrous, that all men are created equal, that we need to learn that truth, know it, and act upon it when necessary. But I was too timid to say anything in Larry's defense. Larry got fired because he's black and openly gay. In the face of such injustice and unfairness, I should not work at this place.

I seethe with anger and confusion. America can be so very strange. Despite the ideals of its constitution, it is a nation of un-equals; there are really only two classes of people in the so-called melting pot: first, the white Anglo-Saxons, and then, everybody else. I recoil in disgust at America's treatment of its native peoples and the descendants of its imported African slaves. When I came to America, I was an observer. I never participated in student demonstrations, sit-ins, battles with the police, student strikes, or political rallies. Now I have become both an observer of the American reality and my own. I fume as I exit the train at Fullerton and descend the stairs, muttering to myself.

"How could anyone help but love you?" I hear Sabina's voice. I look up and there she is, waiting for me. She's wearing a long, sleeveless Indian cotton dress. She looks smashing in purple. "You'll never have a more persistent admirer," she says, smiling.

I loosen my tie. She holds my bag. We walk together to my apartment. I tell her about the incident at the office.

"I'm upset and angry," I say. "I really don't want to talk about it."

"Welcome to the land of equal opportunity," she says. "The rudiments of hatred are everywhere."

"I want to go to the civil rights marches," I say. "Now I know what they are marching for."

"Last year in May, I was in Jackson, Mississippi," Sabina says looking very serious. "We were protesting against the city's segregated facilities. Four black students and a white professor walked in and sat down at a whites-only lunch counter at the Woolworth's downtown. The local radio and TV stations played *Dixie* and called its citizens to arms. This angry white mob converged downtown. When the counter staff refused to serve them, all five of them remained seated for more than three hours, while the mob slathered them with mustard, salt, sugar, anything they could find. The mob would drag them off their stools and onto the ground, but they would just get up and sit back down. Then the mob doused them with spray paint, and started to beat them. And the police just stood there and watched. I thought those folks would never get out alive from Woolworth's, but somehow they all survived."

I feel waves of emotions roil inside me. My own silence depresses me.

CHAPTER 26

Now that winter is upon us, I have learned that we have four cricket teams in Chicago; next spring I intend to find myself a team to play for. In the meantime, I have been enjoying television broadcasts of America's favorite pass time. On Thursday, the St. Louis Cardinals won the 1964 World Series, beating the New York Yankees 7 to 5 in the seventh game. I was rooting for the Yankees.

On Sunday afternoon, Latif is out when Sabina comes to visit and brings a nickel bag of Acapulco gold along with the British release of the Beatles' "Please Please Me." Sitting on the couch in the living room, she rolls a joint. We smoke the gold, take a hot bath, and engage in a matinee listening of the Beatles' "Love Me Do." Afterwards we make an elaborate Indian meal of *mong dal*, okra, and chicken curry. Sabina bakes a pecan pie. After dinner, we watch the presidential debate on TV.

Lyndon "All the Way" Johnson, the man who wears cowboy hats, is debating Barry "Choice for Change" Goldwater, the man who wears dark-rimmed glasses. Lyndon is telling us that the key to peace is to be found in strength. Barry wants us to realize that in our hearts we know he's right.

"In your guts, you know he's nuts," says Sabina.

If elected, "Barry for Change" will turn the clock back by making social security "voluntary" and ending farm price support. He also promises to seek an absolute victory in Vietnam. During his acceptance speech as the Republican Party's presidential nominee, he said, "Extremism in defense of liberty is no vice. Moderation in pursuit of justice is no virtue." During the debate, Barry makes his point with his hands open, his body leaning forward on the podium, his neck and head bent to the right, while Lyndon makes his point standing erect, his head and neck bent to the left.

"Their body language tells more than the words they utter," Sabina says. "I can't trust these two."

The exchange ultimately was dull.

"There were no knockout punches," says the TV analyst. To me there was something honest about the way Barry talked, but I kept that opinion to myself.

Helen Witowski the landlady does not permit girls to stay overnight in our apartment. As a matter of fact, she has a ten o'clock curfew Sundays through Thursdays, midnight on Fridays and Saturdays. Sneaking girls in and out of Helen's house past curfew is a challenge that Latif and I relish. The fact that she promptly goes to bed at nine o'clock after turning on the front porch light and closing the curtains of every window tips the balance in our favor.

On weekdays, Sabina meets me at the L station. We go grocery shopping, and when we go back to my place, she parks her car right across from the old Victorian, where Mrs. Witowski of the "better dead than red" political persuasion sits on the old oak rocker on her front porch, watching the "hippies" move onto her block. "Next the colored people will be moving next door," she often mutters out loud. She is bigoted, but she likes Sabina. She probably does not know that Sabina is Jewish and because Sabina is the only one she sees me with, she thinks we are going steady. She does not approve of Latif's changing cast of maidens. On the nights Sabina sleeps over, just before nine o'clock when Helen Witowski draws her shades, closes her curtains, and turns on the porch light, we go outside and kiss goodbye. I walk her to her car and watch as she drives away. Then I sigh and go back upstairs. Meanwhile, Sabina parks her car a block or two away from Helen's place and sneaks in from the back stairs, carrying her shoes in her hand. The collusion, secrecy, and deception of our routine combine to act as a powerful aphrodisiac.

When Sabina really leaves to go home, I always feel like I'll never see her again. She'll disappear into the crowd; she'll meet a brighter, more intelligent, beautiful, blond blue-eyed guy on campus, and I'll be forgotten. She is too good for me. Besides, I have to marry Leila. I'm losing my mind—I have lost my mind. My mother and father will never approve of an American woman, a white American woman, and my being so "lost in love," so given "in" love. Since I met Sabina, there is always turbulence in my head, a high, throbbing, sharp pain that starts at the forehead and slowly and systematically moves down from the front to the back of my head and explodes. The explosion, like the calm of the rainfall at the end of a storm, brings me some relief, until the turbulence starts all over again.

159

I hate working as an engineer with a slide rule dangling from my waist like an external male organ. The curse of my vocation is that I chose it. I was not confused or lost, I knew what I wanted to be, a civil engineer, or so I thought when I was a student. I was a good student, and I worked hard. The working world is another matter. At times it is a total bore. My ennui and world-weariness, my inner conflict regarding religion, country, as well as love makes me feel out of sorts, not to mention out of place. I go to work on autopilot. I work on my projects like a robot. I know employment is a necessary evil, an obligation, a means to earn our keep, but it does not make me feel intelligent or worthwhile, and it is not meant to be enjoyed or to be pleasant. I keep myself isolated, and have not made any American friends at the office. Sheltered within my own world, with my own kind, living in America on an Indo-Pak island. Not only I am not from here, I'm not here while I am *here*. There aren't many women in my field, and the few who are among us look like amateur boxers and have mustaches. Sabina is bright and beautiful. She could abandon me so fast, so fast, but Sabina is kind and she loves me. The most wonderful thing that has happened to me since I arrived in America is that I have met her, and the worst disaster that has befallen upon me since coming to America is that I have fallen for her. I feel the crazy turbulence in my head.

CHAPTER 27

Before going home for the Thanksgiving holidays, Sabina comes to visit on a cool, crisp Saturday afternoon. A sudden desire overtakes us, and we hurriedly make love in the kitchen before Latif returns from his shopping. Afterward we prepare an early dinner of chicken curry and okra sautéed in garlic, onion, and green pepper. I also make a tomato, cucumber, and onion salad with fresh lemon juice. When we are ready to sit down to eat, we hear Latif walk in.

"I like Latif better when he is not around," whispers Sabina.

Latif joins us for dinner. He piles up his plate with a little too much of everything, and sits down between Sabina and me at the kitchen table.

"I live such a mundane life compared to you lovebirds," Latif says.

Sabina makes a face.

"You guys are so alive, so full of energy, and I am all dud."

"I won't disagree with you this time," I say smiling.

He picks up a drumstick and says, "One cannibal says to another, 'I don't like your mother-in-law.' 'In that case,' replies the other cannibal, 'just eat the noodles.'" Neither Sabina nor I respond, which gives him a floor to talk. "The latest survey shows that ninety percent of prostitutes are not virgins." Latif goes into his joke-telling mode. "How do you seat seventy-one people in a Volkswagen?"

"I don't know," I say, "And I don't care."

"Two in front and sixty-nine in the back."

We eat quietly while Latif keeps talking.

"You stand an equal chance of winning the lottery whether you buy a ticket or not. As a matter of fact, your chances of getting hit by lightning are greater than your chance of winning the lottery, even if you buy a ticket.

"They, who keep the myths and legends alive, whoever 'they' are, *they* say that social life is easy for man: a man can ask any woman out, whenever he wants. But the truth is that most men are shy, it takes courage to ask a woman for a date, and he must be prepared for rejection, every time. And if she says yes, the man has to pay for the

161

evening. It gets in the way of whom a man asks out.

"*They* also say that men talk about women in mean and degrading ways, and make claims of conquests never made, but what can a poor man do when he is not getting any? *They* say men don't respect girls who neck and pet easily. For God's sake, men are not that stupid. While men may not respect girls who are easy, they date them. They take them to go to a drive-in movie, but not to the prom. *They* say men lose interest when women begin to comfort them. That is not true. I always appreciate a girl who cares and is careful and shows an interest in my life." Latif looks around then picks an ashtray and begins to light his cigarette.

"Latif, I'd appreciate it if you don't smoke while we eat," Sabina says.

"I'm sorry," he says, "I thought you were done."

Sabina and I look at each other; we've had enough of Latif's lecture. "Latif," Sabina says, "we shall leave you to continue with your profound contemplation and to puff on your Pall Mall. Rama and I are going to Barbara's Bookstore on Wells Street." We get up, leaving Latif with the dishes.

It's a cold evening with a silent drizzle, still, we decide to walk. Sabina is wearing her long brown embroidered sheepskin coat, collar turned up, and a deep purple Mexican scarf around her neck. I'm in my long, heavy blue woolen overcoat and a matching woolen scarf. We walk briskly and hold gloved hands. Every time we talk, our white breaths drift in the air, a cloud of frozen words, like subtitles in a foreign movie.

" . . . And yes, I would like to understand and listen to your troubles," she says. "I'll be a good friend."

"I'm happy that we're good friends," I reply. She tucks her arm through mine and I look at her. I adore her.

"The moments of tenderness and understanding are our only salvation in this hostile world. I'm not looking to get married or start having children," she continues. "Most important to me is fairness and honesty within human relationships."

"With this I totally agree," I say with much oomph. My own emphasis on personal relationships comes from being alone in an alien world. Moments of tenderness and understanding are sometimes the

162

only things that keep me going.

"I've given up caring about what happens in politics," Sabina says. "We expect the worst, yet the pessimism is never total. I still protest the war, it is politically motivated, violence perpetuated against innocent. The Pentagon always finds a new supply of villains. Today it is Communism, tomorrow it be could be Judaism, or Islam." She looks at me. I search for the right words to express my thoughts. Not finding them, I bite my lip and remain silent. "We always portray our enemy to be evil and of course we are righteous, good, our enemy's reverse image," she continues. "We never ask why does everyone in the world hate us?"

"Not everyone," I say, "I love my American."

"But I'm starting to feel that peace marches stink. Sit-ins and teaching peace just don't work." She shakes her head. "The police invade university dormitories. They knock on the door at five in the morning and drag students off to jail—it's like Nazi Germany. It won't be long before they start firing guns at antiwar demonstrators."

"There's little major change an individual, or a group of individuals, can instigate," I say. "I'm struggling to find myself so I can be free to become someone else, someone new."

"Rama, there's no escape, you'll always be you, you can adjust, accommodate, and learn to contain, but at the end of the day, you have to be you. And there's no escape from social issues either," Sabina says passionately.

"You don't have to tell this to a Pakistani like me. Our national pastime is politics."

Sabina gives me a sharp look. "You vote for the person of your choice and live with the consequences."

"Or you vote for the man of your compromise and live with your choice," I counter.

"That's for sure! But the cultural center of America is the bowling alley, for God's sake. We are pig-headed, arrogant, and ignorant. There's a war going on, and the best thing the mainstream can come up with is 'My country, right or wrong!' Compassion is gone.

"When our president talks about the war, he talks in the royal *we*. It is not, the *we* of the Declaration of Independence, or the *we* of

163

the Constitution. No one scrutinizes his actions and intentions. Our failing lies in our selfishness, wastefulness, and our greed to control the rest of the world.

"We've colonized our own native people, we have race riots. What I can't understand is why we can't treat others as human beings, no better and no worse than ourselves. Much of what we do in our organized activities is a reflection of our sense of self. We fight over the most trivial things, because it serves our egos to see others humiliated, degraded, and proved wrong.

"I ask questions like, can an individual be of any effect in society? Is there such a thing as self-fulfillment? Can I ever understand the meaning of my own existence?"

I think about the monotony of my own job. "I wonder if there are any relevant jobs. The ultimate crucifier of ideals is a job in corporate America."

We come to an intersection with a red traffic light. The questions she asks are timeless. They have always existed. It's too easy to lose sight of what we have if we become obsessed with the chaos of the outside world. Life is a motion picture not a snapshot. *But if I say this she will think I'm making fun of her.* She is such a solemn, serious being. *I need to find a way to make her relax.* But at end of the day, you have to be you. We wait for the green light in silence, watching the cars stream past, listening to the hiss of their wheels on the wet pavement.

Sabina sighs, blowing a great cloud of steam. "The fact is, the capitalistic system is just wrong. Corporate methods of oppressing the individual on a day-to-day basis are just a sophisticated version of slavery."

The light changes, the traffic stops, and we step off the curb. We reach the other curb and turn down a side street. The traffic noise fades, and we walk for a while in silence, listening to the patter of the rain.

"There are times," Sabina says softly, "when I wish I could do something, something spectacular."

"Any which way I look at you," I say, "You are spectacular."

She presses her head against my shoulder briefly. "You are so sweet, but what I mean is that I suspect I work for applause, eccentricity, and not for my own values in many cases. I have too many goals and too many ideals. I'll probably be disappointed by life. Don't you think?"

"That sounds pessimistic," I answer.

"Does it? Maybe one day I'll make teaching literature and writing short stories my business. I don't want to gamble away my escapes too quickly."

"Is someone pressuring you?" I ask. "Your parents?"

"No," she says, "It's just that I often wonder how relevant it is to immerse myself in John Tanner's relationship with Henry Straker. This was something I spent a lot of time thinking about last week. And I'm not talking love."

We turn onto Wells Street. *The problem is that there is no original dilemma.*

"I guess I'm really confused," Sabina sighs. "Perhaps I'm unsure of my own status, but I won't hold you back from what you want for yourself."

"I love you, for setting me free," I say. *I have my own dilemma; I am walking with the woman I'm in love with yet planning to go home and marry another.* The turbulence in my head begins to erupt.

CHAPTER 28

Thanks to Latif and his dinners at hospital cafeterias, an anesthesiologist formerly of Dublin, Ireland, invites Latif and I for Thanksgiving dinner at his house on the lake in Winnetka. Dr. Allen, a short, muscular, broad-shouldered man with a red face and receding hairline, has a wife Clara who has a pale face and a sad smile. Clara plays Irish music on a Grundig stereo as she prepares the Thanksgiving meal while sipping whiskey from a tumbler.

Their five-and-a-half-year-old son Brandon is a carbon copy of his father. Brandon smiles a lot, and like his father, his hairline is already receding. At the large round dinner table, I sit between Brandon and Clara, with a view of the lake. Dr. Allen opens a bottle of champagne and pours everyone at the table a glass, including a small portion for Brandon. *I don't drink alcohol,* I want to announce, but to be polite I say nothing.

Dr. Allen looks into his glass of champagne and contemplates for a brief moment. Raising his glass for a toast, Dr. Allen says, "Let all of us say a quiet thanks for whatever we feel thankful for." I lift my glass, but my lips don't touch the champagne. Dr. Allen drinks his glass of champagne in one gulp. Brandon immediately gulps his champagne just like his father. Clara gets up and puts Christmas carols on the reel-to-reel tape deck.

"Today's Muslims drink, although we still don't eat pork," Latif says, taking a sip of his bubbly. *I still do not drink.* We are all victims of our own shortcomings. At an appropriate moment, I switch my full glass with Brandon's empty one. He promptly gulps it down.

"Last year around this time," Dr. Allen says, "I was monitoring a seventy-eight-year-old patient Bob O'Brien's prostate surgery, when the nurse in charge Janet Robinson burst into the OR and announced that someone had shot President Kennedy in Dallas, the president of the United States blown away by an assassin's bullet, the luck of the Irish; Bob O'Brien died two days later."

Brandon applauds, laughing.

"The lad's got drunk on spoonful of champagne," says Dr. Allen, pouring everyone except Brandon another round.

What am I thankful for? I miss Sabina . . . If you are Christian, you can eat pork and drink alcohol; if you are a Jew you can drink alcohol, but you can't eat pork; but if you are a Muslim, you cannot eat pork or drink alcohol. Yet we are all children of Abraham. Someone once reminded Mullah Nasrudin, the wise fool, just as he was about to take a sip of his wine, "You are not allowed a single drop of alcohol." The wise Mullah immediately dipped the tip of his index finger into his wine and flicked a drop off. "There," he said, "I'll not drink a single drop of alcohol."

"Thank God for Sabina," I murmur to myself. I pick up my glass and drink the champagne in two gulps, my first-ever swallow of the forbidden drink. I am surprised by how sour and bitter it tastes. I thought it would be sweet, like the wine in heaven promised to good Muslims. I know I'll repeat this sin.

On the Sunday after Thanksgiving, Helen Witowski's son Harold comes into the city from Hoffman Estates with his wife Honey and their five-year-old son Harry. With strings of red and green lights, they decorate the front of the house and the large spruce growing on the west side of the lawn. The old Victorian blooms in a blush of red and green, and shines brightly until midnight, when an electric timer automatically turns off the glitter.

Sabina returns from Brooklyn past seven in the night. After a quick dinner that I prepared in advance, we lie in my bed. I look out the window and watch the naked oak tree reflect the red and green Christmas lights. The turbulence inside my head sets in. "I'll never regret," I say, each word slow and deliberate, "meeting, knowing, liking, and loving you. When we get old, we'll think only of our yesterdays."

"Sometimes, I get the feeling that I could ride a train forever and never stop or arrive anywhere. Life can end just like that." Sabina snaps her fingers. "Let's promise to be honest with each other, even if it hurts."

My life is to live with her. Without her I'll die. For me, no one smiles like her, no one cries like her. She has the most enchanting eyes. I kiss her hair and put my head against her shoulder. "As long as I can be with you every day, I want nothing more," I say.

167

"I want hot showers, a Chinese honeymoon basket in the bedroom, and mirrors on the ceiling," she says embracing me.

"Anything you want is fine with me," I whisper, "as long as it's me you want."

She nibbles my ear. "You are the only one for me—for a while."

On Thursday, Sabina leaves for Brooklyn to spend the holidays with her family. On Friday night, Latif talks me into going on a date he has arranged for me. "It's time you get yourself some extra sweets," he says, taking a puff of his Pall Mall. "You are seeing Sabina and Sabina only, you're not being fair to her. I don't date any woman more than four or five times, I don't do a woman more than two or three times, and I don't lead them on. When I feel they want more than I want to give, I'll stop calling them and stop returning their calls." He looks at me for a long time. Latif is looking dashing, splendid, all set to go out in a navy blue suit with a blue oxford shirt and a striped blue-and-red tie. "You are only young once," he says with a smile. "Men drink with women so they can put a move on them. Women drink with men for the same reason. After a few drinks, they expect men to make the move."

Despite not wanting to go out, I yield—to see how it'd feel. Is it love I want or lust? Who am I going to marry, if I can cheat on Leila, why not on Sabina?

I meet Dolores Anderson at John Barleycorn's Pub. She is a student nurse from Peoria doing an eight-week rotation at the Children's Hospital. She sits across from me at a table for two and sips her Bloody Mary. "We all laugh at the same situations, and we all cry at the same departures," says Dolores. "The tide you saw once will not return."

I take a sip of Virgin Mary, put my glass down, and look at her. Dolores is pretty with large brown eyes, long blonde hair, full red lips, and pink smooth skin. She is very desirable. I don't say anything.

"Who is she?" she asks.

Tracing the rim of my drink with my finger, I look down and remain silent.

"You are acting like a baby who has lost his toy."

"I haven't lost anything," I say sharply, looking at her.

"Then maybe someone else is playing with it," she says with a smile.

"Maybe." I look away.

"Tell me," she asks, putting her drink down, "if you can think about her while you are with me, why can't she think about you while she is with someone else?"

That is no consolation, I want to say, but I don't. I should have stayed home.

"You probably think that she and whoever she's with are having more fun than you are."

I smile sheepishly.

"Sometimes, just sometimes," she continues, "one person, one single person, can't meet all your needs and vice-versa." Like an artist's model, she is amazing to look at. She leans forward, closer. I sense the presence of her body, the scent of her aura. She reaches out and touches my hand.

"That's all right," I say. "I am fine."

We order another round of drinks, Bloody Mary for both. *Men drink with women so they can put a move on them. Women drink with men for the same reason. After a few drinks, they expect men to make the move.*

"It has been two years since I've seen Tony," she says. "Tony is somewhere in Indochina and since he left I've met other boys, good and bad, men of all colors and sizes. Some of them I liked and some of them I didn't, but they all wanted to sodomize me."

"Do you swallow love?" I inquire abruptly.

She ignores my question. "Tony is the best for me. You think that because I am with you, he is not in my life, or because I may kiss you, that I don't love my Tony. I am receptive to everyone that I like, but Tony is the only one I love."

"So. Do you swallow love?" I ask again.

She looks at me wetting her lips, her tongue moves slowly one way then another. "I'm a versatile woman interested in English, French, Greek, and Turkish cultures. I can perform Cleopatra like the hands of a dairymaid milking the cow. But I was talking of emotional connection not physical love.

169

"Once you find someone good, your true love, don't ever let her slip away. Love is not something you pick up on the street or buy in a supermarket. Love happens but once. When you find it, save it."

Everyone believes that love happens but once, I did too, but now I know that love happens again and again. Dolores and I were strangers in the night. I think of Leila, I miss Sabina.

"Or at least the memory of it," I reply.

"No, don't settle for memory." Dolores leans across the table, bristling with earnestness. "Demand all of it, everything, all of it!"

"You talk like someone in a movie."

"Speaking of movies, would you care to go to a show?" she asks, "I love making out in the movies, ah, picnic on the second balcony."

"I'm tempted," I say. "But if I'm at the movies, I have to watch the show."

"You can watch, but you need to learn to act as well,"

Looking at Dolores, I consider it. To desire her is one thing, to do her is another, I decide not to do her. I want Sabina and no one else. I wish Dolores good luck with Tony and walk her back to her dorm on Orchard Street.

※

December turns cold. Time seems to stand still, frozen in the cosmos. The days of togetherness are gone and back are the days of loneliness. Nothing stays put and nothing sits right. Love makes one possessive. Happiness is such that no one wants to part with it, but an eternal state of joy might be boring. Every day shouldn't be Sunday.

On Saturday, the weather turns warm. I take a train downtown for holiday shopping. I get off at Washington and State Street and walk down to the corner to admire the Christmas decorations in the windows of Marshall Field's. I stand under the clock, where I often wait for Sabina, then walk eastward to Grant Park. In the park by the Art Institute, I sit down on a bench next to a noisy electrical transformer. Young men and women occupy the benches, kissing passionately while others walk around holding hands. I enter the Art Institute and wander aimlessly. I stand for a long time before

170

the painting of a country butcher standing in his shop with slaughtered hens hanging everywhere. I walk out.

The Clark Theater is showing *Lust for Life* (1956, 122 min.) about the life of Vincent Van Gogh. Anthony Quinn was on the screen as Gauguin for a total of eight minutes and won the Oscar for supporting actor, but just like in life, no awards for Vincent, played by Kirk Douglas.

This is the longest I've been separated from Sabina. I miss her more than I thought I would, and at times I feel very insecure. What if she meets someone else better? I bet she is having more fun than I am. I am uncertain about everything. I'd like to make Sabina happy. I'd do anything for her. I love her, but there is little else I can promise. She is the one I absolutely cannot live without. Yet, I have to leave her one-day soon, that exactly is the current plan. There is something I've been meaning to tell her ever since we met. Although the time we spend together was brief, it was fulfilling, and I'll always treasure it. I want her to come back soon. Sometimes I am still lonesome, even when I am with her, knowing that it is all temporary—a good time that shall pass into a better time—home, family, Leila. I should be happy thinking of the future. Joy is so elusive—when you catch it, you feel it, and it slips away.

Living is ordinary again; time stands still. I'm at the crossroads of lost and found. I need to decide which way to turn—unless *goris* are just to fuck, as Latif says. Why do I continue to want to be involved with Sabina? Is she just a lay? I love Sabina surely, deeply, and completely. I have never loved any woman like this before, and I probably never will again, and yet one day I'll have to leave her. My mother will not approve of this relationship, my father will not accept it, my sister will not support it, my brother will not sanction it. I should not be involved like this. I'm at the crossroads of lost and lost . . . And there is no way out. Sometimes I walk from point A to point B without having a conscious recollection of my movement. The turbulence in my head . . .

I write Sabina a letter:

So, once again, dear love, you have left me, never to return. And with your departure, the old lesions and the old harms

171

are turning green. Knowing that you and I will not grow old together is a source of agony. Still, when you grow old, having lived six dozen years, when your dark silky hair begins to shine like the glow of a silver moon, your rosy cheeks have a wrinkle or two, your hazel eyes lose their twinkle, sitting with your grandchildren, telling them wise old stories, you should then reflect for a moment on your own youth and how your eyes were full of life, passion, and Eros. Remember how your eyes were bright and spellbinding—and you were stunning to look at, how your dark wavy hair often fell over your eyes, yet your eyes kept looking at me, kept inviting me like flame to moth, day to night, sun to moon.

You were once dazzling to look upon; you were the dream of this devotee and the fantasy of a heathen. How beautiful you were and always will be! And your smile, yes, your smile was what I loved most and still do. No one else has your smile. I see myself reflected in your eyes and I see only you and that smile.
My house is empty without you, but my mind is filled with thoughts of you. In any event, don't let your concern for me get in your way. You and I must be completely and totally unselfish. Give me an abundance of love, dear love, or an abundance of despair, for I know you'll be gone one day. Think of me, then, when we are no longer together. Think of me as the one who worshipped you and loved whispering your name. How enchanting were the moments I spent with you and, dear love, how splendid was our love. I love and love to remain, although I may not live and live beside you.
Yours truly,
Rama
Sunday, December 21, 1964

After I finish my letter, my turbulence ceases, melts away like a snowflake on a windshield. I sit for a long time, wondering if I haven't sent another such letter before, perhaps in another language, to Leila. I know the heroes in Shafiqur Rahman's stories always write this kind of letter. Maybe I'm just repeating it. I mail the letter to Sabina anyway.

On Christmas Eve, I receive a letter from Sabina, with a five-cent William Shakespeare commemorative stamp on it.

172

I am waiting, for the hate to die.
I am waiting the sun to set, for the moon to rise,
And for the winter to depart
I am waiting for the tree to blossom
I am waiting for the shade to be drawn
And the night to begin
I am waiting for the child to be born.
I am waiting.
Dear Rama, Yesterday I went with my brother back to our old house where I spent the first sixteen years of my life. The house was boarded up. We parked the car and walked up the driveway to the front of the house. Under the broken porch, I saw an old deflated white soccer ball. I picked it up and recognized that it was mine, my childhood soccer ball! I got it on my seventh or eighth birthday. My mother gave it to me; she thought girls should be athletic. My younger brother Victor mostly kicked it around.

Driving away from my father's old house, I looked back and saw myself nine or ten years old, dressed in a periwinkle cotton dress, sitting carefully on a cracked cement bench in the back yard, feeling every inch of the surface. I inscribed "Sabina Dubin" in blue ink on my white rubber soccer ball.

I can't recall the day I first uttered "Mama," but I already miss her. It's been only a short time since I've met you, but it feels like I've always known you. My father is still a doctor and my mother is still my mother, and the tree of their life will only add new rings. No new branches will sprout. Watch and try to understand space and time and cycles.

Love,
Sabina

P.S. My brother Vic is leaving on a boat tomorrow for Nova Scotia. He's going to live in Canada because he doesn't want to be drafted. I pretend I am sailing away as well.

How one letter can cheer me so much! It came and it's from her and it's full of flattery, human kindness, and simple delight. My day has some meaning at last; I am complete.

173

CHAPTER 29

Sabina returns the afternoon of New Year's Day. I go to her apartment. Dressed in a blue turtleneck sweater and a blue denim skirt, she is making dinner. In the background, the Beatles sing "Please Please Me." Sabina looks at me smiling, and my heart jumps. I can't get enough of her touch. We rush to the bedroom, to her big brass bed. "Your eyes have the soul of a dove," she tells me. *Mind me not, oh happy day,* I say to myself. I know this will not last.

Later, we sit in the kitchen drinking tea. I look out the window. The sky has changed from blue to gray. I make myself another cup of tea and tell Sabina about my date with Dolores.

"You are the only one for me for a while," says Sabina. She gets up from the table and walks to the kitchen counter. She reties the knot in the sash of her kimono, picks up her empty cup, and recites, "Thou must give, or woo in vain, / So to thee, farewell! / Love me little, love me long."

I take a sip of my tea. "Are you jealous?" I ask.

"Am I jealous?" she echoes. "Of course I am! What kind of a question is that? I am a jealous gal, my love is possessive, and we love the ones we love, for who they are, with their foibles as well as their excellence."

"Life is like an onion. You peel one layer at a time, and sometimes you cry," I say.

She laughs.

"I don't want to lose you already," I tell her. "You are my best girl." . . . *and to love her is to love her for always and forever.* "I hope you'll be my last girl, too."

"Loosen up, Rama," she says, still laughing. "You are too much."

"If you cannot forget / Let it be unforgotten," I recite with fervor. "I associate each letter of the alphabet with a specific color."

"S," she says.

"'She took away the sun,'" I say. "'Lemon Tree,' Peter, Paul and Mary."

"You can be so profound," she teases.

174

"'Thank you very much, you've got a lucky face' was John Lennon's entire acceptance speech at the Foyles Literary Luncheon held in his honor. Carry on."

Sabina smiles at me, shaking her head.

"I've got an idea," I tell her. "Why don't I take tomorrow off, and we can have a three-day weekend together?"

"I can't tomorrow. I've volunteered to work at the Student Peace Union."

"Can't you choose another day?"

"I can, but this is something I wanted to do," she says. "Why don't you work with me? It's right here on University Avenue, between 60th and 61st Street. We can walk down after breakfast."

"Maybe another day," I sigh, disappointed.

"There is a major contradiction in the justification that the way to peace is through war. The war is a business, and our weapons of extermination are the merchandise. Peace is necessary for our survival, and we need to make peace a permanent state, not a state we arrive at after the end of a war, after assessing the efficiency of our latest weapons of inhumanity."

"Life is rare, my dear one," I say, "but life goes on!" *She's such a child. I don't want to talk politics.* "You probably think that ecumenism and the liberal ways and tolerance for all can resolve all issues without war."

She stops chopping onion. "Rama, I'm serious!" she says. "People who say 'In God We Trust' do not trust other people, and somehow, we always declare ourselves above the law. We've got to stop the production of nuclear weapons. We already have enough to destroy the world four times over."

"I am not so sure about that," I say. "As free citizens living in the world's largest democracy, you have an obligation and a commitment to world peace, and peace comes with strength. I think there are times when war is the answer. War may not be a virtue, but I believe in Machiavelli's advice that princes should spend most of their time preparing for war. War is the necessary evil, it is not 'anti-progressive.'"

"Yes, wars have become necessary because men and their societies are moved by avarice, greed, and lust for power," she says

175

forcefully.

"If that's the case," I claim victoriously, "then it would be a delusional folly to expect that one day wars will cease."

"And obviously you have no problem with the destruction and killing of innocent civilian in the war?"

"Carnage and chaos are elements of war, the collateral damage," I say. "Courage and strength are needed to protect justice, freedom, and truth, and if war is not the answer, what is?"

"So, you're telling me that men are evil and peace is not the normal condition, but since we want peace, we must go to war, and it's better to be feared than loved?" Sabina exclaims. "The arms race goes on and on, the world is led closer and closer to nuclear destruction, and meanwhile, we've got people starving to death right here in Chicago, not to mention rest of the world! We have to stop this insanity of going to war to 'preserve' peace. One more war to stop all wars."

I say nothing.

She continues, "We've got to stop this muscle flexing. America doesn't have to police the world. Weapons of destruction should be abolished, not admired."

"You are talking in idealisms. Real life is very different," I say.

"I am talking real life! Militarism is glorified. We impose our ideals, our ways, upon the world community. Freedom of speech and the right to dissent are repressed." Her voice rises. "America—love it or leave it! The fascists in Washington are trying to force us to act like robots to display a false show of national unity. The military-industrial complex is ready to exterminate unnumbered millions in the name of national security. Instead of seeking peaceful solutions to our differences, we always choose war. We the citizens need to refuse to pay taxes slated for armed forces. More than 50% of the federal discretionary spending in our national budget is military cost. So whether you join the army and fight or just pay your hard earned dollar for someone else to fight and to have weapons produced is an issue of morality and conscience."

I don't like to be on the wrong side, and I don't want our evening spoiled either. "This is not my war," I say.

She explodes. "Where do you come from, Mars? War is a

global issue, Rama, not a local one. It's immoral not to search your own soul."

Suddenly, unexpectedly, I am engulfed in a wave of loneliness, sinking in emotional quicksand. The turbulence in my head begins to erupt. I am caught in a skin that is getting too tight. "No, I am not from Mars," I tell her, "but sometimes I feel like I've landed on Mars. This country can be so foreign—so alien." *Indians and Pakistanis have roots in the past. Americans have their roots all over the world, but the only ones that count are European. You take pride in your mobility, at being ready to relocate at a moment's notice. You change apartments, houses, jobs, and spouses without a second thought. You don't know your ancestors, where they came from, and the languages they spoke, and the foods they ate. Some of you don't even know where your grandparents are buried. You have little knowledge of nature and even less respect for the earth beneath your feet.* "I am uncertain of everything, and it is not easy to rebel against my parents, my basic upbringing."

"Holy Dickens! You don't understand anything, you don't ask anything." She flings a knife in the sink and snatches at the knot on the sash of her kimono. "You don't seem to have a problem rebelling against your parents while you're in bed with me."

"Please, Sabina," I plead. "Let's not argue."

"But when it comes to taking a moral stand publicly, you hide behind your goddamned family traditions and 'This is not my country, this is not my war' bullshit! But just remember: I'm committed to the peace movement, to building bridges, resolving our differences, and finding common ground. There is nothing else I can do, I cannot sign off."

I fall back in my chair. Fighting with Sabina is the last thing I want to do on the first day of the New Year. I know that she is a bohemian, a part of the beat generation, someone from the subculture, the anti-culture, and that she is against war, violence, and degenerating humans. "You are carrying the weight of the world on your shoulders," I tell her. "We all have our share of old, jaded ideals that no one else cares for or remembers."

Sabina's eyes widen with fury. "Don't you dare patronize me!" she shrieks. "Old, jaded ideals! Is that what you think of the principles I live by? Well, let me tell you what happens when no one cares or

177

remembers." Sabina's voice grows suddenly quiet, and her face is dead white. "Someone like Adolph Hitler comes along and six million Jews go to the gas chambers because of the complacency of people like you. In 1942, in this country, people like you stood by while Roosevelt signed the executive order that mandated the incarceration of more than 120,000 American citizens of Japanese ancestry in concentration camps."

"But that was after Japan attacked Pearl Harbor."

"Those Japanese Americans had nothing to do with the attack; there is not a single documented act of espionage, sabotage, or fifth column activity committed by them, but they were rounded up without due process and despite their demonstrated loyalty to the United States, a case of monumental historic injustice. How would you feel if a rogue Islamic State bombed Disneyland, and the U.S. Government decided to round up all the Muslims living in America and put them in an internment camp?"

I say nothing. She leaves the kitchen. I watch her back disappear through the bedroom door. I feel beaten, slapped across the face. *Allah, Allah,* I repeat to myself. I squeeze my eyes shut, and suddenly, completely unexpectedly, I see the yellow dust of the Sepri Bazaar hanging in the air like dirty curtains.

ૐ

September 1947, I was eight years old, walking home from Saraswati School as I did every afternoon, swinging my books bag and humming happily, "Of all the lands in the world, the best is our Hindustan." At the end of the school day, I always stopped at Opal Cha-Cha's tea stall to buy myself a treat. Opal Cha-Cha was old. His hair was white, and his dark brown face looked like cured leather. When he smiled, which was often, only two teeth showed, but they were as dazzling as the midday sun. He was always pleased to see me. Opal Cha-Cha, in addition to tea, sold lemon soda in thick green bottles with dark green marble stoppers to keep the fizz in. He also sold glucose biscuits, my favorite, which he kept in a big clear glass jar. As I approached the stall, I started to dig in my pocket for the paisa my mother gave me every morning. One paisa bought two biscuits.

178

Opal Cha-Cha was very busy, snatching things off the narrow counter and placing them out of sight. When he saw me, the greeting I was about to offer died on my lips. Opal Cha-Cha was not smiling. He reached under the counter for the big glass jar and quickly extracted two biscuits, ignoring my paisa. Pressing them into my hand, he said urgently, "Rama, run home immediately."

I stared at him, uncomprehending.

"Rama," he repeated, "go home *now*, child! There is trouble in the city. I am closing up."

Until this moment, I had been totally absorbed in the simple pleasure of my anticipation. Suddenly, I was aware of the street around me. Everywhere along the bazaar, shutters were slamming. There were no late-afternoon shoppers, no bustle of activity, no carts, or vendors, or peddlers crying out their wares, no housemaids haggling prices at the vegetable stall, no astrologer drawing up horoscopes, no men arguing with the barber about who will win Sunday's cricket match. The surrounding silence was saturated with foreboding.

I turned toward home, hurrying along the familiar street that now looked strange, malign. Fat drops of sweat rolled down my forehead. I sensed eyes glaring at me from behind the shuttered windows. I had overheard whispered tales of Hindus killing Muslims. Was someone going to kill me for being a Muslim?

The narrow street seemed to stretch endlessly in front of me. There was an acrid smell in the air. Smoke hung over the rooftops in the direction of my house. I walked faster skirting what I thought at first was a mud puddle, the kind you made when you smashed a balloon full of water on hard ground. But it was not water. It was dark red blood turning brown. Struck with terror, I imagined my mother and father, my brother and sister, lying slaughtered in our courtyard. Somewhere there was a shout and a scream. In the heat of the blazing sun, I saw dark shadows approaching. I ran and ran. I heard only the rasp of my own breath and the thunder of my heart. My schoolbooks lay abandoned in the road behind me. My glucose biscuits were crushed and soggy in my clenched fist when I got home.

A week later, we fled to Pakistan, and we never saw our home again.

On Saturday June 21, 1964, I walked through a group of

179

marching protesters on my way into the Wieboldt's on State Street. I took an escalator up to the men's shop. At the landing, I found myself sandwiched between two men in light gray flannel suits and felt hats. They flashed their FBI badges, and the shorter one of the two grabbed my arm. His grip was so firm that any thought of freeing my arm was out of the question. He pulled me aside. I turned to face this man. Agent Wayne was about ten years older and six inches shorter than me but looked strong with a wide torso and broad shoulders. He had a tanned face and dark tortoiseshell glasses. "Let's move away from the escalator," he said. "We need to talk."

Once again, I thought about jerking my arm loose and walking away, but his powerful grip got tighter. I nodded and followed. He led me to an isolated corner with no exits and demanded to know what I was protesting, why I was marching. I remained silent. Despite the sunglasses that hid their eyes, I could feel their stare. There was no way I could shake loose; his hold on my arm was perfectly measured.

"Are you a citizen of this country? Do you have identification on you?" Agent Wayne did all the talking while Agent Price kept the watch. I knew any false move on my part would bring Agent Price into action as well. I needed to free my arm to pull out my wallet and take out my driver's license. I did nothing.

"This is not your country," said Agent Wayne. "You are not from here, you have no right to protest the policies of this country. This time we are going to let you go. If you are seen at another protest march, you will be arrested and deported back to your country." He fell silent and stared at me. Still gripping my arm, he continued, "Do you hear me? Do you understand me? We are the FBI. We can do whatever we need to do. We know who you are. We know where you live." They never raised their voice. I knew they were trying to intimidate and harass me, and they were successful. I was so shaken by that encounter that I turned around without shopping and took the first train back to my apartment.

I press the heels of my hands against my eyes. Tense, I grind my teeth. There is an explosion at the base of my skull. *I will control my feelings towards this woman,* I instruct myself, *and go back and marry the girl I'm committed to marry.* It is getting dark. I see my reflection in the kitchen window, a man in confinement, his face pale. Inside my head, I listen to Phil Ochs sing "There but for Fortune." Sex is well and good, but it's time to pull up my pants and apologize for myself. Sabina walks back. She turns on the overhead light. I snap back to alertness and look up at her warily. Her face is still without color, her mouth tense. I can see the pain around her eyes. She puts a package loosely wrapped in green tissue paper on the table, than sits down beside me.

I hear in my head a verse from Ghalib. *Among the houris of heaven, I should but see your face.*

"Sabina, I am so sorry," I say. "I have made you angry and sad. Tell me what you want from me, and I'll do accordingly." The moment I say it, I hear my lie; I think one thing, and I say the other.

She rakes her hair back off her face with her fingers, not speaking, then leans toward me and kisses me gently on the lips. "I love you," she says shakily, a tear rolls down her cheek.

I pull her to me, onto my lap. "I wrote this poem for you." Putting my head on her shoulder, I recite it with my mouth close to her ear.

If I am not here
I must be there.
Look for me, Dear Love,
Please do not lose me.
The night is young,
And I'm lost,
Waiting for you somewhere.

"Dear Rama, I know you think you love me, but perhaps you won't always." I just look at her; I'm out of my mind. Do I have any control over love?

"Open it," she says. She struggles to sit up. Moving back to her chair, she thrusts the package at me.

"I have something for you, too," I announce. I have bought her a Lady Remington shaver, on sale at Goldblatt's.

I open the package, carefully removing the clear plastic tape. I hold out a gray woolen sweater. It has blue bands at the cuffs, along the bottom, and around the V-neck.

181

"This is great!" I exclaim. "A cricketer's sweater! Where did you find it?"

"Try it on," Sabina says, her face flushed with pleasure. "I hope I got the size right. I tried to measure it against your yellow sweater."

As I get up and put it on, it dawns on me that she has knitted it herself. I am awestruck. "You made this yourself?" I ask.

She nods, wiping the tears from her cheeks with the back of her hand.

"I didn't even know you could knit," I say. I put the sweater on carefully. The sleeves are perfect; it fits loosely, the way we cricketers like. "Now that I'm not playing cricket, I play a fool," I tell her. I hug her tightly. "It's wonderful! You are wonderful!" I kiss her eyelids, then her mouth. She tastes of cinnamon and salt.

We eat our dinner cold then go to Orchestra Hall for a special New Year's Day concert given by the Freedom Singers, Dave van Ronk, and Phil Ochs.

"'Fare you well, my only Love," I say as I leave Sabina after the concert, "And fare you well a while! / And I will come again, my Love, / Although it were ten thousand miles!'"

I take the number 11 bus northbound from downtown. It begins to snow. The first snow of the winter is the most beautiful—so quiet and tranquil, peaceful, enveloping. It's late and the city is asleep. I get off the bus by Town Theater at Lincoln and Armitage, before my usual stop, so I can walk in the snow. It's coming down in big, lacy flakes at an accelerating pace. I walk lazily down the quiet street.

When I get home, my hair is wet and melted snow runs down my neck. My neck is where I always feel the cold. I walk upstairs. Latif has already gone to sleep. The blue flame of the space heater burns brightly in the living room. It is warm and quiet in the dark apartment. An unfamiliar joy sweeps over me—*Sabina, Sabina, Sabina*, I chant silently.

I take off my jacket and hang it on the back of the Lazy boy. I take off Sabina's sweater. It is a bit wet, so I spread it over the space heater and walk down to the bathroom to dry my hair and neck. When I walk back to the living room the sweater is burning—not with flames, but smoldering, smoking. "Hell!" I cry. I grab it off the stove.

182

There's a scorched spot on the back. It reminds me of when I lost the quilt my mother made for me. How could I have been so stupid? Sabina will never forgive me!

After a close examination, I decide it is not that bad. The spot is on the backside. If I wear it under a jacket, I calculate frantically, no one will know. Then, to my surprise, I recover my good mood. I sing to myself, "Mind me not, joy of the day / There are moments when the untrue seems true."

CHAPTER 30

On a cold, frigid Friday in February, I arrive home to find a letter from Leila sitting in the mailbox. I'm annoyed with myself. There is no pleasure in receiving her letter any more. It is about time she knows the truth and learns of my ways. I open it quickly and read it fast before Sabina arrives for the evening.

Music of My Life,
Each of your letters brings a different rhythm to my heart, a drum with a different beat. It raises questions I cannot answer. All I know: my love is here to stay, forever. You love only once—after that it's repetition. The first time it comes naturally, like falling asleep. Later it's like riding a bicycle—you get up and move on.

The night when our two hearts beat with a single resonance will be ours soon! Our love has touched everything with its magic—looking at a red, velvety bir bahuti in the grass for the first time, the night of our first embrace . . . the birds and the sky, the spring rain, a bud opening into a flower. I long, I yearn for us to be together, for our love is true—love like ours happens only once.
Truly yours,
Leila
February 1, 1965

Stressed, I grind my teeth. There is a detonation setting off, spreading in my head. How long do I intend to keep the poor woman in the dark, how long?

Affected, infected, anxious, it is impossible for me to behave naturally, to be relaxed. Sitting on my living room couch, Sabina and I watch the *CBS Evening News*. Walter Cronkite reports: "Vietcong attacked the U.S. air base near Pleiku, killing eight American servicemen and wounding over a hundred. In response to the severe attack by Communist guerrillas, President Johnson has ordered forty-nine U.S. planes to bomb Vietcong barracks and staging areas. Guerrilla fighters killed another twenty-three Americans during a raid on the U.S. Army barracks in the port city of Qui Nhon. The U.S. retaliated with a 160-plane raid." A black-and-white screen shows planes dropping bombs on trees, swamps, and lowlands. Clearly, the war is escalating. A solemn President Johnson appears onscreen saying, "We did not seek a wider war."

"This is an arrogant abuse of power," Sabina fumes. "How can we forgive ourselves for the things we are doing in this war?"

I say nothing. I want to watch the rest of the news.

More than 2,000 Vietnamese and Chinese Communist student demonstrators attacked the U.S. embassy in Moscow in protest. An Eastern Air Line plane plunged into the Atlantic killing all 84 abroad.

Sabina gets up and snaps off the TV. "This war is between two giants, the Communists versus the U.S., why should good men die for a bad cause?" she asks, pacing back and forth in front of the couch. "When I'm ready to kill, I want it to be hot-blooded murder, well-calculated and carefully planned. Shooting at strangers is like a zipless fuck!"

The only time I ever fired a gun was when we lived in the house across the *mandir* in the city by the River Betwa. During a hunting trip with Baba, I watched as he loaded his single-barrel rifle with gunpowder and a lead bullet and packed it with an old cotton rag. He cocked it, put a cap on the nipple, aimed, and fired. I always prayed for the safety of the game—a pheasant, a duck, or a deer. But Baba was a sure shot; he never missed. I'd feel sorry for the animal and would refuse to eat the meat my mother subsequently prepared. Then I'd get hungry and eat the sauce only, with rice.

Baba thought I should learn how to fire a gun. I was curious, but I didn't want to learn; I never played soldier or wanted to be a policeman as a child. To please Baba, I complied with his wishes and followed his instructions. Baba loaded his gun, and I pressed it against my shoulder. Baba's shoulder was pressed firmly against mine.

It was quite a jolt, the shock behind action and reaction, but Baba absorbed most of it and I was deadly accurate. Like in a cowboy movie, I hit the Dalda Vegetable Oil can through and through, "You're a dead shot," said Baba, but I was aware that it was Baba who was the dead shot. I aimed and I fired, but he showed me where to aim, how to take a long, deep breath and exhale slow and easy, and when to pull

185

the trigger. I also knew, I wanted to kill no one, not even an enemy or Ahab the Arab.

The last time I remember my father firing a gun was in Munno Mia's compound. He was asked the favor of shooting Munno Mia's mad dog, a German Shepherd called King. Baba didn't want me to go with him, but I insisted and he relented. Munno Mia and his family lived not too far from us in a large white house with an eight-foot-high brick wall enclosing a large front and backyard with tall mango trees and their sweet water well. King used to guard the small mango orchard and the house, but he also protected the stray men and women stealing the water from the well. On this day King was tied to a huge neem tree. King barked violently, then attacked the tree, first tearing at the bark with his teeth, than smashing his head repeatedly against the trunk, snarling and growling. Baba stood more than twenty feet away and shot King cleanly through the heart. The dog arched up into the air, then fell on the ground, blood gushing out of his chest. I looked the other way, but it was too late, I had seen much too much. "You shoot mad dogs and Englishmen," cried Munno Mia, large tears rolling from his eyes.

"You have to shoot mad dogs and Englishmen," I say softly.

Sabina stops in the middle of the living room. "I don't know what you mean, but I don't like what it implies."

"Dear," I say, trying to amuse her, "I know you are blue, but don't make yourself miserable."

"Stop it!" she says furiously. "Every time I try to have a serious conversation with you, you slide away from it with stupid jokes. This fucking war is not something to make light of."

"Fear, pity, and humor are appropriate reactions to tragedy," I say, trying to salvage the moment.

"I don't see any humor in war."

"No," I reply, "you don't see any humor in anything these days. You are both wasted and falling apart trying to get inspired spiritually, chemically, smoking dope."

"People are dying over there, damn it! Not just the Vietnamese, but Americans—*kids*, eighteen, nineteen years old. Seventy-three of them this week, *if* the Pentagon can be believed, and how many will die next week? And next month and a year from now?"

186

"Sabina! "

"Don't 'Sabina' me! This is not World War II. This is a stupid, blind, ego-driven gunfight at the O.K. Corral, except that the cowboys sit safely in the Pentagon and send out kids—fucking *kids*, Rama—to fight their goddamned 'limited' war! The Vietcong pose no threat to the United States. We provide arms and weapons to one country while banning them from another. We create an uneven balance of power and an arms race around the world. In North Vietnam, Americans have killed more civilians than the Vietcong. North Vietnamese don't see our freedom, they see the 'Made in USA' stamp on our bombshells and tear gas canisters."

Peace marches are very Bertrand Russell, and of course, anything good enough for Bertie is good enough for her. "Please, Sabina," I plead, "I'm not in favor of the war."

"You are not a cold person," She interrupts me with a kind of cool detachment, "But you refuse to get emotionally involved—not with this immoral imperialistic war and not with me either."

I'm self-conscious of my feelings, and I do not want to get hurt. There is a part of me that I keep in a world of my own, a world of my losses, sketches from memories that others cannot see because others cannot feel what I feel. I remember all things, all contents: past, present, and future, conscious, subconscious, unconscious. I don't give and I don't let myself go. Sabina is the best thing that has ever happened to me, yet it seems I'll do whatever I have to in order to lose her. "It's just that I am experiencing something wonderful for the first time," I say, "Maybe I'm selfish, but I don't want anything to cast its shadow on us."

"Right," she says bitterly. "You lust after me, yet you have no real passion for life. The scented pink letters keep coming. You correspond with this poor woman you claim your family chose for you. I may be giving, or carefree, but I'm not a fool. You want to be the hero in an Indian movie, singing songs in the moonlight and stealing forbidden kisses in a perfumed garden." Sabina shakes her head. "I'm not real to you. I'm just the other woman in the movie playing a short-lived role in your head."

"That's not true!" I protest. But even as I deny it, I know that it *is* true. I use the truth of my engagement and my lie—the so-called

187

woman of my mother's choosing is a woman I chose and supposedly loved—and the necessity of my ultimate departure from America as ways to create distance from Sabina! I squeeze my eyes shut. *Oh, God.* "Objectivity is not a concern to your subjective passion!" I shout. "You act as though I'm supporting Chang Kai Shek and you are supporting Mao."

"What do we have anyway," she finishes, her voice quiet and flat, "except this thing for each other in bed?"

I don't know what to say. "Do you really believe we don't have anything in common?" I ask after a few moments.

"I know I don't have time for bullshit," Sabina replies coldly. "There is a war going on, both in Vietnam and on the streets of America. And by God, this is *my* country and these are *my* issues."

My issues, I think. How am I going to deal with my issues? I know what *my* issues are, but I don't want to look at my issues. Denial is an island. The thought of leaving America fills me with sorrow. How sad I will be to leave Sabina. How much I'll miss her smile. "It's not true that you're not real to me," I say. "I create distance because I do not know what is right, I'm lost and confused, I do not know what to do."

"If you love me as you say you do," Sabina says savagely, "then how can there be any doubt about what to do?"

"Love wins in the end in the movies, but this is life, my life," I snap. "You make it sound so easy. Have you ever tried to put yourself in my place? Have you tried to imagine what it would be like to leave your family, your culture, your language—everything that is beloved and familiar to you and go to live in another country where you feel like a stranger twenty-four hours a day, seven days a week? Where nothing looks or sounds or tastes or even smells familiar?"

She opens her mouth, but I won't let her speak. Turbulence rumbles in my head; a scowl hardens my face. I feel rigid and immobile. All at once my loneliness and pain and anger boil up and overflow like a pot of rice forgotten on the stove. "You ridicule my obligations and responsibilities to my family because you are so deep into the cult of individualism that you have no sense of connection to anything but your own pleasure and convenience."

Sabina looks disconcerted. She is much too smart to be

influenced by a given policy, personal advice, or my guidance. "All I know is that I can't say or do anything right by you!" I shout. "Maybe we should not be an item any more. Perhaps you should go out and meet your own kind of men."

"How can you talk about me that way? You tell me to meet other guys. Honey, let's get one thing crystal clear: I don't mess around. If I were with another guy, I wouldn't be with you, but maybe you're right. Maybe I should go out with other guys. There are times when I wonder about your love and lovemaking."

"My dear, you've hurt me beyond repair," I say, sarcastic. "I don't have anyone to compare you with, and, definitely, I'm not as experienced as you in this game."

"Why is it when I know a man too well, I begin to hate him?"

"All your relationships are reflections of your relationship with yourself," I say. "It's horrible to become disappointed in your idolized self."

"I should have been less truthful with you. It's my fault. I already know that. I picked you up—the man who can't make commitments, the guy who withholds." She snatches up her purse and jacket from the couch. "Don't lose any sleep over me," she says, her voice icy. "If I ever want a wedding band, I know I can get one." She pauses a moment. "Everything that was good between us is gone now. I want to go away. And we are both free to do what we want." She slams out of the apartment, leaving me stunned and defeated.

I hear Sabina start her car and then the put-put of her departing Volkswagen. *There is absolutely no reason why she should call me or be with me. I should go back to where I belong.* But where *do* I belong? I am lost, wandering in the cosmos, and I am not being honest with Sabina, Leila, or my mother. Am I still in love with Leila? Where do I want to live? Whom do I wish to marry?

This is going to hurt more than I thought, I think grimly. I know I need Sabina badly. I yank myself back from the verge of this thought as if it were the edge of an abyss.

There is nothing wrong with sadness, I lecture myself, *it's just another feeling, and it all fades with time. There is always pain, love lost, and suffering. Then there's the Beatles for popular distraction.*

I hate relationships based on insecurities and lies. I am

insecure, and I tell lies. I have not told Sabina the truth about myself: I am the one who is committed to marry Leila; I'm the one who once loved and wanted to marry Leila. I want to scream out loud. I tell myself that I should call someone and go out and do something, but I'm immobilized on the couch. Finally I get up and put on a Beatles album Sabina gave me and sit listening to it in the dark. In the middle of John Lennon singing "Bad Boy," Latif walks in. He turns on the light and turns off the music. I look up, squinting irritably.

Latif stands there, dressed in a gray gabardine suit. "What are you doing home so early without a date?" I ask him.

"All dressed up with no place to go," he says. "My blind date didn't show."

He looks around and finds an ashtray, the one he brought back from the Playboy Club, an orange square with the outline of a woman drawn in black. Sabina hates ashtrays full of cigarette butts, and Latif always leaves the ashtrays brimming.

"Maybe your blind date saw you first and escaped."

"Very funny," he says, sitting on the La-Z-Boy across from the TV. He takes a pack of Pall Malls from his pocket, pulls out a cigarette, taps it a few times on his Zippo lighter, and lights it. He takes a long drag and exhales with a noisy breath.

"I think you're seeing too much of Sabina," he says abruptly.

"I don't recall asking your opinion."

Latif goes on as though he hasn't heard me. "Unless a woman is a whore, you cannot fuck her more than once without saying 'I love you.'" He takes another drag and spits out a tobacco cram from his tongue. "On second thought, even if she is a whore, she would want you to say 'I love you.'"

"Sabina is not a whore," I say quietly. I am dimly aware of an immense pressure building up in my head.

"It is very simple. You don't spend every weekend, Friday evening through Monday morning, with the same woman for six months unless you plan to marry her."

"I thought it was 'you don't buy a pair of shoes without trying them on.'"

"Yes, there is wisdom in that," Latif says, smoothly exhaling, "but you don't try the same pair of shoes on over and over again. What

190

you need is fresh pussy to eat, a new vagina to fit into, and another tight ass to kiss. *Goris* are to fuck and forget, not to marry."

I open my mouth to protest, but Latif continues, "Don't lead her on, you carry your fiancé's photograph in your wallet, and you receive those pink envelopes from her on regular basis. Like you, one day I'm going home to marry the woman of my mother's choosing. Our women may not give blow jobs, but you can always flip them over and fuck them in the ass, and you can teach them to do anything."

"I don't believe you think like that."

"Don't forget your own roots." He takes another drag of his cigarette. "And don't forget that you are an Indian, and not even a Native American Indian. In any event, a quail's marriage to a pheasant never works."

"Don't lecture me on love and marriage," I say, standing abruptly. "You disgust me." I see with satisfaction that I have shocked Latif. The intensity of my anger distresses me. Without another word, I go to my bedroom and shut the door.

I lie in bed staring at the faint rectangle of light filtered in from the window. *It's never truly dark in the city,* I think. *And I'll never sleep tonight.* I run mathematical equations through my head for a while and then reflect on the way changing weather makes me feel. Am I really affected by the full moon? *My soul is adrift in the pursuit of its own destiny. I can never love the same way again.* Yet, I do love Sabina; she'll always be a dream away. I sigh noisily and punch up my wilted pillow.

I am going to have to choose. This thought pops into my head as though a gong has been struck beside the bed. I sit up in a wild panic and turn on my reading lamp. I sit in solitude. After a while, I turn off the light and lay down again. I fall asleep watching raindrops on the windowpanes turn into snowflakes.

Five or more inches have fallen by the time I wake up, and it is still coming down. The roofs and streets are paved with white. The morning is windless, the snow silent.

I lie in bed remembering dreams of Sabina. In one dream, she goes away to Paris to join a student protest march, and her plane crashes. In another, she gets arrested in Badshahi Masjid Lahore because her knees are exposed. Dan Rather reports it live from the scene on the evening news.

I get out of bed, aching for Sabina. I shave in the shower, an act of efficiency I have mastered and am quite proud of. It saves me ten to fifteen minutes every morning, and Sabina loves hot showers.

I finish my cup of tea and take out the black army combat boots that lace all the way up my ankles. I bought them at the Army-Navy Surplus Store on Lincoln Avenue. I dress in jeans, a blue work shirt, and the gray sweater Sabina knitted for me. Then I put on the army boots, a long gray scarf, and an army overcoat. I walk down to the Fullerton Avenue L station.

From my coat pocket, I pull the small notebook and pen that I always carry with me. Riding my train, I write: *If you want love, give love. If you want to be loved, try loving. I need to practice giving what I seek, what I want* . . . In my fury to capture my thoughts on paper, I almost miss my stop. I leap through the closing doors and onto the platform. The wind is calm, the sun peeking above the gray clouds, beginning to wake people up. Some are shoveling the sidewalks, others cleaning the snow off their cars. Walking to Sabina's apartment, I'm aware that between last night and this morning something within me has shifted. The effect is gradual, my features soften, my scowl melting, and my movement becomes fluid again. I am at Sabina's door. I press the bell.

"Is that you?" she calls down through the intercom.

"It is I who is sorry," I call back. "It is I who loves you." She buzzes me in.

I mount the stairs, tracking melting snow on the blue-and-gray-striped rug all the way to the third floor. Sabina's apartment door is ajar. She is not waiting for me at the entrance. I sit down on the top step and efficiently undo the laces from one boot then the other. I place them on the brown jute mat. Then I walk in and close the door. Sabina stands in the living room in front of the fireplace, her back towards me. Embers glow from a dying fire. Her books lie on the Chinese rug; ashes from last night's incense fill the incense holder. An old blue-and-green double wedding-ring quilt is still spread out on the brown cut-velvet couch. From the look of the room, I can tell this is where she spent the night.

"I am here, Love," I say in an effort to amuse her, "and I'd

192

like to stay. Stay forever."

She doesn't look at me. She sinks to her knees in front of the hearth and carefully arranges a couple of logs. Patiently, she blows on the embers until a flame erupts, and the logs catch. She holds out her hands to the fire to soak up the heat. "You look at your predicament a hundred different ways and find yourself perplexed at your dire straits," she says in a low voice, clearly enunciating each word. "There are reasons to split up and reasons to stay together."

She goes on like she is talking to herself. In a whisper she says, "I see around me the sorrow and the sadness of the world over and over again, and try as I might, I cannot turn away."

She turns to face me for the first time. Her eyes look sad and tired, her gaze contemptuous. "Why are we unhappy more often than we are happy? Why are there wars? I want sunshine, blue skies, and peace every day. I always want Mama and always want love."

"I have not been good for you," I say.

Sabina puts some music on; Bob Dylan sings, "You're No Good." She sits down on the couch. "What bothers me is that you express no emotion. I never know what you are thinking or what is on your mind, and you never respond to what is being said. You speak in clichés, in advertising slogans. You're all style and no substance."

"That hurts," I say. It is hard to be spontaneous when you are carefully considering what you are going to say next. "But when you care for someone, you worry about her feelings, and you do not go about doing things the way you want, like you don't care or don't understand. I accommodate, and I try not to hurt you, and that's when the question of understanding comes in."

"Rama, you are not making sense," Sabina sighs.

"What I'm trying to say," I repeat, "is that I don't know what the future holds, but I am here right now, and I'd like to stay. Forever!"

Sabina shakes her head and stares at me blankly. "You don't know what the future holds, but you are here to stay forever."

Dylan sings "Man of Constant Sorrow."

I go to the couch and sit beside her. She is slipping away. She is going to leave me. I feel the abyss beckoning again.

"My dearest lotus blossom," I say, "what the devil is the matter with you?"

193

She ignores my question. "No one knows what you want, and no one understands you," she says, ice-cold. "Poor Rama! Doesn't it bother you, or do you think it adds to your cachet?"

"Look, Sabina," I sigh, "I create distance because I do not know what is right and I do not know what you want."

"Right and wrong are not the issue here, and what *I* want is not the issue either. I'm talking about your life and what you want for yourself."

"I am confused and unsure of everything," I tell her. "These are major life issues—love, marriage, home, country. Everything is up for grabs!" The fire burns brightly in the fireplace. "Can you possibly understand that, Sabina?"

"I *have* been trying! But when I begin to think that we're getting closer, you become reclusive and demanding at the same time." She looks into my eyes. I look away. "You're fair, but you fight dirty. You're manipulative, deceitful, and controlling. You may claim to forgive, but you don't forget anything. And you live in the past, no matter how miserable it was."

"I cling to the past because it holds everything familiar, not because it was miserable," I reply with a sad smile. "But this morning, on the way here, I began to glimpse some clarity. I wrote down my thoughts." I reach for her hand, and holding it in both of mine, I kiss her open palm. "May I share with you the wanderings of my soul?"

Slowly, Sabina lets out her breath. "Yes," she says simply.

I retrieve my notebook from my coat pocket and read aloud, "If you want love, give love. If you want to be loved, try loving. Everything comes from the unknown, and in the realm of the unknown, everything is possible. Your destiny compels your deed, and your deed your desire. The essence of life breathes without breath, that's what the soul is and that is what death is as well . . . Karma is both action and the consequence of action. Everything that is happening in the present is the result of the choices one has made in the past . . . Even unconscious decisions bring consequences. We all pay our karmic debts. For one to transcend karma, to become independent of it, one needs to find oneself—soul and spirit. Breathing without body, out of body . . . When one begins to know what the gods are thinking, when everything is in balance, suspended in equilibrium, one needs to surrender to the moment, relinquish the need to defend one's point of view. One has no need to convince or persuade others to one's own point of view. Past, present, and future are all part of our consciousness. The future is created in the present. And the present is awareness of the moment. The past is recollection and memory, and the future is anticipation, expectation, and hope. Consciousness is rooted in the past, connected to the imagination of the future. When one can free oneself from the anticipation of the future, detach oneself from the end result . . . uncertainty is the path to freedom. Everything is possible—that's the road to independence. I am free."

I don't dare look at Sabina when I am finished. After reading it now, I wonder if it really means anything beyond some conceptual mumbo-jumbo, gibberish, nonsense. She puts her hands on my cheeks and tilts my head up, and in her eyes a hundred emotions flit. "I'm not going anywhere, Rama," she says softly. "You're the one who must ultimately decide. And I don't know if I'm capable of the kind of detachment you write about. Life is short, and I've always felt that I will die young."

"Please don't say that, Sabina. It frightens me. I want to love you without fear or desperation." I hold both of Sabina's hands in mine. "My commitment to honor my mother's choice is always hanging over me." I continue to lie. I should tell her who Leila really is, someone I think I might still love. No, no, no. No more lies, no more lies. "I have previous commitments, but I have to make a decision. I know it casts its shadow on our relationship. What I am learning is that what is to happen will happen. And when you think nothing is going to happen, that's when things happen, and they happen even when you prepare yourself for the unavoidable. And no matter what you prepare yourself for, it's never the thing that actually does happen. And when you think you have lost all that you could lose, you can still lose something more, I never thought I'd feel this way about you, that I would fall in love with an American woman. But I did. I am experiencing something wonderful. I am happy when I am with you, sitting beside you!" I put my head on her shoulder, I have a sudden sense, a fantasy, a fancy, that I could inhabit parallel universes: In one, I stay with Sabina; in the other, I return to my family and do what is expected of me. With my fingertip I trace the lines on the palm of her hand. I tell her, "I am conflicted, but I know exactly what I want." *I no longer know what is true and what is a lie.* "I know I cannot go back home and live happily ever after. My future is with you. When and where and how only time will tell."

Sabina's eyes search mine. "All I can say is that I'm not going anywhere. I can wait," she says. "Do what you must."

"Thank you for setting me free," I say. *I've just knit a web and trapped myself in it.* "I may be rough, tough, carefree, and indifferent upfront, but deep down inside I am insecure and uncertain about everything."

"Show me the rough, tough, upfront side," she says, breaking into a grin. "I may not be the marrying kind, but I'll stay with you as long as you want, and definitely tonight." Sabina leans toward me and settles against my chest.

"I love your morning caresses the most," I declare, sliding my hands up her spine to the bare skin at the nape of her neck. As always my pulse goes crazy at the smell of her hair. "I feel being rejected by others the most when *I* reject others," I volunteer, "like I am rejecting myself. I can never say no. That also means rejecting others, and I could never take a no because that means I'm being rejected, but I think it's better to be a rejecter than a rejectee."

Suddenly, I have no idea what I have just said.

She slides out of my hands to the floor and lies down on the purple part of the Chinese rug. "My love for you is unconditional. Like a watermark, it will always be there," she says. Sitting on the cut velvet couch, I watch her another moment. Then I lie down beside her.

CHAPTER 31

On a sunny day in March early in the spring, the temperature rises to eighty degrees. I walk home dressed in a woolen suit and tie, feeling the heat. When I arrive at our apartment, Latif is already there, sitting on a rocking chair in the living room. All the windows are open, the curtains drawn, and the window shades flap in the breeze. On the radio, Frank Sinatra sings "Don't Wait Too Long."

"I've decided to go back home next month," Latif announces.

"That's rather sudden," I say, sitting on the couch across from him.

"When I begin to fall asleep at work and start missing my coffee breaks, I know *it's time to go home.*"

He looks happy, smiling from ear to ear.

"What can I say," I shrug, "finding a roommate in the middle of the school year is like finding a bride through the classifieds."

"When your new year begins to look like a used year, its time to pack and move," says Latif. He starts telling jokes without punch lines. If I sit here, he'll tell jokes nonstop through the night. I get up and head to my room.

"When I think of you as a normal person, it's out of guilt," Latif says. "It's your turn to sing me a song."

I keep walking. *If you already don't like someone,* I reflect, *at least you know where you're starting.* I change clothes and go to the kitchen. I put red lentils on one burner and rice on another. From the kitchen phone, I call Sabina. She answers on the second ring.

"Let's get married so I don't have to find another roommate," I say.

❦

Sabina and I take Latif out for a farewell dinner at The Bakery on Lincoln Avenue. A tiny Japanese lady with a marvelous smile greets us and leads us to our table. Sabina and I sit across from each other with Latif in the middle.

Our table is covered with linen. A single fresh red rose sits

197

meticulously among an assortment of plates and silverware. There are no menus. Dinner begins with a *pâté maison* and homemade French bread with sweet butter. Soup is ladled from a tureen at our table, next we're served salads made from the freshest greens followed by our choice of entrees: *filet de boeuf en croûte* for me, duckling with cherry sauce for Sabina, and chicken paprika for Latif.

We enjoy our meal, drinking Perrier.

There is an element of civility among us. Sabina is amazingly graceful, and Latif is charming and polite. "You shall visit me in Karachi," Latif tells Sabina. "It's a nice place to visit, but you will not want to live there."

Latif departs at the end of April, leaving his blue '58 Chevrolet Impala parked in front of Helen Witowski's house for me. I like having all the space to myself. I enjoy living alone; it can be a growing experience. Everyone should try it, at least for a few days.

I lie around listening to the Beatles and the Brothers Four, watching *I Love Lucy* reruns, and reading Jack McDonald mysteries. In reality, I am not alone much. During the week I drive to Sabina's and sleep over at her place Tuesday and Wednesday nights. I fix dinner while she studies. Then on Fridays Sabina comes over to my place and stays until Monday morning. When we are not together, we are talking on the phone.

"My dear, the part of me that is you is not with me when you are away," I tell Sabina on the phone.

"I miss you when I am hungry, and I miss you when I eat alone," she says.

Pity this poor immigrant. I am going out of my mind filling out all the forms to become an alien, a green card holder, so I can leave and re-enter this country as I please. I'll still not be allowed to vote, run for political office, or work for the federal government, but I could be drafted into the armed forces. My company has sponsored me to apply for the green card. When I went to Bill Wright, my supervisor, to have him sign the papers, he looked at me suspiciously for the longest time and then said, "Rama, given the way you feel about America and her foreign policies, why do you want to join a sinking ship?" Maybe, because I'm already on it, I think. Before I could come up with an answer, he signed my forms. He thinks I'm some kind of hippie because he's seen me reading Jack Kerouac's *On The Road.* Politically, we don't see eye to eye. To become a permanent resident, I have to swear that I have never been a communist, trafficked in drugs or women, or committed adultery. I also have to produce evidence of exceptional ability in the sciences or the arts. I am doing all of this for Sabina, because nobody smiles like her and nobody cries like her, and she has the most enchanting eyes of any woman on earth.

I ask, "What has four eyes but cannot see?"

"Mississippi," she replies without hesitation, giggling. "Rama, you are so funny. That joke is so old, I can remember it from grade school."

"Well, it's new to me, and I'd like to go to Mississippi with you and work to register voters."

Sabina sighs, "Anyone can say they don't care what other people say about them. I don't think I can believe that. Sometimes I get this feeling—I get chills down my spine just thinking about it."

"What feeling?" I prompt her.

"Sometimes, " Sabina says, "if I want to see myself from an observer's point of view, I can be sitting in a classroom, and all of a sudden, I'm watching myself move and think. It makes me wonder what we actually are sometimes. I had a revelation today. I found out that my Renaissance literature teacher is human after all. It's ironic that we're in school to learn, yet, we forsake knowledge for grades. To work on the school paper, I may have to sacrifice my grades. Why do I get so concerned about damn grades and tests? Who'll care ten years from now whether I got an *A* on a test? Nobody, probably not even myself!"

I love hearing Sabina talk; I love everything she says. My Sabina is an extraordinary woman, and I love her so.

199

CHAPTER 32

In May, just before Sabina graduates, she finds a job with Channel 7, an ABC affiliate, as a news writer.

"I thought news just happens," I say. "How do you write news?"

"Very accurately, not allowing more than forty-five seconds for any given incident," she says. She is excited. It's a great beginner's job, and it could lead to becoming a news editor, a news reporter, even an anchorwoman.

"This calls for a celebration," I say. "Let's do something fancy, something special." Blues may have been born in the Mississippi Delta, but Chicago is where it came to mature. The same is true of jazz. Chicago is a great music town. I wanted to go to Mister Kelly's, a sophisticated supper club on Rush Street. Today's top echelon of entertainers—comedians like Shelley Berman, Mort Sahl, Shecky Green, and Woody Allen and singers such as Carmen McRae, Dorothy Loudon, and Lainie Kazan—perform there all the time. I've always wanted to go to Mr. Kelly's, and this weekend the Smothers Brothers are performing three shows Friday through Saturday at 9:00 p.m., midnight, and 3:00 a.m. I'm a big fan of the Smothers Brothers, their comedy, the way they sing, and since I am a member of the Gourmet Checks Plan, I can purchase two tickets for the price of one.

"I don't care for that kind of hoopla," says Sabina, "but if you want it, we'll do it."

So on Saturday night, Sabina and I go to Mister Kelly's for the nine o'clock show. Sabina wears a black silk Chinese dress her parents brought her from a recent trip to Hong Kong. She looks elegant, like she walked out of a Jane Austen novel, with her dark hair combed back and tied with a maroon silk ribbon. The tiny silk buttons climbing up her collar complement her long neck, and the long slits baring her thighs make her look a little naughty, like Suzie Wong.

I wear my navy blue gabardine suit and oxford blue shirt with a red-and-blue-striped tie. Together we are handsome, tall and slim, more like a couple in a French film than an Indian or English movie.

It is still light outside when Sabina parks her VW on Oak

200

Street. She takes pride in knowing her city so well that she can always find free parking in downtown, Gold Coast, or Old Town. A pleasant breeze blows us gently in the right direction. She carries her black purse like a book. For a brief moment, we're young, happy, and carefree. Before we're aware of it, we walk holding hands.

We sit at a table for two covered with a leopard-spotted padded plastic tablecloth and order a bottle of red wine. I look at Sabina. When you are in love, you sense the moods of your love, her fears, her anxieties, and her joys. Something is on her mind.

Before I can ask her, Sabina looks at me. "Would you like to live with me?" she asks.

"Is this a proposal?" I ask with a smile.

"No," she says, "I meant strictly as roommates!"

"I thought so," I say. "It may complicate things."

"It might not," she says. "I'm not the marrying kind."

"I am."

The show begins.

"I never will marry, I'll have me no wife," sings Dick Smothers.

"But I may fool around a bit," adds brother Tom.

"I am enjoying this in spite of myself," Sabina declares, laughing.

After the show, driving towards my apartment, I ask again if it's a good idea for the two of us to live together.

"I know to live with me you have to lie to your mother and fiancé, but I'm not exactly announcing it to my parents either, and I know they will support me if I tell them. In our case nothing much is going to change, everything will be fine for a while," she says. "We'll live together until you go back home and do your thing."

I feel sad listening to Sabina talk like this. "I'll never be able to leave you," I say.

"Then we'll live happily ever after."

"It can't be as simple as that." I feel a dark cloud of sadness cross over me.

"But that's exactly how it is," she says. "We live together as long as we are happy or until you leave to go back. Whichever comes first? I'm happy for now."

"I'm happy for now as well, but I have to think of our tomorrow. I have to go back home and resolve my dilemma. I'll have to set the other woman free to set me free, or I'll have to set you free."

"So we should make ourselves miserable today because we have concerns about tomorrow?"

"I'm sorry I can't share your enthusiasm," I say. "Living with you could change my life for ever."

"Just share my joy. Live with me. As long as it doesn't ruin your life."

I'm twenty-five now. I'm not looking for another, I'm all committed, all taken, there is no end to my desperate, reckless, gallant, imprudent ways and tonight will be fine for a while. Life is short, long is my journey. What do I have to lose? "It's better to have lived together and parted than never to have lived together at all," I recite.

"That's the spirit. What do we have to lose?" she asks.

I take a deep breath and jump.

Helen Witowski will not allow Sabina and I to live together in my rented flat out of wedlock. Sabina calls and sets up an appointment to see a two bedrooms apartment on Mohawk Street in Old Town. She has to lie and tell the landlady that we were married. When we arrive at the appointed time and ring the doorbell for the landlady, she comes down, a middle age flabby, stout woman with pale face, and salt and pepper hair. She examines us briefly from behind a closed glass. She refuses to open the front door and calls out that she does not rent her place to mixed couples and she does not rent to people of color. I am in a state of shock beyond words. An outraged Sabina pounds the glass door with her fist. "Go away, before I call the police." Says the landlady and walks away leaving us on the outside of the closed glass door. Sabina finally finds us a two-bedroom apartment on Deming Place. It's the top floor of an old three-flat brick building and has a large sun porch facing east. We have to lie to the landlord and say that we are married, explaining that Sabina uses her maiden name since she is a reporter at ABC News.

I have little to move other than my clothes and a portable Magnavox turntable with attached speakers. I have few records and fewer books. Sabina, on the other hand, has the dowry of an eagerly sought wife. She brings her apartment full of personal belongings—old oak dressers, a round oak dining table with two extra leaves and six matching chairs, a brown cut velvet couch with six handsomely carved legs and goose down cushions, her brass bed, the green Chinese rug with a purple border, silverware, and china jars full of pasta and spices.

There is a story behind each and every one of her antiques and all her rhymes and reasons for her attachment to it. We rent a U-Haul trailer, attach it to my recently acquired Chevy Impala, load it up, and begin the move to our new dwelling. It takes an entire trip just to move her plants. She introduces them to me: the fourteen-inch *Dieffenbachia* a friend left behind for temporary care but never came back to collect, the coleus, asparagus fern, begonias, purple passion, rubber plant, cypress, wandering Jew, spider plant, and oxalis. She talks to them, murmurs sweet nothings to them, congratulates them on their new leaves, and commiserates with those that aren't looking well.

When we finish at last and take the trailer back, we're exhausted. We hang up a new plastic shower curtain bought at True Value Hardware and take a long, hot shower together. I wash her back, and she washes mine as well, releasing my tension. She combs her wet hair back, and we go out to dinner to our favorite Mexican restaurant. Afterwards, we hang an Indian print cotton sheet over the two windows of our new bedroom. We are too tired to put the bed together, so we simply lay the mattress on the floor and fall asleep cuddled together.

The next day Sabina leaves to visit her parents in Brooklyn for a week before starting her new job. Day after day, I sit among her boxes in the kitchen, drinking tea in the morning, and returning in the evening, tired and exhausted, to eat Swanson's Mexican TV dinners. I sleep on the mattress on the floor, waiting for Sabina to return. I begin to feel lonely again.

I've lived in this city for almost a year now, and I haven't made many friends. I live like a foreigner who is passing through on his way to a worthier destination. At work, I ignore everyone and keep myself constantly engaged, task-oriented, to maintain a certain distance, acting like an alien not just from another country, but also from another planet—Krypton, perhaps. I eat lunch every day with Ali Masavi, a civil engineer from Iran. Jax Pope, an electrical engineer from Poland, and Hans Maier, a mechanical engineer from Germany via Argentina, occasionally join us. I maintain an aloofness from them at all times.

On the fourth day of Sabina's absence, upon returning from work, I receive a letter from her. I also find, redirected from my old apartment, a letter from home. I change quickly into a white cotton shirt, trousers, and water buffalo sandals. In the kitchen, I put the kettle on for tea.

While waiting for the water to boil, I read the letter from home. It's from Amaji, dictated to my sister. My mother, like many women of her generation, was taught to read but not to write, although with lot of practice she did learn to sign her name.

As always, the letter reports the same things—the weather, the latest cricket scores, happenings in the lives of our extended family—and concludes with "Come back soon, we miss you." But there is something else this time. She informs me that Leila's parents wish to settle their daughter's betrothal as soon as possible. My head begins to throb. On the one hand, I'm learning that I cannot, absolutely not, live without Sabina, and, on the other hand, I'm finding out that I will not be allowed to live like this. The hole that I have dug myself into is getting deeper. I must be out of my mind.

I make myself a cup of tea, sit down, and open Sabina's letter.

Dear Rama,

> *If my joy doesn't last long, then why should my sorrow? I don't believe happiness is a state that I can strive for, achieve, and keep. It's an occasional blessing that befalls me now and then. Why is life so complicated?*
> *Love is an understanding, and, my dear Rama, the letter you sent was beautiful.*
> *"Watching the screens of rain."*
> *I remembered how you love the rain.*
> *I read:*
> *"And not the letter in any written shape to send . . ."*
> *and I remembered the moody letters you will not send me.*
> *I read:*
> *"I cross the river . . .to be with you."*

and I remembered our walk to the lake.
  I read:
  "The bush you wanted could not be planted . . ."
and I remembered the cruelty of love.
  I read:
  "The places, faces, frontiers and landscapes, and days
that went away ages ago . . ."
and I remembered our wonderful summer, and, yes, I
remember, too.
  I read:
  "Who will you and I be in a year?"
and I remembered my hopes and doubts.
  I read:
  "This stream of wanting, cumbersome in words,
lame."
and I remembered how much I want you.
  I read:
  "Come"
And I remembered our mornings, days, and nights.
  And I will come
Someday soon.

Life is slow, and I've made it dull. I have nothing to do, no friends to visit. The headache that started four days earlier is still fresh and only growing more intense. I've lost interest in cooking, and there seems to be a conspiracy in the neighborhood theaters. They are showing *Wild on the Beach, Beach Party, Beach Blanket Bingo, How to Stuff a Wild Bikini, Girl Happy*—all flat, flavorless, and totally forgettable. At least there is *The Pawnbroker* (116 min., 1964), an engrossing C-rated melodrama condemned by the Catholic Legion of Decency, but I have already seen it.

Beatles records and James Bond adventures—speeding trains and helicopters, sex, violence, and campy humor—keep me occupied. I watch *Help!* one night and the *Dr. No* and *From Russia with Love* double feature the next. Movies always take me beyond my worries and fantasies, but where I am, there is little to imagine. I eat dinner, meat loaf, the special of the day at Frances's on Clark Street. I take long walks on familiar streets, feeling alone and wondering what I am doing here.

Life torn by inner conflict, is not either or: left or right, right or wrong, strong or weak, awake or asleep. I am feeling pulled in opposite directions. I hold on to the tension and resist the temptation to choose, to give myself over to one side or the other. The wholeness of being demands both, and living with my opposites provides a new balance. In this way I do nothing. I leave things undone. I need to develop the courage to live with my opposites, yet I must make decisions and abide by the consequences.

On the seventh night of Sabina's absence, I dream of climbing endless hills. I wake up early on Thursday morning, exhausted. It's a warm day, and the weather is fickle. One minute it's raining, and the next minute the sun is out. High winds blow, and then there is sudden calm. Everything seems temperamental. At the end of the day, though, the sun finally comes out to stay. It's a beautiful day to dream and to bring a box of chocolates and a long stem rose to your love. Sometimes, I wish there was a way to tell her how I love her without diluting its significance. Sentiments expressed over and over again lose their magic.

Today is the day! Sabina returns tonight. I can't wait. After a long day at work, I arrive at our apartment with a bag full of groceries, sweating in my gray-and-white seersucker suit. I put the bag of groceries on the kitchen table and undo my tie. I change quickly and begin working on dinner. I chop onions for the beef dish I'm preparing along with curried eggplant. Once the meat is simmering, I start to put the brass bed together. *What am I doing?* I ask myself. This equation is not balanced. I am making dinner for Sabina; I am sleeping with this American woman whom I claim to be in love with, and I am expected to marry Leila.

I look out the window. A quarter moon hangs. I close the half-open window to within four inches from the sill. I am always cold, and Sabina is always hot. Winter through fall, she sleeps with the window open a crack. We both like leaving the curtains partially open. Night is beginning to show, a street lamp flickers dimly behind a lush green maple tree. The hot summer breeze feels good against my sweating body. I have only one life to live. I want to live in peace and in love with Sabina.

I go back to the kitchen. The art of Indian cooking is in the long slow simmer over a low fire and in stirring frequently. Everything is under control. Dinner is cooked, the bed is made, and I'm ready for my woman to arrive. I take a shower and dress for the trip to the airport. *What would happen,* I wonder, *if she decided to remain in New York!*

I love train stations, seaports, and airports. They are full of nervous, melancholy energy. Chicago has a modern airport, little over two years old, with four passenger terminal complex buildings linked by walkways. They say Chicago's airport is the busiest. O'Hare has parallel runways, northeast to southwest and southeast to northwest. The traffic is continuous with simultaneous landings and takeoffs. Between 4:00 p.m. and 8:00 p.m., the rush hour, planes land and take off every two minutes. There are two observation decks. For a dime, you can watch all the action and some of the world's most glamorous jets. People come from all over to O'Hare Airport for plane spotting.

Sabina's flight arrives twelve minutes ahead of schedule. I'm there waiting with a single red long stem rose in my hand. One, two, three . . . Tall and magnificent, wearing a long tan raincoat and carrying a dark brown leather bag over her shoulder, she is the twenty-seventh passenger out of the arrival gate. Combing her long hair back with her fingers, looking straight ahead, she spots me.

She smiles and walks toward me at an accelerated pace. Without saying a word, breathing in sync, we embrace, holding each other tightly for a long time.

"I missed you," I finally whisper.

"I love you," she whispers back.

I frame her face with my hands, and I see the only eyes I want to see every morning. "Don't ever leave me again." I tell her. *My loneliness tells me that I have sinned.*

CHAPTER 33

We wake up early the next morning. I've taken the day off from work to help Sabina set up our apartment. She starts with the kitchen. She washes every cupboard and then goes to the hardware store, returning with white paper to line the shelves. She also buys a metal rack to hang up all the pots and pans. She unpacks, cleans, and re-labels the spices, and we arrange them in alphabetical order—black, red, and white pepper next to one another, followed by salt and sugar. I am a good helper; with little difficulty and few tools, I manage to hang the pot rack over the kitchen sink. With the pots and pans hanging, the silverware in the drawer, the knives, spoons, and forks in their proper slots, the kitchen is finally done. The table is set for two with placemats and matching cotton napkins.

It is her show. I watch her with absolute awe. Next she goes to Crate and Barrel on Wells Street and buys purple, blue, and white Marimekko fabric. She sits at her sewing machine on the large oak desk in the study and sews the entire weekend, making curtains for the living room, dining room, and bathroom. After the curtains are hung, she sets up her study. I continue to play helper and assist Sabina whenever she asks. I also cook, serve, and clean. In three days, Friday through Sunday, she transforms our apartment into a home. *Why aren't men as creative?* I wonder. *They never sit down on weekends making curtains, setting up kitchens, bedrooms, or bathrooms for their homes, unless, of course, they're gay. Or tailors. Or gay tailors maybe.*

On Monday morning, when we are ready to leave for work, our apartment looks as though we have been living there for years.

I get up first in the morning. I shower, shave, and before getting dressed, I start the water for tea. Making tea is an art in itself. If you over-boil the water, the water loses hydrogen, and that will make the tea gray instead of brown. You can see the difference, especially if you add milk to it. While Sabina showers and gets ready for work, I'm already dressed and set out the morning tea with French bread from Toscana's Bakery and fresh orange juice. We have breakfast together.

On Sundays and Wednesdays, Sabina cooks dinner. She makes pasta, linguini, eggplant Parmesan, pot roast, and Cornish hen, among other dishes. On Mondays, Tuesdays, and Thursdays, Sabina works late writing the news, and I cook dinner. I make chicken curry, onion beef, broiled lamb chops, spinach with potatoes, dill, and fenugreek satiated with onion and garlic, okra, or eggplant. I always make three dishes: a meat, a lentil, and a vegetable to go with steamed rice. Every Friday and Saturday, we see a movie, a play, or a concert; we love going to see sneak previews. And for dinner, we go to Bratislava, Istanbul, Casbah, Ann Sather's, Matsuya, or Mama De Luca's—Slovak, Turkish, Moroccan, Swedish, Japanese, or Sicilian—all within walking distance. Sometimes we drive all the way to 183rd Street on South Halsted to the Dragon Inn for Mandarin food, or to the Serbian Club on Evergreen for *chabab-chaci,* and to Ashkenaz on Morse Avenue for homemade blintzes and cabbage soup. And then there's our favorite, Taqueria Mexicana. We have special dinners at The Bakery, and every so often we meet downtown for lunch at the Berghoff and go shopping at Carson Pirie Scott & Company.

On Saturdays, we do our grocery shopping, cruise rummage sales, or go downtown to look for bargains in Bond's and Goldblatt's basements. Some Sundays, we go to Maxwell Street then to a peace march. Other Sundays, we sleep in late, and Sabina makes us a large breakfast—pancakes, or French toast, and omelets with onions, cilantro, and peppers. Time passes at an accelerated pace.

Suddenly, the summer is gone. "It's incredible . . . that someone so unforgettable . . . thinks that I am unforgettable too . . ." sings Nat King Cole. The million-and-one-dollar question keeps haunting me—why be so happy when your time together is limited? *Go home. Leave the poor woman for her well being, for my own good.*

Sabina sits up in bed with her back against a large pillow, reading *A Summer Bird-Cage.* The lamp at her side burns brightly. I walk to the window and look out. A dim streetlight flickers from behind the sprawling maple tree that glows red with the declining year.

Fall used to be a happy time for me. I found pleasure in going back to school, seeing old friends again, and looking forward to meeting new ones. I am an engineer now. Engineering is exact: things either work, or they don't. Life for me is not exact. It almost never works. I am uncertain of everything. I'm supposed to be living in peace and harmony with Sabina until I leave to go home. On the surface all is well in our lives, I'm happy, acting happy, but inside I'm torn. My calculations suggested that after living with Sabina, my path would become clear and lead me to my destiny. It has not been that simple. I'm constantly fighting an inner turbulence, serious headaches, knotted stomach, stiff neck, and severe shoulder pain. At the same time, the outside symmetry and balance seem to have no effect. I'm nervous, jumpy, lost, and confused. It is not going to go away because... something inside of me has been severed. There are no acceptable losses. I'm going to be broken to the point of no repair. I need to rescue myself from myself. I need to free myself so I can become someone else. Something needs to be synchronized.

I love being anonymous, a stranger. I have been suspended between two worlds long enough. It's been almost six years. I have a green card. Now I can travel back and forth. It's time I went back. I can no longer rationalize staying in America to myself or anyone else. I fight a losing battle, yet I fight. *Fall of my life, oh melodious, colorful fall, why must I go home?* The sinking feeling started early this evening, a longing, a sadness I cannot shake. What a fake I am! What do I want? Where do I go from here? I have to go home, but I don't know where that is.

"What are you pondering?" I hear Sabina. I look at her. She smiles, putting a marker between the pages, closing her book.

"I was wondering where I shall live, who I shall grow old with."

"I'm twenty-six now, and I still catch myself prefacing what I say with 'when I grow up,'" Sabina says. "What really amazes me is the disappointing realization that we never grow up."

"But you can always go home," I say.

"No, you can't." There's firmness in her voice. "You have to leave home to find it, but once you leave home, you cannot go back. A cliché, but true, because I think there is no home and you can never be sure of the definition." She lays the book on the bed. "And the questions that need answers will never stop plaguing you."

"If I continue to live here, I'll always feel an uncanny foreignness. And if we lived in my home, you'd be a total outsider."

"I am searching for my home in my own consciousness," she says. "I can wait until you can make up your mind, and then we'll worry about where we live."

"I don't know who, where, or what I am. I live a double life. I am a contradiction." I look at her. She says nothing, so I go on, "I'm stuck between intimacy and isolation. I may state my feelings, but I don't fight for them. I give in quickly, retreat fast."

"Have more faith in you," she says. "It's not if I go this way, I'll get there." She looks at me. I say nothing. She continues, "I know, to be with me you have to lie to your mother and your fiancé. I hope that I haven't ruined your life. Marriage licenses should be signed like a lease, with an option to renew." She smiles. "My family is not religious, but I know my mother would be happy if I got married, and happier yet if I married a Jew, a professional." She shakes her head, and her hair bounces. "A professional Jew," she laughs.

"I am a professional," I say, "and Muslims can be like Jews."

"Religions don't bring people together, nor do they create universal understanding," she says. "Religion at times teaches the unreality of life more than the reality of it."

"You are talking about global consciousness while I am concerned about individual survival," I say.

"I'm content with where we are."

Again, I look out the partially open window with the curtains half drawn. I walk over to her and sit down on the bed. Love does not have to be confining. Love does not require that you hold on or be withholding.

"Home is what I want. Home is where I need to go. One thing I do know for sure, if I can't get out of my predicament and break my commitment, if I get married there, I'll stay there. I have to resolve this issue once and for all."

"I know," she says softly. "Do what you must. I can wait."

"With you so giving, it makes it even more difficult for me to leave," I say in a low voice.

"In you I trust," she says, "but freedom of choice must not suffer."

"Do you believe in free love?" I ask.

"No, love is never free or easy."

I lie down beside her. "Chestnuts will be in season again."

A ray of light falls onto our bed through the partially open curtain. She puts her head on my shoulder and says, "Love is both selfish and altruistic at the same time, and that makes it complicated. One thing I now know is that I love you so much that I could let you go."

"I love you too," I say and close my eyes to go to sleep.

"Goodnight, moon," she says.

"And goodnight to all the silences in the room," I say.

Lying beside Sabina, I dream my recurring dream. I am at a train station, dressed in a long gray overcoat, wearing Baba's gray felt hat. My mother is there, dressed in a nun's habit, black with a white collar. She wears thick brown tortoiseshell glasses with lenses that make her look cross-eyed.

I keep searching for a train ticket in my coat pocket. I don't have a ticket, and I can't remember where I am going. Looking at the departing train, my mother insists that since it's my wish, I must go.

Home

for Sabina,
who never was—
yet still is

CHAPTER 34

I write a brief letter to Leila:
Please do not sadden, woe-be-gone, do not despair.
What happened was not meant to be so.
   Yours,
   Rama

To Sabina, I recite Tagore: "The lamp waits through the long day of neglect / for the flame's kiss in the night."

ॐ

On a cold and cloudy Thanksgiving Day, Sabina and I take a Yellow Cab to the airport. I am on my way to Karachi via London, Sabina to Brooklyn via Newark. We ride quietly.

There is so much to say and nothing to say. Everything is uncertain. If I get married to Leila, I have told Sabina, then I'll just stay there. If I'm a man of my word, then this is it. Hello, goodbye, have a good life. But I'm not a man of my word. I have already broken my word; I've lied to both Leila and Sabina, not to mention my mother. Can I really leave Sabina? Can I leave Leila? Can I leave my family, my mother?

It starts to rain.

"I am not sure of anything," I say, "and I am scared. It is the return of the native, except I don't know where I'm going."

"This is no time to get into an existential monologue," she says in a low voice, tears rolling down her cheeks. "I'm at home when I'm with the one I love."

"That sounds like a country-western song. I'm leaving on a jet plane for Karachi, Pakistan, so I can live the rest of my life."

I want to be gone. But Sabina believes in proper goodbyes.

"I want this moment to be real, so I can play it back whenever I want," she says, her eyes red with sorrow.

We walk together holding hands to the Pan American Airlines in the international terminal. I am aware that I'm holding Sabina's hand, and despite my reluctance to display intimacy in a public place, I do not let go. I know we look good together. I embrace her for a long time. I kiss her on the lips. She kisses me back, our tender kisses salty. I look at her as if for the last time, and my heart skips a beat. We kiss one more time.

I pick up my bag. "Goodnight, moon," I say.

Before I make my turn toward the departure gate, I look back at her. She stands there, beautiful, body and soul, long and tall, wearing a gray trench coat, a silk scarf wrapped around her neck, tears rolling down that she keeps wiping with the back of her hand. She waves at me. I want to run back to her. She waves again.

I'll remember her smile the most. My eyes are moist. I wave and back away toward the departing plane.

On my Pan-Am flight from Chicago to London, I try to sleep with more turbulence in my head than in the air. My Pakistan International Airlines Flight from London lands in Karachi on Saturday at 4:05 a.m., an hour later than its scheduled time. I return one day ahead of my announced arrival date to avoid the hoopla of parades, bands, and garlands that are accorded to passengers returning from overseas. I have brought back gifts for all my relatives. I've arranged through a shipping agent in Frankfurt to send directly to Karachi: a Siemens washing machine for my mother; a Grundig radiogram, a tape recorder, and a nineteen-inch black-and-white television for the family; and a brand new forest-green Volkswagen for my father. The prodigal son returns with a dowry worth his weight in gold.

When Sabina started making jewelry as a hobby, I got her a twelve-square-inch slab of stainless steel that was an inch thick. It weighed a ton. Sabina said it was the best gift anyone had ever given her.

During the customs inspection and the immigration procedures, I don't miss a beat. I feel like I never left. I am amazed at what a bilingual person I have come to be.

When I walk outside the international terminal, carrying two suitcases and a handbag over my shoulder, I'm jolted by the heat. I'm hot in my jacket and jeans. It is muggy, sultry, oppressive. I am overwhelmed by the spectacle that confronts me, the cacophony of taxi

215

drivers screaming, "Where would you like to go, Sahib?" I hand my suitcase to a young driver who stands quietly, dressed in a white shirt, brown pants, and flip-flops sandals.

I was a young man, once, with dreams. I follow the cab driver and get into the back seat of a yellow-and-black Morris Minor. I roll down the window. The night is beginning to peel off, and as the taxi moves past the airport compound, a welcome breeze blows in from the sea. Birds perch on the telephone wires. The street lamps dim with the growing light; a new day has begun. My mood too grows lighter despite my apprehension. I'm excited to be back, exited to see my family. I hum along with the music on the radio. In the middle of Mohammed Ali Jinnah Road, on the median, a family of four—mother, father, a tiny boy, and a little girl—sit around a small fire, their faces lit by the flames as they look up at the passing traffic. In America, the streets are public domain and the houses private, but not so in Karachi, where the streets are neither quiet nor uninhabited. The streets are an extension of life lived on the sidewalks. They are the setting for social gatherings. Here, streets get cordoned off for days, colorful tents stretching from one side of the road to the other, just to stage someone's wedding, and a flat stretch of a road is the perfect place to play cricket at the end of a school day or on Sundays.

I think of the time when we left our home by the River Betwa. The SS Pudma left Bombay with a thousand and one people on board. Amaji spent the entire trip lying under her embroidered green shawl on the metal deck, paralyzed with motion sickness. When the SS Pudma finally docked three days later in Karachi, Baba put on his jacket and felt hat before disembarking. Amaji was grateful just to get up. It was a bright sunny day. A hot, sandy wind blew from the land towards the sea. Other than a few palm trees in the distance, I could see nothing green. No trees and no grass. I was glad to be off the boat. I asked Amaji when we could go back home.

"This is home," Baba replied.

There will never be home again, I thought.

I watched as a huge crane unloaded the last of the passengers' possessions from the *Pudma*'s hold. Baba ran around, still in his hat and jacket, collecting our luggage. The back and underarms of his jacket wet with sweat, he looked ridiculous. Amaji looked pale, dark patches under her eyes.

"Amaji, where are we going to stay?" I asked.

She touched my shoulder. "Your father will know," she said with the utmost confidence.

At last, every piece of luggage was collected. Baba counted them twice.

At the pier, there were large carts pulled by camels. Baba removed his jacket and handed it to Amaji. A tall, dark-skinned camel-cart driver in a white short-sleeved T-shirt with a large gold-and-white striped handkerchief hanging over his neck approached Baba. He asked Baba in broken Urdu if he could take us to our destination.

"That would be very nice," replied Baba. He took off his hat and fanned his face with it. "How much would it cost us?"

"It depends on where your destination is," said the camel cart driver. He pulled the handkerchief from his neck and wiped his shining forehead with it.

"How much would it cost to go to your house?" asked Baba, putting his hat back on.

The camel cart driver smiled. He had a tooth missing. That night we slept in the camel cart driver's shack. *There will never be home again*, I thought.

My cab moves erratically at high speed, then slows down on a speed bump. The crows and roosters are awake; the shades of night merging into day play games with my memory. I think of Shaukat's mother who faithfully came to beg each Thursday on Mission Road. Shaukat ki Amma, a middle-aged widow, also read palms. Her front teeth stuck out over her lower lip and gave her a sinister appearance. Once, she read my palm and told me that I would travel to a faraway land, never to return home again. That made my mother very sad. I look out of my cab, all is familiar, but nothing is the same. When the taxi turns right on Mission Road and arrives at Ali Manzil, a golden bright light is beginning to show. The wretched mosque on the sidewalk appears as spiritless today as it did twenty years ago when it was hurriedly erected with bamboo, straw mats, and a tin roof. Men are walking out from the mosque after saying the *Fajr* prayers.

I hadn't changed my money into rupees at the airport. I pay

the cab driver generously in dollars. Carrying my suitcases, I quickly walk up to the second floor, apartment number two, and knock on the door.

"My Rama is back! My Rama is back!" I hear Amaji announce before she opens the door.

She cries with joy, with uncontrollable tears. "I knew it was you by the way you knocked on the door!"

She looks older. Her dark eyes seem sadder, and she has gained weight. She hugs me. I put my head on her shoulder. I smell jasmine and perspiration.

Baba and Yasmin come out of their rooms.

Amaji dries her tears with the cotton shawl she is wearing.

Baba says, "I thought you might do this; arrive a day or two earlier and surprise us."

"I can't believe you are here!" says Yasmin with a smile. My big sister is married now, her husband away working on his FRCS degree in Dublin. She teaches microbiology at a women's college. My brother Kamran, a final-year medical student, is working at the hospital.

In the living room, a double bed with a canopy is neatly made up with red sheets and a red satin quilt. Silver and gold garlands decorate the canopy. It is a wedding bed, a honeymoon bed. I get situated in the living room. A fluorescent light hangs from the blue ceiling, humming in a monotonous whine.

The word of my return spreads fast—family, friends, and neighbors keep pouring in to visit and pay their regards all day long. Exhausted by jetlag, I watch them helplessly and say little. In the evening, after a long sleepless nap where I keep falling asleep and waking up abruptly, I sit on the honeymoon bed that faces a sofa-sized canvas Baba painted. The painting shows a black dog with a white spot on its face sitting contentedly inside a large brown beer barrel, shielded from the falling rain. Beneath the painting, Amaji and Baba sit on a blue velvet covered couch. On the two matching stuffed chairs sit Yasmin to my right and Kamran on the left.

With the fluorescent light burning brightly, the discussion immediately focuses on how soon I shall be wed since in my letter I said that I'd be here on short leave.

218

"According to your wishes, your mother has arranged your marriage to Leila," My father reminds me. "Her parents do not wish to wait any longer since their daughter is highly sought after."

"There is a cardiologist, a classmate of Leila, currently working in Dar-us-Salam who really wants to marry her," Yasmin informs me.

"I am not ready to get married," I hear myself say immediately. I am amazed at myself, at the candor I am able to express. There is a pause. The fluorescent light hums furiously.

"Rama has just returned from a long trip," says Amaji, saving the day. "He must be tired and exhausted. Let him sleep now. We'll discuss this matter another time."

One after the other they get up, Baba first, and walk out of the living room through a side door that opens into the dining room. I change into my sleepwear of a t-shirt and drawstring cotton pants. I set the table fan on low and turn off the fluorescent light. I lie awake under the canopy of the honeymoon bed. Something bleak and heartbreaking is in progress, settling into my head. What do I really know of love? I have had two or three sweethearts in my life. I'm intoxicated now with the love of sweet Sabina, but it's a zero sum game. Someone is going to get hurt. Someone has to lose. To feel joy, I must betray one woman for another. I sit up in my bed. I want to go for a walk, but I'm fatigued. Distress overwhelms my heart, saps my soul. If I can live without Sabina, I shall marry Leila. You get used to your life, whatever it may turn out to be. If I have to, I can live without Sabina. Do I want to marry Leila? What do I hope for? What do I wish for? Someone is waiting for me there, and someone is waiting for me right here. Someone will remain waiting, living in an empty room, sad and alone, in a room that no one else will enter but her, and it will be my wretched doing. We all want to live happily, to live with that special person, who loves you, cares for you, and tells you those charming foolish words. But that room is always there—lonely, full of regrets, with no conversations and no echoes. Here I'm at home with my family, and here I'm more alone than ever before. I lie down again, with my eyes open.

CHAPTER 35

I sleep late and wake up with a supersonic jet roaring through my skull. I sit on the edge of the bed holding my head. I must tell my family about Sabina. Until I left Sabina, part of me was sure that if I needed to, I'd be able to leave her. I meant every word when I told her that if I got married here, I'd stay here.

Latif comes to visit. We drive to the Intercontinental Hotel for a drink in his brand new, 1965, red Chevrolet Caprice. Latif had it shipped to Karachi from Detroit. LEFT-HAND DRIVE it says over the license plate. Latif is married now. His wife Zulekha, a doctor, is expecting.

We sit in the International Lounge amongst the mostly foreign guests staying at the hotel. The room is carpeted in red and has red tablecloths and napkins. Waiters dressed in short red vests and red turbans promptly serve us. Latif orders himself a gin and tonic. I order a pot of black coffee.

"Do you know," asks Latif, pointing his finger, "that reading the Quran and reciting 'Allah, Allah' reduces tension, particularly among those who suffer from dejection, misery, and gloom?"

I look at Latif with amazement—a good Muslim speaking of Allah with a gin and tonic in his left hand. He is outlandish, so-out-and-out, unqualified. I think of V.J.

He continues, "The first letter 'A' in Allah when pronounced the Arabic way with the tongue slightly touching the upper part of the jaw helps release more air from the respiratory system. Also, pronouncing 'H' the Arabic way makes a contact between the lungs and the heart; this contact controls the heartbeat, which affects breathing."

"The state of the Islamic world is such that we can use all the help from Allah," I say.

"I'm sure even non-Muslims can benefit by calling out 'Allah, Allah.'"

"May Allah help all men." Looking into my cup of black coffee, I add, "I am ready to break the news to my family that I am going to return to America and marry a—"

"To be with your own kind is what you need," prescribes Latif, looking at me and gulping his drink down. "Come back home, *bhai*." He signals the waiter for another.

"There is no home for people like me," I say in a low voice. "I'm an expatriate, a once-upon-a-time Indian, currently a Pakistani, and a future American. Now I'm a member of a community that is a blend of many religions, languages, cultures."

"Don't talk that existential bullshit with me," says Latif. "There is always home, and there certainly are people of your own kind."

"Maybe your kind." I force a smile. "Having been born under the *Raj,* you have conveniently become a brown gentleman, complete with all the social snobbery and class consciousness of the oppressor."

"Those of us who remain citizens of the same country inherit its shame and its pride," Latif replies coldly. "Religion does not block or hinder development; it is the lack of education that leads to the political use of religion."

"I consider myself fortunate to have grown up in India and Pakistan when things were different," I say.

"If I change my name to Prince Charming, would every woman in the world be looking for me?"

"As you wish! You are a prince all right, charming is another matter," I say.

"So what is there to admire?" he asks.

"Despite all its follies, America is still struggling to do the best that it can. It strives to be civil *within,* and Americans are good people."

"The fact is," says Latif knowingly, "when you emigrate, you reject a part of yourself, the island that is you."

"You're a fool if you think that I will ever be able to forget my Indian childhood, my Pakistani youth, my *desi* memories, my Urdu poetry, my Indian movie songs. My Indian features will always be with me, and my brown skin will remain brown. I may leave India, but India will never leave me." I pause. "America is a country of many people, and being an American is an attitude, you are as American as you wish."

Latif's drink is served. He takes a sip and puts it down.

221

Shaking his head, he looks at me and says, "Now you are talking like a Republican."

I can't believe that Latif would speak with such ignorance. I think about walking out.

"The fact is," I say, taking a sip of my coffee, "I cannot live without Sabina. Not only do I love her, I admire her. I am proud of the person she is." Latif stares at me as though I've turned into a ghost. "Now that I think of it, it astounds me how much I owe to Sabina's philosophy on life for making me a better person. Until I met her, I kept my heart locked up. I always denied my feelings." I feel sadness inside, but on the outside I smile and add, "She loves me so much that she could let me go."

"You sound like you are talking in a movie," Latif says, making no attempt to conceal the contempt in his voice. "So do you love her enough to let her go?"

He stares at me. I stare back. Once again I focus and act tough; I lean back in my chair, pretending to be enjoying myself. "Did you ever love anybody?" I ask, looking him in the eyes.

"I'm a married man, happily married, life is good if I may say so myself. I'd like you to meet my wife and have dinner with us."

"Latif. I must say, I can't wait to see Sabina again."

"You should marry the woman you have been committed to marry," insists Latif. "She is beautiful, has a great body, and has been waiting for her hero to return." With a wink, Latif drains his glass and begins to look around for the waiter. There is something furtive and at the same time smug about the way he does this, and I find myself quite unexpectedly furious.

"Of course, I could still choose to live without Sabina, but then my life would be much different, unprincipled, perhaps even vicious and arrogant. The gift of Sabina is the freedom she has given me. She has taught me openness and honesty. She has made me feel full of life. The reason I want to be with her is not because of how much I love her, it is for how much she loves me."

"How honest are you with Leila, but never mind—whatever happened to building bridges in a developing country?" asks Latif.

"I have no idea," I reply. "For God's sake, there isn't even a system in place here for me to fight from within. I find life here profoundly depressing." Latif stares at me as though I have been speaking Eskimo. Not building bridges in the homeland and betraying Leila, my first love, will be the everlasting regrets of this stranger, but they are regrets I have to live with."

"You don't know what is going on," says Latif cracking his knuckles violently. His drink is delivered to the table. "You are possessed by Amadeus, and you are made lazy by love."

"I am lost in love, maybe. I know no one loves me like she does."

"*Desi* women," he says with a smile. "Especially native Pakistani women, can be very resourceful in love. We men need to show them the way. They can learn to live with what you want."

"I'm conflicted, not confused," I tell him. "If you want a wife for sex and childbearing and housekeeping, that's your business, but I am walking away from that. Maybe I feel guilty, but I know what I want."

"Fuck the guilt. If you don't marry Leila, you'll put your mother and the poor girl through a lot."

"I will seek their forgiveness. Besides, life is uncertain." I put down my coffee cup.

"Isn't she Jewish?" he asks, smiling. "Jews in America are outsiders."

"You are among outsiders when your friends refuse to accept you for who you are," I reply.

"No," says Latif, looking me in the eyes. "You are an outsider when you exile yourself and refuse to accept who you are. You are too sentimental. Men do not hurt. They distance themselves."

"Latif," I sigh, "you should be more frugal with your limited wisdom."

"Your homeland needs you. You don't want to be part of the brain drain by living in America." He finishes his drink. "One more," he says, signaling for two. "Let's have a drink for old times' sake. America is great, we all want to live there, but here is where you are needed."

When our drinks are served, I lift my glass to him. "Please don't give me all that bullshit," I tell him. "I am not ready to get married and honeymoon in the living room under the blue ceiling."

223

"One thing I have to tell you," Latif says with a vicious smile, "your parents know about Sabina. I've told your brother Kamran."

I stare at Latif for several seconds. I think how great it would feel to wipe that self-satisfied smirk off his face, but I don't stir.

We finish our drinks in silence and walk out.

Outside, evening has begun to show. A soft breeze ruffles the palm trees. That's one thing I love about this city—regardless of how hot the day is, there is always a cool breeze in the evening. "I'll just walk home," I tell Latif. "I need to have a long conversation with myself."

I walk down a familiar avenue. A slope on the polo ground toward Noor Jehan Garden. It is very quiet, red-gold light filters down through the trees, and I can feel the left-right impact of my own feet from my heels to my head. The sky is radiant, the road behind me empty. Ali Manzil was home once upon a time, and before that, home was across the *mandir* in the city by the River Betwa. How much my life has changed! Further down, by the ice factory where the road bends, flowerbeds and green grass are turning brown. Dry leaves skitter and crackle on the tarred road.

The evening glows in an incredible orange, descending into imperceptible degrees of violet dusk. Behind the Blue Mosque, *kababs* are being sold by the same vender from days long past. Kazi and I used to eat here. Those hot and spicy *kababs* made with secret recipes passed down from one generation to the next. The secret spices are mixed with the right amount of green papaya to tenderize the toughest meat, rendering it so light that it becomes a part of you as you chew it. Kazi and I used to order the whole works, the grilled *kababs* with onions deep-fried in *ghee* and topped with brain and marrow from goat bones. Afterward, Kazi and I would walk to the corner *paanwala* where Kazi bought his *paan* laced with lime and sweet tobacco. I chewed a sweet mixture of betel nut with clove and cardamom.

The *kababwala's* beard is mostly gray now. The prayer mark on his forehead, earned by years of humility and proclaiming "glory to my Lord Who alone is high," glows like a medal. To my amazement and delight, the old man recognizes me. I sit down at a wooden table in front of his stall. For a brief moment, sitting behind the Blue Mosque, eating *kabab* and *paratha,* and drinking Pakola, I feel at home.

I smile and ask *kababwala* if he remembers my friend Kazi. He nods with a sad smile and says, "The earth has claimed what was hers." I tell him that I have been away studying in America, that now I'm going back to live in the United States and marry a Jewish woman. Strangely, I'm relieved to learn that my family knows that Sabina exists.

He wipes his forehead with a small white towel draped over his shoulders. "May God bless your marriage, in Allah we are at home no matter where we live." He serves me a fresh cool bottle of Pakola.

I am capable of taking charge of myself, and dealing with my situation head on. The hardest part will be breaking the news to Leila. Where has my love for her gone? I admire Baba for his energy and zeal and for the way he maintains an uninvolved posture. He is arrogant and distant, and sometimes self-centered, but that probably comes with the territory; after all, he is an artist. He is becoming more and more religious with age, but somehow the sincerity of my mother's piety is lacking in Baba.

I hope that if and when I grow old, I won't fall into any of this hocus-pocus to save my soul.

"*Allah-u-Akbar, Allah-u-Akbar!*" I hear the muezzin call for prayer from the mosque. Living in the West, I missed not hearing azan five times a day.

Leaving his assistant in charge, the *kababwala* goes to say the *maghrib* prayer. I sit quietly, chewing my food in small bites for a long time, savoring the taste, listening to other people talk. The *kababwala's* assistant has a long nose, long and thin enough to wear an engagement ring. There is a constant hum around here, the hum of a different world. A couple of young boys, still in their school uniforms—blue pants with lighter blue shirts—study me frankly and call out in English, "Hello, hippie! What is your name?"

"Gunga Din," I tell them quietly.

"Gunga Din, go home," they say aloud.

My world is changed. I'm 25 now, and I've already left home more than once. I'm always going to be half empty. The change, the exile, my action, is not an isolated happening; it has affected every facet of my existence.

I want to wait for *kababwala* to return from his prayers so I can say goodbye to him, but it feels too final, like the end. I can't bear it. I pay his assistant and leave.

I walk to Noor Jehan Garden instead. It is turning dark now; a dim yellow bulb burns on the lamppost. I sit quietly on the bench where I once used to sit with Leila. For a brief moment, I expect her to walk out from behind the bushes. *This is where I should meet Leila for our final meeting.* The End. *What perfect symmetry!* Looking down, I see a child's plastic wristwatch, red numbers on a blue dial, lying on the grass. I pick it up. The blue plastic strap is broken and the time frozen at 10:10. I hold the watch for a long moment, thinking about what it means for time to pass. Lives are measured in time, as well as pain and pleasure. May there always be Sabina, and may there still be time. The toy watch, I toss it back on the grass.

CHAPTER 36

For the next two days there is a simulation of truce; they all leave me alone. I sleep late adjusting to the jetlag. "There is ten hours time difference," they acknowledge, "day and night." I think I know what I need to do, but shall I begin with seeing Leila first or talking to my mother instead? On the third morning of my return, a butcher arrives with a white male calf to be sacrificed to give thanks to Allah the Magnificent for my safe return. The sacrificial calf has large black eyes and tiny gray horns. The butcher ties the calf to a pole erected in the patch of unpaved earth in the otherwise concrete backyard of our building. It is offered a meal of chopped garbanzo beans mixed with finely cut dry hay.

In the afternoon, following the *zuhr* prayers, the calf is given his last drink of water. The butcher ties its front and hind legs with a rope, then lays the calf down on its side next to a freshly dug foot-deep hole to collect the blood. The butcher holds the calf in the proper position, its neck at the right angle to slash. I am asked to slaughter the calf. There is no way I can perform the required task, so I symbolically touch the calf while the butcher chants the proper prayers and slits the throat in one quick, continuous motion. He immediately jerks the rope off the calf's legs, setting it free. The poor beast shakes violently, gasping for its last breath. I can't watch I walk way.

Later, sitting on a straw mat with a butcher's block, a cleaver and sharp knife, he slices the sacrificial calf, chopping into pieces, each weighing about a pound and a half, to be given away to the poor and destitute. The liver and heart are saved. A large dinner is prepared: lamb korma and biryani, chicken tikka, naan, ladyfingers, and all the other dishes that are supposed to have been my favorites. The heart of the fatted calf is cooked in a red curry and the liver in yellow curry for me, the guest of honor. I enjoy the dinner more than I thought I would. To my amazement, even the heart and the liver taste delicious.

After dinner, the second session of marriage talk begins under the blue living room ceiling. Once again, my mother and father sit next to each other on the blue velvet sofa. Kamran and Yasmin sit across from each other on the stuffed chairs. I sit on the canopied honeymoon bed.

"I don't know where to begin," I say, looking down at the carpet. For the first time, I notice the interconnecting patterns make a four-way lotus flower. How can I explain this love between Sabina and me? I look up at the faces of my parents and see the smallest beginnings of wariness. "The first thing I want to say is that, besides my family, there is another person in my life that I care for and love dearly. There is a woman in my life."

The room soaks the silence like a sponge.

"You mean besides Leila?" my mother asks at last.

"Yes," I answer, "I am in love with a woman I met in America." I draw a deep breath. My face feels numb. "I want to marry her and spend the rest of my life with her."

Amaji immediately begins to weep—large, uncontrollable tears roll down her cheeks as she snatches at the end of her shawl. "I was afraid this would happen!" she wails between sobs. "I knew you stayed away too long!"

Yasmin and Kamran are red with outrage. "What do you mean 'I want to spend the rest of my life with her'?" Yasmin shrieks. She is straight and rigid in her chair. "Are you mad? You were in love with Leila, and honoring your wishes, you have been betrothed to Leila for almost two years. How can you even think of this? And what do you think Leila will do?"

Amaji tries to hush Yasmin but my sister pays no attention. "She might as well throw herself into a deep dark well!" She, too, bursts into tears.

Now Kamran is on his feet, all too dramatic like a bad actor, waving his arms. His face has gone from red to blanched. "This is an issue of honor. If your brother will not live up to his own commitment and marry someone's sister," he yells, "how can you expect someone else's brother to marry *your* sister?"

"The shame of it!" cries Yasmin.

"What is to become of all our sisters?" demands Kamran, staring daggers at me. "This is a disgrace." He turns to Baba. "How would we feel if Farhad, your son-in-law, returns from Dublin next year and announces he met the love of his life in Ireland? Ramzan Bhai has to marry Leila," he declares, his voice tight with fury.

Baba's face is like stone. He just looks at me, saying nothing. Somehow this is much worse than all the shouting and weeping. My insides feel as though they are turning to water and full of sharks.

"Look," I say, suddenly on my feet, playing my role, "I did not do this deliberately in order to hurt or disgrace anyone." I search from face to face, seeing the pain and fear underlying all the tears and anger. My own eyes fill with tears; I feel like an assassin. "I have been grappling with myself, trying to reconcile my change of heart. I am profoundly sorry for the wrongs I have done in both word and deed, but I simply cannot marry Leila. This woman—Sabina—did not seek me out. We met by chance and fell in love." I sit down with my head in my hands under the canopy of my bed.

"What you are describing," my father finally speaks, "is not love." Slowly, he sinks back onto his chair. "Real love does not strike one like a bolt of lightning or a flowerpot falling off a balcony. It grows between a man and a woman as they build a life together." He looks at Amaji for a moment, thoughtfully, and returns his attention to me. "You have been very foolish, my son, and I am sorry for the great suffering that you are causing for yourself and for this American woman. But you agreed to your betrothal to Leila, and she has honored you by waiting for you to return home and marry her. You cannot simply turn your back on her and walk away from your commitment and responsibilities."

"But *can* I marry her knowing that I love another woman?" I ask. "How honorable is that? 'Sorry, Leila, you're a wonderful girl, but I'm no longer in love with you because my heart will always belong to Sabina.'"

"All things pass," Kamran snaps. "You will forget about Sabina after a while."

"No, I'll not," I say.

Amaji sits with her face in her shawl. Yasmin clenches and unclenches a wet handkerchief, her face stricken and sorrowful. Kamran stares at me.

Baba, sad and hard, looks at me briefly, "You will marry Leila as you promised. Your mother will begin the wedding arrangements tomorrow."

"With all due respect to all of you," I say, "I can't."

229

"It is not you can't," shouts Kamran, "you won't."

"So, I won't," I respond.

"There is nothing more to discuss," declares Baba. "You will marry Leila as planned, or it will be hard for me to call you my son, you will have to leave, get out of here."

His words are like a fist in my stomach. *He's right*, I think wildly. I can't even speak. It's clear that this conversation is over. *Oh god, oh god, oh my god.*

"Rama," says my mother, "this is your home, you are our son, and you are not going anywhere until everything is resolved."

"There is nothing to resolve," declares Baba again, "Rama will marry Leila, or he is not my son." Baba moves toward the door.

CHAPTER 37

Yasmin and I sip hot tea companionably as though not a single angry word passed between us the night before. They all act as if nothing is at stake. I smile, and she says, "So, dear Romeo, when do you plan to see Leila?"

I raise my eyebrows in mild surprise. "Oh? Yes, yes," I answer, "that is the million-dollar question?"

"Who knows, maybe you are still in love with her," she says teasingly. "Absence makes the heart grow fonder."

I take another sip of my tea, wondering if I should explain to Yasmin. *Why not?* I decide. *No more secrets!* "I need to resolve my relationship with Leila," I say slowly. "I don't want any of the dead weight of the past pressing down on my future relationship."

Yasmin stares at me intently. "Dear brother," she says at last, "I understand what you mean." She waves away my attempted apology. "No ghosts on your wedding night. As you know, Leila works at Civil Hospital, where Kamran is interning."

"I'll visit her," I say.

"Marriage, a crucial decision, is not a personal decision made by consenting adults in this part of the world, but made by your family in your best interest." My big sister informs me of my country's customs as if I don't know them. "Every girl has an image of her Prince Charming. Before I consented to marry Farhad, I considered what was most important in choosing my life partner—religion, family, and education."

I nod my head and listen.

She continues, "Our parents are kind, loving, giving people. They let you choose Leila just as they let me marry someone I love. My religion is what I am. It provides me direction, guidance, and it represents my values. It tells me how to respect my spouse, fulfill my responsibilities and obligations, and how to raise children. My second concern is my family. My parents, they worked hard, made sacrifices, gave direction, and provided all the best they could. I will be happy and proud if I am as good a mother as our mother. My third criteria: education, since it is the only wealth you never lose, and it buys you all the good things in life. I don't have to tell you the value of it; you became acceptable to Leila's family because of your American education."

"I'm certainly very happy for my dear sister," I say, a tinge of guilt and sorrow penetrating my heart.

The new strategy at home seems to be trying to win me over with their love, affection, and tenderness. They think they can wheedle me back into my own people and my former ways, my values and culture, my best interests. We are all scheming, them versus me. I play along. I quietly know I'll be all right once I leave.

On Wednesday, six days away from Sabina and counting, I'm forlorn, lonesome. I cannot think of anyone or anything else but her. At 3:00 PM, dressed in my olive green corduroy jacket and a blue Oxford button down shirt with a matching blue-and-green striped tie, like a ship without a rudder in the sea of anxiety, I walk toward Civil Hospital. I'm not excited. Breaking up is hard, particularly when you are the guilty party. Leila still loves me. She may love me more than I know. Having her love was once the best thing in the world. It makes me feel terrible and selfish that I no longer have that longing. It is not fair for her to be with me if I can't return her love. I know my leaving her will hurt her. It is never easy to leave a love. I may regret leaving her. I need courage to do the right thing now and be ready to face her disappointment. *And I'll be there before the next teardrop falls* is just the failure of the song. It is not simple. Sometimes things change, and things don't work out as one may have planned.

A pale day moon hangs low in the sky; sand and dust swirl through the air like dire yearnings. It's eighty-two degrees Fahrenheit —in December—and the heat totally exhausts me. Hot in my jacket and tie, I feel like I'm on a movie set but not wearing proper attire for the scene. I arrive at the hospital at the appointed time to the Beatles sing, "Everybody's Trying to be My Baby," in my head.

Leila is waiting for me at the emergency room nursing station. She is as gorgeous as ever, and in her white coat, with a stethoscope writhing from one of its pockets, she looks more like a doctor in a movie, like Ingrid Bergman in *Spellbound* (US, 111min., bw). She greets me with a smile, as if we last met only a few days ago. Without exchanging a word, we walk to her car, a white Mercedes, parked in a nearby lot. She gets in and unlocks the passenger door for me. The handle is burning hot.

The inside of the car is hot enough to bake bread. She starts the car, opens her window a crack, and turns the air on. Settling in the passenger seat next to Leila, in spite of hours of internal rehearsal, I cannot think of a beginning or how to explain what has happened. My mind wanders. *In November of 1939 the first air-conditioned automobile, made by Packard Motor Car Co., went on display at an auto show in Chicago.* Leila sits quietly, looking calm. Glancing at herself in the rearview mirror, she combs back a loose tress of hair with her fingers and then puts on her sunglasses. There was a time when only movie stars or people with eye infections wore sunglasses, I remember. She takes off the sunglasses and looks in the rearview mirror once more. Other than the *kajal* lining her eyes, she wears no makeup. I take a slow, deep breath. The strong smell of antiseptic floats in the air. Only moments have elapsed, but it seems like it's been an eternity, and I still do not know where to start. Leila adjusts the side view mirror as though she is ready to drive off.

"What's the perfume you're wearing?" I finally ask, attempting a smile.

Looking at me, she purses her thin lips. Without saying a word, she puts her sunglasses on again, gets out of the car, and goes to stand in front of it with her back towards me. I wait a moment. *Can I still be in love with her?* This is the moment in an Indian movie when the misunderstanding that separated the lovers is finally resolved. They sing a heart-wrenching duet that ends in a warm embrace against a spectacular Technicolor sunset, never to part again. I get out of the car and walk to Leila. Her starched white coat crackles in the blowing wind. She shakes her head, takes off her sunglasses, and looks at me. I see anger in her face.

"I haven't seen you in five plus years, and all you ask is what perfume I am wearing?"

"What is it, anyway?" I ask with a teasing smile. "I really would like to know."

"For your information," she says in a brisk voice, "I wear no perfume to work."

I gaze at her for a moment. She stares past me. I'm silent, searching for the right words. I have lost faith, and I have betrayed Leila as well as my mother. I finally blurt out, "I feel like I no longer know you."

"Let me refresh your memory then. I'm still an only child, lonely. When you and I met there was no television in the country, no telephone in every home. It was all less than six years ago, but it all seems so distant. Everything is different now, and you have found someone new."

I nod. I want to deny Sabina and come back to Leila. I feel awful.

"And there is nothing you can do about it."

I nod again silently. What kind of a man am I? I can still redeem myself. Everything could be fine. There is no longer a carefully crafted castle in the sky. I need to separate myself from this time and place. I need to decide now. I need to move on, but I feel absolutely deflated with no energy to move. Leila is pure, there is an innocence about her, while mine is lost. I'm no longer pure. But then I was living someone else's life. It takes a long time to become real. I came here to confess everything, but she already knows. With Sabina, I can be honest. I can be me. I need to set Leila free. I'm not her man. She is still romantic, I no longer am. Something is holding me back. Was it all an illusion? Was it real? Did she really love me? Did I even love her? Standing in front of Leila, my thoughts are with Sabina, and I cannot stand the thought of never seeing her again. Without Sabina my life will be without meaning.

"Rama," Leila says softly, "there is no middle ground. You need to decide, and you need to decide now. I no longer want to wait."

I came to talk about myself, but she is equally needy. "I never wanted to hurt you," I say, carefully selecting my words. "I truly believed that our love was to last, but... it will always be a fine memory. We will not work out anymore."

"This I know," she says, surprising me. "You know, it's hard to go backward. You are no longer pure. I don't mean to be taking a moral high ground; I thought you might have cheated with your body, and I was ready to accept that. But you cheated with your heart, you cheated on love, and it probably still would have been all right but for

234

your lies." Her tone is calm, and she seems perfectly in control. "And by the way," she concludes, her voice breaking, "thank you for making it so absolutely unambiguous that I'm not here and that you are already gone. And, yes, our special thing will always be there for us to remember."

Leila is playing tough, like she does not care, and making it easy for me to walk away. Sabina would have said, if something is bothering you, you can talk to me, tell me about it. This is Leila all grown up, lonely but proud. She also loves me enough to let me go. I think of ways I can make it up to her. A long time ago, we went to see *Love In The Afternoon*. I held her hand in mine, fingers interlaced, clasped, and I never felt touched like that before. I stare at my hand, believing that feeling would always be with me. How far have I traveled, and how things have changed. I look up and see Leila gazing at me. "You are right," I lower my eyes, "I'm no longer pure."

She squints her eyes; there is too much light, and she puts her sunglasses on again. Looking lost, she slips her hands into her tunic pockets. I want to hold her in my arms for a long time, until she forgives me.

"You don't seem to know right from wrong, at this point in time, it would be hard for me to take you back even if you...."

Don't dwell on what has passed away, I remind myself. "Until now," I tell Leila, "I was living someone else's life in someone else's country. My brain...." This is the turning point and possibly the point of no return. It is all too painful to be real, to be my life.

"There is nothing more I want from you, there is nothing more I wish to know," Leila declares. She is ready to leave.

There are several ways to look at it. She never really loved me. She loved me at the time and still loves me. She didn't love me then, and she still does not. She is too proud to be humble and wishes to remain a puzzle. I stare at her for a moment. Standing in front of her car, the engine running, I look at my dear lost love. Words fail me and there are no deeds that will comfort her. I would have liked it to have ended with love, to have ended my life loving her. I won't forget her. I want her mercy to spill over me like light from a distant star.

She stares past me.

Still, our situation feels unresolved, so I provoke her and ask,

"Did you ever love me?"

"No," she says bitterly.

"I thought you did."

She puts her sunglasses on once again. "It was a flirtation, a trifling affair. Now I can't even remember why I did it." She shrugs impatiently. "Why did you say you loved me when you didn't?"

"I was young," I say, trying to look in her eyes now covered by her dark glasses. "I thought I loved you," I continue smoothly. "Maybe I still love you." I pause. "You did not know me, I did not know you, we, just thought we did."

"Let me see if I follow your reasoning," she says. "Since my love for you was merely a youthful infatuation, then the pain you inflicted doesn't count. Is that it? Perhaps it was even my own fault for becoming infatuated in the first place."

This is the moment of forgiveness. Now I shall look into her eyes with love. She will put her head on my shoulder, and we will embrace.

"At the time I was in love with you, and I felt tenderly towards you," I say hurriedly, "but with time this thing called love has faded like a watermark."

"That's all you felt? Tenderness?" she asks angrily.

"I'm sorry," I say, looking away from Leila for the first time. "I know I failed you, and I have caused you pain."

"A watermark is never there, and a watermark is never gone," she says. She waits for me to respond. I say nothing, so she continues. "If you want to know the truth, you were ungiving, withholding, and you were not generous, with either your compliments or your commitments." She shakes her head in anger. There is sadness in her dark eyes. "You didn't even write passionate letters. You lacked warmth, and you asked redundant questions. You kept seeing life like an Indian movie. I think you love only yourself. I could have been yours, but you could have never been mine." All of a sudden the sky has grown cloudy and dark. "You are free, you can go."

I look at her, stunned. "Either you are mocking me, or this is a joke, or you are busy being an only child," I say. "We are on the threshold of the theater. The drama is about to begin. Evolution means unfolding—of time passed and of time yet to come. It is not over between us. I can make it up to you," I declare, suddenly fervent. I know she no longer wants me. She no longer will take me back, so I challenge. "I am not married yet. Will you marry me?" I ask. "I'm right here. It's not too late."

The sun dodges back behind the clouds. I stand there, watching Leila walk around to the other side of her car. I follow her.

"No, it is way too late," She answers quietly, "and please stop playing mind games with me."

"Then what are you doing here if you don't want to marry me?" I explode.

"I came here to let you go," she replies. "Do you have the slightest idea of what a...?"

A dozen emotions pass through my heart. There is confusion and anger in her eyes. I see the college girl I so adored. My heart melts. Leila looks beautiful, lonely, vain, and proud. Suddenly I am swept by a wave of sadness. *Oh, Sabina, Sabina, look what has happened, what did I do?*

To Leila I want to say, "I am grateful to have seen you today. My love for you is like a watermark that is never there and never gone; it will keep us connected, and it will keep us apart. You will be in my thoughts and in my heart. I'll remember the times we laughed and cried, and I'll always remember loving you."

Without looking back at me again, she says, "Good luck to you." She gets back in her car and drives away. I stand there watching until her car makes a right turn and disappears from my view. There is no limit to the cruelty inflicted by lovers. Things almost never begin, and they certainly never end. I do not look back. One of the hardest lessons in life to learn is to know which bridges to cross and which ones to burn. If all were fantasy, this would be nothing more than a lovers' quarrel, but what has happened is for real and forever. She once was my true love. *Love, dear love, don't leave me,* I want to cry out, but she is gone.

The cow jumps over the moon, and it gets instantly darker. What could be truer than the truth itself? But no one tells the truth. False promises, broken windows, open doors, and closed hearts. Everyone talks to himself, but when your lips begin to move as you talk to yourself, and the people around you begin to hear you, and you

237

yourself begin to hear voices, then you should start worrying about yourself. Oblivious I am, but not unmindful—I hope.

Only yesterday, I was there, with her,
  And now I do not know where I am
Or where she did go.
  Whatever happened?

It's been a long, long time now
  And I feel fine.
Like a wounded
  And crippled pilgrim could feel.
On a long journey to the unknown,
  in the kingdom of yesterday.
And god knows, and the gods know not
  Where I am.
Today I am going, I am going,
    And I am gone, to the dark side of the moon.

I don't know if I am breathing a sigh of relief or vomiting lava!

Walking home, my head is heavy with regret, but all I can say is that it's about time I take charge of myself. I play the victim, but that must end. *All suffering is caused by emotional failures, unresolved issues, unexpressed feelings, the failure of being,* I tell myself. *Suffering is like a sad melody; it can produce growth. Pain is like a toothache that makes you lie down and howl. I'll bear my fair share of suffering, but I won't carry unnecessary pain.*

I try hard to be a good son and a good brother. It's all right to play this role during a vacation, but it's painful to play it for an extended length of time, to pretend to be someone I no longer am. In reality, I am no longer a part of this world and most of its values. Men need firm beliefs to have a sense of grounding, but there is nothing I would kill for, this I know.

I see everything through a different lens without the rosy filter: this place is depressing; people are arrogant, ignorant, and aggressive; they have as many faces as they need to keep on top; they all have a sob story; they all are victims, or so they want you to believe.

238

I hate seeing things this way, but then maybe I am wrong. Besides, right now I am getting angry with them all. I refuse to feel sorry for them. There is no way they are going to make me feel guilty. In my zeal to be a tough guy, I have not acknowledged, even to myself, how hard it all has been. I wish Kazi had not died. I know that he would have accepted me without judgment. Tears roll down my cheeks.

Wedding dress for sale, never worn. Say something Alice, it's getting late. I weep for my lost home. I weep with the knowledge that I can no longer be part of the life that is here. I weep for betraying Leila, not being there for her, and for everything I have done wrong and to leave behind. The real tragedy is that our love is gone, whether I stay or leave. I need to walk away knowing that it is over.

CHAPTER 38

I take my time walking home. When I arrive home, Amaji, Baba, Yasmin, and Kamran are waiting for me in the living room slash bedroom slash potential honeymoon room with a canopy bed. The fluorescent light is burning brightly, its hum drowning in the whispers of its occupant. All the characters sit in their appointed seats, in their respective positions, assigned roles, waiting for our hero to walk in. And as soon as I sit down on the canopied bed, Baba looks at me face-to-face, eye-to-eye. The drama begins. Sound! Camera rolling! Action!

Baba begins immediately, "I allowed you a few days to think and cool off. Dear boy, I cannot permit you to marry a non-Muslim; your only option is your mother-mandated, chosen by you, your self-proclaimed love, Leila."

"I have been thinking about this for the last few days, and today I have met with Leila. She is love lost, a thing of the past. I can only marry Sabina. I know I've done wrong to Leila and Amaji. I may not be a good Muslim," I say with a detached calm, "but I consider myself to be a good person. I know religion is important to all of you. I not only love my family, I respect you. But to think that Leila marrying me would have been better, better for whom? Better for me? Better for her? I hope my family can respect my wishes."

"Men do not walk away from their commitments and responsibilities," Baba says forcefully.

"You are right, still, it is just something we men say and like to believe. Ideally, I'd love to marry a Muslim woman, a woman of my mother's choosing, but I can't. I want my parents to look at the character and the decency of the woman of my choosing, as well as her family, her culture, class, looks, and career, before passing a judgment on her. But perhaps Baba is right. All good children should love and respect their fathers and do the honorable thing. Abraham claimed to love God above everything else. So if it will make all of you happy, I'll take my losses, leave Sabina, and choose to live my life in misery. I'll do what is expected of me and marry whomever you wish me to."

I can't believe my own words.

"People live and die every day, Sabina, like Leila, will be a love

240

lost and a thing of past," says Kamran.

"No, Sabina will never be a thing—"

"Let us not start that dialogue all over," interrupts Baba. He looks at me coldly. "Your mother will proceed with your wedding arrangements immediately." He gets ready to walk out of the room.

It's clear that this conversation is over. Like a little helpless boy, I look at my mother, pleading wordlessly. *Please help me, rescue me...* My mother looks back at me, her eyes welling with tears.

"*No!*" The word comes out so forcefully that we all look around baffled. It is Amaji on her feet, and even Baba turns to stare as though a stranger has spoken. "No," she repeats more softly. Drying her eyes with her cotton shawl. She stands very straight, almost rigid, as though she is trying to keep from trembling.

"I will not force my son to marry a woman he cannot love. After all, it is his life, his decision."

Kamran and Yasmin begin to stutter, and Baba continues to stare, amazed. Amaji makes a hard, dismissive wave of her hand. She looks straight at me. "I wish with all my heart that this had not happened. It is a loss, like death to me. But this is a risk I took when we sent you to Amreeka. I knew it then, I saw it coming, but I could do nothing." She glances at Baba. "The only way we could have possibly prevented it was to forbid Rama from going to study abroad. I could not break my son's heart just to keep him close to us. Children are like birds; they fly away." She looks at me, her eyes full of compassion. "So we let you go to a world so strange it might as well have been the moon and hoped you would remain unchanged. How naive we were. There is no room for matchmaking in Rama's world."

This is a side of my mother I have never met before, capable not only of tenderness and caretaking, but also of wisdom. I realize suddenly that my mouth is open. I close it abruptly.

"Marriage is not like buying a suit. We shall not drag Rama from store to store—Does he want this one, or that one—until he selects one. This is a sad state of affairs," she says briskly, "but it is not the end of the world. Surely Leila deserves a better chance at marriage than a man who no longer loves her. After learning of how Rama feels about it, I spoke to her family right away. I told Leila's family that Rama has a girlfriend in America that he smokes and drinks, and he is not the boy his mother has asked their daughter to marry. I talked to Leila myself and told her the truth that Rama does not wish to marry her and that he wishes to meet her in person and apologize for his betrayal. She is a girl of honor and dignity. She told me that she would like to meet Rama as well, see what he has to say. But she would rather die a spinster than marry a man who does not wish to marry her. Her family is supporting her. They want to break this engagement. I was hoping that if Rama saw Leila, and they talked, maybe he'd change his mind… Obviously, that is not the case."

It can't be that simple, I say to myself.

"There is no reason to believe that arranged marriages don't do as well," says Kamran. "Look at the divorce rate in America. Half the Americans who find their own sweethearts let them go."

"Let us not think that way," says Baba, "if we are giving Rama our blessing to marry Sabina."

I sensed approval in his voice.

"What would be the religion of your children?" asks Kamran sharply.

"The religion of my children," I say very carefully, "of course, would be that of their father." I no longer have a religion. That much I knew.

"And that would be?" challenges Kamran.

The moment suspends in the air and they wait for my reply.

"And that could be," I say, "no religion too."

"Kamran," says Amaji, "you shall be more respectful to your older brother."

It's been very difficult, but maybe it's over now. I'm beginning to feel good inside.

"Marriage is a lifelong commitment," Baba says thoughtfully. "We are blessed, you and I. But it is not so with everyone."

Something I cannot quite identify flickers across his eyes, and Amaji drops her gaze. "Let's all go to bed," Baba continues. "It looks as though we have a great deal to face in the morning."

Everyone in our apartment is in bed. I am exhausted but unable to fall asleep. My wandering thoughts keep me awake. Finally, I give up and go down to the enclosed back yard. A pale yellow three-

242

quarter moon is on a slant; except for a silver beam of light that falls on the concrete floor, the yard is dark.

In the middle of the garage wall, the faint outline of a wicket drawn long ago still shows. I sit down on the platform by the water pump. In the summer time, after playing hours of cricket in the back yard, I used to push the pump handle up and down furiously. As soon as the water splashed out, I would stop pumping to stick my head in the stream. After a few seconds, the water would stop, and I would resume pumping, dousing and pumping, dousing and pumping, until drenched and dazed by the cold water, I could no longer find the pump handle.

Sitting there, I think about my childhood dreams of adult life. Until now, I have persisted in thinking that I can have everything. There are, in fact, just too many possibilities, and no matter what I choose, I will lose something and hurt someone.

It is strange to be a stranger in your own land. I am leaving and I know with a sinking feeling that something is missing. Something very special will always be missing from now on. I am choosing new love over old love, unfaithfulness over commitment. I know all decisions bear consequences. May Allah have mercy on me! I have betrayed my mother, but she has forgiven me. She has set me free. I hope one day Leila would pardon me as well. And the best thing my father has done for me is to let me be.

A *muezzin's* voice from the nearby mosque calls out for prayer. Prayer is better than sleep. I watch lights come on in random order throughout the apartment buildings as the believers begin their day.

I get up from the concrete platform and walk back upstairs. I stand in the doorway and watch my mother worship. After she finishes, she sits on her prayer rug holding her rosary in her hands. Her green embroidered shawl covers her head and shoulders. She looks so serene, so tranquil. She looks up and sees me standing there.

Without saying a word, she beckons me to sit next to her. I join her on the prayer rug. "Did you pray this morning?" she asks.

I wish I could say yes, but I cannot. "No, Amaji, I no longer pray."

"One needs to pray to calm the soul," she says softly. She puts her rosary aside and massages my head. The music of her bangles is

243

soothing. I put my head on her lap and close my eyes.

"Will you recite *Sura-e-Fatiha* for me?" she asks.

With my eyes closed, I can see my mother's radiant face. I recite:

> *In the name of Allah*
> *The Compassionate, the Merciful:*
>
> *Praise be to Allah, Lord of creation,*
> *The Compassionate, the Merciful,*
> *King of the Judgment Day!*
> *You alone we worship, and you alone*
> *We pray to for help.*
>
> *Guide us to the straight path,*
> *The path of those whom You have favored,*
> *Not of those who have incurred Your wrath,*
> *Nor of those who have gone astray.*

I open my eyes. My mother smiles down at me. I close my eyes again. She kisses my forehead and whispers, "You're a good boy. I love you very much." She covers me with her shawl, and I fall sleep.

I dream that I am at summer school, a large yellow stone building surrounded by a thick, lush forest of ancient maple trees. The summer term has ended, but I am not allowed to return home. I sit inside the yellow stone building, looking out at a cold, drizzling fall day. The leaves of the maple trees turn from green to red to brown. Black-and-white photographs begin to fall from their branches, photographs with faces of total strangers and people I know well: Amaji, Baba, Kamran, Yasmin, Leila, Kazi, Latif, V.J. The wind catches them, and they curl and blow away like dry leaves across the wet ground.

CHAPTER 39

Today I return to the States. Yasmin and I drink tea together in the morning. We sit quietly for a few moments.

"Do you ever think of us," she asks abruptly, "when you are in your new world?"

"I am like the washer-man's donkey," I reply. "I belong neither in the house nor at the well."

"That doesn't answer my question," says Yasmin. "I mean, do you think of us? Miss us?"

"I miss you already," I say. "But it is not the end of the world. In fact, it is the birth of a new world for all of us."

"Dear Romeo, don't try to charm me. Just a straight answer—yes or no?"

"I love you dearly," I say, "and of course I miss you. Do you know what I wish?"

"Tell me."

"If all was equal, I'd like us to return to our home by the River Betwa, across from the little *mandir*, to Amaji's vegetable garden… and wait for you to return from school in the late afternoon on the bullock cart, and live in the soft light from the oil lamps at night."

"Don't!" Yasmin says suddenly, covering her eyes with her hands. "I can't bear to remember, Rama." She lowers her hands and looks at me. I can see tears in her eyes. "We were like trees in a cyclone, ripped from our roots and flung all the way to Karachi."

I reach across the table for Yasmin's hands. "That was home to me," I tell her softly, "and that is what my leaving feels like now. Only instead of leaving a house and our possessions behind, I am leaving my family."

Yasmin withdraws her hands and produces a handkerchief from the folds of her sari. She blots the tears on her cheeks and then passes the handkerchief to me. "Rama," she says, "sometimes I think you are over-romantic, sentimental, affected by emotional matters to the point of mawkish nostalgia. Look at Baba—he continued to be his strong self."

I smile. "I once wanted to be just like Baba."

"And then you saw too many American movies," accuses Yasmin.

"The America of my movies was not only beautiful, but honest and rich. Everyone was always clean, everything was transparent and open—there were no smells, no odors," I say with a smile.

"Dear God," she laughs, shaking her head. Her face suddenly sobers. "In the future, you may only spend a week or ten days of the summer with us. You will never come home. You have no idea what a hole you leave behind. I'll wander around in a lonely daze. Amaji will cry every day, sitting in your room, smelling your pillow. Baba and Kamran will act as though nothing is different, but they won't smile or laugh."

"When we first arrived in Karachi," I say, "I used to wake up in the middle of the night in a sweat, wondering where I am. And then I'd remember what had happened and realize that we could never go home again."

Yasmin's eyes soften. "I remember you weeping in the night. One day, I too will leave. But the woman, from day one, is told she will marry and leave."

I stand up from my cold tea and gather my sister into my arms. "You'll be in my heart," I tell her fervently. "I'll carry you with me wherever I go."

"Little brother," Yasmin says, seizing my ears and kissing both my cheeks, "loving thoughts will always keep you near. You'll be only a dream away." Her eyes sparkling with mischief, she adds, "And please do make lots and lots of money in America. You'll need it for all the plane tickets you're going to be buying."

From a metal trunk, Amaji takes out her silver wedding anklets with tiny bells that tinkle, the pair her own mother wore at her wedding. She wraps them, tying them into a perfumed red silk handkerchief, and hands them to me. "For my daughter-in-law, Sabina," she says with a sad smile. "Bring her home soon."

A gray day turns into a dark evening. The sky is ragged with gloomy clouds like the filling of a worn-out quilt. The rain that started in the afternoon stops falling. We drive through flooded streets on the way to the airport. I sit in the back seat of the car with my mother and Yasmin. Kamran and Baba sit in the front. All the way to the airport, like my mother, tears roll from my eyes. At first, I wipe them off with a white handkerchief that I keep in my pocket, but after a while, I let them flow unattended. *This is another point of no return*, I think. I will never live here again. That much I know. My heart skips a beat.

"It must be nice to leave it all behind," says Kamran.

I nod my head in agreement. There is no time to explain to my brother that there will never be any leaving it all behind.

"When you live in exile," says Baba, "your roots are grounded in memories."

At the airport, Kamran promises to visit me after he finishes his internship.

Yasmin says, "Come back soon, Rama."

Baba says, "Why leave if you're planning to come back?"

"I fear that I will never see you again," says Amaji between sobs, her eyes laced with red threads.

"It will never be so," I assure her fiercely.

I walk to the waiting plane, weeping. When I left this place six years ago on a steamship, I was a boy, a student going off to college. Now I'm leaving on a jet plane as a grown man, and I know they never will accept that I am gone for good. And it hurts to know how much they care, and how much my departure means, not just to me, but also to those I'm leaving behind. *What has happened? What have I done?* Only the day before yesterday, I remember feeling excited, telling myself, *only two more days before I can go back to Sabina!* And now... It is so easy to err, so easy to go wrong, to slip, to descend, to fall, and it is so easy to do nothing at all.

I recall the story of a king who died in exile. He willed that his body be cremated but that his heart be removed from his body and returned for burial in the land of his birth. Home is where the heart is buried.

I board my plane. I sit next to an empty seat. *Life was supposed to have been a certain way—like marrying your own kind in your own religion, living in your own country with your own family, eating your own native food, listening to your own music, contemplating hundreds of everyday happenings in your own mother tongue. If I observe*

247

a moment of silence for every place I have left, for everyone who is gone and everyone absent, I tell myself, *I'll never speak again. I think I have contemplated long enough.* I take my book, *The Stranger*, out of my bag. Turning on the reading light, I open to it page one and begin to read. I can't keep count of how many times I've read this book, but I like how it makes me think and feel. Long live, Camus!

❧

Out over the Atlantic Ocean, moving westward in the darkness that comes with sleep, I dream that I've written my autobiography. I am sitting in a group therapy meeting, and there are twelve other group members discussing my life. Someone, in reference to my book, says, "There are too many unexplained moments in it."

I say, "Yes, you are right."

She says, *"Gone with the Wind* isn't that way."

I know I'm supposed to feel hurt, but I reply, "It is kind of you to say so." I press my face against the cold window glass and weep.

The word "Chicago" awakens me as the captain announces that the plane is descending to land at the O'Hare. "Bless me, dear God," I say, rubbing my eyes. "I know I'm imperfect, transcend me, make me nonpareil." A bright sun shines over the silver clouds. The plane sinks beneath them, and I can see the curve of the south end of Lake Michigan, the gray-brown December landscape patched with snow. As the plane drops lower, I pick out Lake Shore Drive, the downtown skyscrapers, and further north, below Belmont Harbor, the neighborhood where Sabina and I live. A sense of excitement begins to overtake me as the plane glides west toward the O'Hare. Sabina waits for me there, and the thought of her smile, her eyes, the wide and generous expanse of her love, draws me down from the sky as surely as the earth's own gravity.

The End

About the Author

Syed Afzal Haider was born in India, grew up in Pakistan, and was educated in America. He studied Electrical Engineering, Psychology, and Social Work. After twenty plus years he forsake all of the above and escaped to writing. His short stories and essays have appeared in a variety of literary magazine including Saint Ann's Review, AmerAsia, Rambunctious Review, The Journal of Pakistani Literature, and Indian Voices. His short stories have been nominated for Pushcart Prize and won best short fiction awards; Oxford University Press, Milkweed Editions, Penguin Books, and Pearson, Longman Literature have anthologized Haider. He has stories forth coming in Marco Polo and Trajectory. He lives in Evanston, IL, with his wife and is the father of two wonderful, grown up boys. Visit the author's website at: www.sahaider.com